Delivery Girl

Lily Kate

Delivery Girl
Copyright: Lily Kate

Published: January 20th, 2017

Interested in receiving *Love Letters from Lily*?
Sign up for her new-release newsletter at: LilyKateAuthor.com!

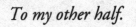

To my other half.

Acknowledgments

Scarlett Rugers for the fabulous cover design.

Caitlin for her fantastic edits.

Virginia for her sharp proofreading eyes.

Next Step PR & Kiki for helping to spread the word.

All of you, **readers**—beta readers, ARC readers, bloggers, and the entire book community—each and every one of you are fabulous!

And, of course, to the very **best of friends**... you know who you are!

Chapter 1

Andi

"I need one order of a smiley face pie," my dad shouts. He's known around town as Papa Peretti, and he runs our family-style pizza joint. "Let's go, Angela. Don't keep the happy couple waiting. Spit out your gum and get to work."

I raise my eyebrows at Angela, who rolls her eyes back. As always, it's a hectic work environment here at Peretti's Pizza. It's a family-run business and, unfortunately, I'm part of the family.

Angela's also part of the family. She's my cousin, and we've developed a sort of silent language with our eye rolls to communicate. It's necessary with a dad like Papa Peretti.

"I call delivery on this one." I raise my hands in a truce. "You're cooking, Ang."

Angela spits her gum into the trash can, scrubs her hands clean, and dives into fresh dough. "Smiley face pizza? Who orders a smiley face pizza?"

Papa Peretti puts a hand on his hip. "Some guy who probably wants to surprise his girlfriend, so make it extra romantic, please."

Angela sets to work arranging a combination of sausage, pepperoni, and basil into a face. Angela is short, stout, and brash. If they held auditions for a remake of *Jersey Shore*, she'd be first in line.

1

Under most circumstances, her orange-ish skin tone would be alarming, but I happen to know she spray tans twice a week, which explains the glow. Then there's her hair—or more accurately, her helmet. Her hair has enough product in it to set this whole place on fire and is hard as a rock.

"There," Angela says as she surveys the grinning pizza. She looks at me and winks. "You think that'll get a girl turned on, Andi?"

"Angela, watch your mouth," my dad says. "This is a family-run business, and I have zero tolerance for that sort of talk."

I have no desire to listen to an argument in which my dad and Angela argue about whether or not she's allowed to say *turned on* at the office, so I grab the pizza and hightail it out of there as fast as my legs will go.

I plug in the address listed on the receipt and climb into the old Toyota Camry my dad donated as the company car ten years ago. It's basically my own personal vehicle, but my dad pays the insurance, so he makes sure I know it's a business car first. It's parked in the alley out back, which is a moderately safe place for it.

Our little shop is located in an old, crumbling brick building on a block that averages three robberies a week, but the Peretti family is not terrified by this alarming statistic. In fact, it doesn't faze us at all because we've started leaving an extra pizza on our back steps most nights. This creates goodwill between us and the criminals, and because of this, we haven't been robbed once.

As I wait for the directions to load, I peek under the lid and survey the smiling marinara face. The pepperoni eyeball is winking at me, and I hate to admit that this is the most action I've seen in months.

I wink back anyway.

Finally, the lovely lady inside the GPS points me in the direction of Los Feliz, an expensive neighborhood on the outskirts of Los Angeles. For the hundredth time, I debate switching the voice to something more reasonable than a clipped English accent, but I leave it be. My mom died a few years ago, and my dad is so lonely that I suspect he likes the soothing sound of this woman's fancy voice.

I drive like a madwoman. It's my last delivery of the night, and I have a show after this. The sooner I finish delivering this pizza, the sooner I can get to the comedy club.

My whole life, I've wanted to become a comedienne, a lady comic—it sounds glamorous, doesn't it? Well, let me assure you, *it's not*. I have yet to see a whiff of success, which means I play seedy bars, late-night shows, and extra parts in movies that will never see the silver screen.

Forty minutes later, I've crossed the hellhole known as the 405. I park at the curb of the address listed on my GPS. Then I double-check the numbers…and I check one more time, because this can't be right.

This house is a freaking mansion. Nobody in a freaking mansion orders from Peretti's Pizza. We're good at what we do, don't get me wrong—my family has been in the pizza industry ever since great-grandpa Peretti came across the pond from Sicily—but we do basic pizzas, none of that fancy Santa Monica shit with salad and avocado and kale on top.

I pull out my phone and call Angela. "Hey, can you read me the address again?"

She rattles it off. "Are you lost?"

"No, that's what I have. I'm here. I just parked."

"So what's the problem?"

"This place is *huge*. I don't even know how to find the doorbell."

"Do me a favor: if the guy's hot, can you get me his number?" She chomps her gum for a bit longer, and my dad yells at her in the background to spit it out. "Scratch that—if he's rich and ugly, I'll still take his number."

3

"He probably ordered this pizza to impress a girl, Ang. I'm sure he's taken." I look up at the ginormous house. "And if he's not taken, I saw him first."

Angela screeches a retort, but I hang up before she finishes. I grab the pie and check on the cute little smiley face. The pizza really is adorable, except somehow, he lost his smile. Now the poor guy looks disgruntled. I push the row of pepperonis back into a grin with my finger.

"Stay," I instruct, feeling like an idiot. "Good boy."

The pizza doesn't respond, but I'm pretty sure we understand each other loud and clear.

Chapter 2

Andi

Navigating my way to the mansion's front door feels like I'm stumbling through an African safari. Then again, it might just be me. You see, I'm not exactly the world's best athlete, but I *do* have a very good excuse for why that is: my boobs shrink when I exercise.

I have a decent amount of boobage, but not a whole lot extra, and I cry a little bit inside when I think about them shrinking. It's a gradual thing, sort of how Hawaii is disappearing into the ocean. One day, they'll be *poof*, gone.

This is why I feel the best exercise is accomplished in the bedroom—or at the ice cream parlor. I figure raising a spoon to my mouth burns the same number of calories as the elliptical machine in some parallel universe.

Finally, I reach the front door. I raise a hand to knock, but a movement through the window catches my eye, and I hesitate. It's a good thing I do because not one second later, the words begin—well, not so much *words* as noises…noises of…pleasure, and…a squeal?

It all becomes clear to me when a female voice yells, "Harder, baby, yes!"

I admit, I'm a little curious to see this couple, the one who couldn't wait to have sex until *after* their pizza arrived. It's not that

I'd turn down sex for pizza, but if a pizza was on its way, I could probably hold off for twenty minutes.

Unfortunately, my opinion doesn't matter here, and I'm put in a strange spot.

Do I knock on the door and interrupt their incredibly loud lovemaking?

Do I set the pizza outside and leave a note with my PayPal information?

Should I just walk right in, set the pizza down, and applaud them on their performance?

So many options, and none of them sound good. Instead of making a decision, I hunker down in some bushes and call Angela; she'll know what to do. She always has answers, even if they're the wrong ones.

"Ang, I need help," I whisper. "I'm standing outside his front door."

"Okay, so knock."

"I *can't.*"

"Why not? That's your job." Angela blows a loud, snappy bubble. "That pizza's gotta be cold by now. Just deliver it and get out of there—I don't need his number that bad."

"You don't understand, I *can't.* They're having sex. In the living room. Which has floor-to-ceiling windows and open shades. It's *loud,* and…creative."

"Well don't interrupt them, that's bad for business."

"I don't think they're stopping any time soon."

"Well, is he hot?"

"I'm not *watching.*" I pause. "Angela, I am *not* watching."

"What sort of sex are they having?"

"What are you talking about? You're crazy."

"You know, what's it like? Dry humping? The real deal? Are they into costumes and kinky shit? I bet you there's a whip involved."

"I don't know, Ang. I'm just trying to deliver a pizza."

"Well, your dad is yelling at me to get off the phone. If I were you, I'd pound on the door and ask to join."

"You wouldn't!"

"No, but I knew it'd make you uncomfortable to picture that. Okay, bye."

She hangs up. I'm just as confused about what to do with the pizza as I was five minutes ago, so I just wait patiently in the bushes. My knees crack like popcorn, and I'm afraid this active couple is going to find me paralyzed in their front bushes holding a pizza. My fear is so strong that I finally step out of the bushes and march forward to deliver the goods. It is my job, after all.

I luck out—the session has now come to an end, although whether that's a pun or not, I can't say. I tried not to listen too closely.

Raising a hand, I knock on the door before the excitable couple begins round two. I'm a little bit angry and extremely frustrated; this delivery is a reminder of all the fun things I'm missing out on with my latest dry spell. At this point, a man could cough in my direction and I'd probably be halfway to an orgasm.

I brush a few stray leaves and branches out of my hair, straighten my clothes, perfect the smiley, and pound on the door. Now that the moans have stopped, this area is actually quite peaceful. I think I hear an owl hooting a few trees over, and I wonder if the birds enjoyed the show too.

I knock again, and before I can draw my hand away, the door whips open and I topple through. This is a problem because I don't have time to catch myself before stumbling headfirst into a half-naked man. I reach out, my hand clapping against his bare chest.

"I'm really sorry," I say, pulling back. My face must look horrified. "I just high-fived your nipple, and I apologize."

This isn't the worst of it.

As I step back, my cheeks burning like a nightlight, I discover that I *know* the man standing before me. I don't know him personally, nor do I know him professionally. However, I do know him intimately because he's been in a few of the magazines I stash in my nightstand.

His name is Ryan, and he's not just any old Ryan. He's *the* Ryan Pierce, hockey star extraordinaire for the Minnesota Stars. He's young, attractive, and new to the scene; the hockey universe is predicting big things for him in the upcoming years.

Furthermore, his face messes with my girl regions. He's not handsome, he's *hot*—a shaggy hot mess of dark hair, dark eyes, and a smile that is now quirking up in my direction.

"No need to apologize," he says carefully. "I didn't mind, but I'm sorry to have startled you."

Next, I make the mistake of looking down. Another wave of horror and odd fascination washes over me as I blurt out, "Where are your pants?"

Most of the time I wish I had a filter, and this is one of those times. Sadly, I do not—a trait I inherited from Papa Peretti.

He looks down, his gorgeous torso on display. Around his waist hangs a towel, and I can't think straight. My mind jumps straight to all the dirty thoughts it can muster. Honestly, he is asking for it.

What man answers the door with a towel around his waist? With his body, it's a sin for him to do that to my heart. I could die. I mean, it's not like I'm an exerciser, for reasons I've already covered.

"Sorry, I just got out of the shower," he says. "Is that my pizza?"

"Smiley face, extra cheese," I say. "Boner is served." I don't know why I say this. It makes him smile, but it makes me want to die. "I meant *dinner*. Goodbye."

I shove the box into his hands and turn around. For once, I *run*. I fly down that path like my life depends on it. Only when I reach

8

Papa Peretti's car do I realize I haven't been paid.

I sigh, and then I climb into my car. I'm late for my show, I owe my dad money, and I just hid in the bushes for what felt like an hour. The only positive in all of this will be the look on Angela's face when I tell her the story.

Chapter 3

Ryan

Damn. I'm standing here in a towel, holding a stack of bills and watching the most adorable delivery girl run away without her money. I can't exactly go chasing after her because, well, I'm wearing a towel and nothing else.

"Ry, where's the pizza?" my brother calls from the living room. "We're hungry. Get your ass in here."

As I turn to head back inside, the sound of a car starting on the street stops me in my tracks. That *can't* be her car. It hardly sounds like a motor vehicle at all; it's more like a fucking tractor with a digestion problem.

Sure enough, it's hers. The delivery girl—Andi is her name, judging by the receipt—is behind the wheel. Her vehicle clunks as it pulls away from the curb, spluttering black smoke that's going to kill someone. She's hunched over the wheel, looking like she's seen a ghost, doing her best not to make eye contact with me.

Scratching my head, I walk back inside, still not quite sure what just happened. All I know is that a few minutes ago, I was taking a shower and the doorbell rang, so I put on a towel, thinking I was the only one home. I came downstairs expecting to find my normal delivery guy: a fifteen-year-old pimply-faced dude, the sort of kid who doesn't care if I'm in a towel or a fucking suit because all they want is a few bucks to buy more video games.

So when I find the pizza waiting for me, I'm not surprised, because I *ordered* a pizza.

However, I *am* surprised to find her. She's every man's fantasy, a gorgeous woman—big green eyes, soft lips quirked upward in a smile, a curvy little body underneath that horrible red company shirt. She's holding a pizza, and it's for me.

By God, I love pizza, and I love beautiful women, and there on my doorstep were two of my favorite things. I must have done something right in this world to deserve that much beauty in one evening.

What I *don't* understand is why she seemed so surprised to see me. Isn't it her job to deliver pizza? Meaning she shouldn't be shocked when someone opens the door to *collect* said pizza? Sure, I wasn't wearing a ton of clothes, but I didn't show her my junk or anything—I'm not a complete animal, nor am I a nudist.

Then she high-fived my chest and things officially turned weird, but she was adorable, which made the whole thing cute. I'd be willing to bet if she took off that stupid red polo shirt, which I'm sure her boss probably makes all the staff wear, she'd make for one helluva knockout.

The way her legs filled out those tight jeans, the curve of her ass as she leaned forward to hand over the pizza…let me just say, I'm not sorry I looked as she walked away.

I am sorry, however, that I'm stuck waiting in the entryway for a minute of my reaction from her touch. How long has it been since I've had sex? Weeks? A month maybe?

Whatever the count, I'm long frigging overdue for a good roll in the sack, and I'm ready just thinking about her again—that whole delicious, irresistible package, and I don't mean the pizza.

I daydream, remembering how her bright pink lips had twisted into a horrified sort of smile at the sight of the towel, while I wished I could wipe that smirk off her face with my lips, drag a kiss down her neck until she couldn't help but follow me inside. I lean against the doorframe, the image ripe with possibility.

Screw the pizza; I want the delivery girl.

And that says something, because I fucking love pizza.

"Ryan, bring the pizza inside!" It's my brother again. "We're starving."

Since he scored his latest deal, Lawrence believes he's the king of the world. Sports agent extraordinaire, my big brother likes to think he can yell at me the way he used to when we were kids. Most days, I'd refuse to do what he said on principle, but not when it comes to pizza. I'm starving too, and my desire for the delivery girl only frustrates me more. I think I understand why people stress eat.

I'm frigging stress eating. Pathetic.

I round the corner and come face to face with two half-clothed individuals, my brother and his fiancée. I shield my eyes with a hand. "Aw, *shit*, you guys! What did I tell you about screwing each other in the living room when I'm home? I'm only here for a few weeks. Get ahold of yourselves."

My brother grins. "Look at her, bro. My fiancée is hot. We're in love."

We're this, *we're* that. The last six months I'm not sure my brother has used the word *I* once. See, my brother used to be a big, huge, hairy, ugly, fatso dick. He wasn't *actually* fat—he prides himself on looking all shiny and slick—but the other parts are true.

Then he met Lilia, and he changed overnight. It's almost cute, but I've said the word *cute* so many times in the last five minutes while thinking about that delivery girl that I'm about to hand over my man card.

I'm using the word *cute*, and I'm stress eating. If I don't get laid in the next week, I'm retiring from life. I'm serious. It's that urgent.

My brother is lucky, however. Their relationship works because Lilia's an angel, pure and simple. She's perfect for Lawrence. How she puts up with his temper, I don't know, but it seems to work for them. Maybe they screw enough that he doesn't get angry anymore. Stranger things have happened.

Plus, she's gorgeous—in a platonic sort of way. Lilia's not my type, which works out well, since she's exactly what my brother needs.

"Here," I say, handing the pizza over and taking a seat on the couch. I reach for a paper towel in the center of the table, averting my eyes as my brother and his fiancée double-check to make sure their clothing is straightened out. "I didn't know you guys were going to be home."

"Us? We live here," Lawrence says. "This is *my* house."

"Sorry, Ry," Lilia says with an easy smile. "We didn't realize you were here. Otherwise we might have taken things elsewhere."

I roll my eyes. "Yeah, right."

Lilia laughs, looking completely unapologetic while running a finger along her soon-to-be-husband's cheek. It's sickening. "You might have a point."

I take a slice of the pizza and shovel it into my mouth, shaking my head as I do so. One thing I love about Lilia is that she's unapologetic about what she wants and who she is. It's probably the reason she can go head to head with my asshole brother and put him in his place if he steps out of line. Like I've said before, they're perfect together.

If Lilia wants sex, she is going to get it, wherever she wants it, whether I am home or not.

"I think you terrified the delivery girl," I say. "She mumbled and smacked me in the chest. I think there were leaves in her hair. She probably heard your sexfest."

Lilia wrinkles her nose. "Oh no, poor thing."

"Poor thing?" Lawrence raises an eyebrow and then reaches over, pinching his fiancée's butt playfully. "If the sounds coming out of your mouth were anything to go by, she got quite the show."

"Lawrence!" She swats at his hand, but there's that post-sex, shit-eating grin on her face. "Sorry, Ry. We're not used to someone else being around the house. We'll be better, I promise."

"Maybe," Lawrence says, a pained look on his face, as if he doesn't really want to be better. "But I don't think that's necessary."

Lilia gives him a look, and he falls silent. As I've mentioned before, he'll do whatever Lilia wants, within reason.

"Why are you guys home so early, anyway?" I eye my brother nonchalantly. "Things go well with Jocelyn?"

He gives me a glance that says he knows I'm fishing for information. "Look who's curious now."

I shrug and shovel more pizza into my mouth. I hate asking my brother for things, but the whole reason I'm out here in Los Angeles, staying in my brother's sex-crazed house, is because Lawrence has managed to snag me a meeting with the one agent hotter than him at the moment: Jocelyn Jones.

Her enemies call her the Blonde Bitch and her clients call her the Ice Queen. The one thing everyone can agree on is that she's cold, she's ruthless, and she's freakishly smart. She's also interested in taking me on as a client, and she thinks she can get me a trade to the LA Lightning, a team destined for the big trophy within the next few years. It's the opportunity of a lifetime.

"You're young," my brother says in answer to the question. He's noncommittal, which doesn't bode well for me. "She's being cautious. You don't have a reputation yet."

"That's a good thing," I say. "And I'm not a child—I'm twenty-six. I just fly under the radar."

"It worries her. You're a good player, smart, but you haven't seen the limelight in a big way yet. The Minnesota Stars are a great team. Good solid coach, respectable captains—they're a good influence on you."

"Okay," I say. "So what?"

"What happens when she throws you a bone with the LA Lightning? Are you going to run around with Cohen James?"

I shrug. It's my own business who I run around with, and if I choose to associate with Cohen James—Hollywood's hockey playboy, a man constantly in and out of court, drinking, drugs, and worse—that's my business. "Cohen is a great player."

"But he's a shitty human being."

"You know me," I say. "I'm not like that."

"I know that, but *she* doesn't."

I exhale a sigh of frustration. "Well, how do you want me to prove to her I'm not a dickhead?"

"Spend some time with her," Lawrence says with a smile. "You're welcome, baby bro. I've booked the two of you dinner and a show next week. Be on your best behavior. If things go well, you might have a shot at a brand new agent."

"I don't like her," Lilia says. "She's got those crazy eyes."

"It doesn't matter if he likes her or not," Lawrence says, rubbing his hand along his fiancée's leg. "It just matters if they can do business together."

She frowns. "I suppose."

"And that's a good thing, baby," he says. "Because if Ryan signs with her for a big salary, he can buy his own damn house and leave us to bang wherever we please."

"Babe!" Lilia swats him again, but he wraps his hand around the back of her head and sticks his tongue down her throat so far I wonder if he can taste what she ate for lunch yesterday.

I stand up, grab a stack of pizza slices, and head toward the door. "Next week?" I say. "Just dinner and a show with Jocelyn, and then I'm good?"

Lawrence nods without removing his tongue from his fiancée's throat. I take my pizza and leave, my thoughts caught somewhere between the delivery girl and Jocelyn Jones.

Chapter 4

Andi

"Hi guys, Andi Peretti here. Thanks for making it out tonight." I squint against the bright lights, taking in a grand total of three—count 'em, *three*—customers in the bar. The bar itself is located on Hollywood Boulevard. It's dirty, loud, and dark, and it's the only place where I can try out my new material without getting judged by the real professionals. "Sorry I'm running a little bit late, but I have a good reason, I promise."

I wait for the reaction, but it never comes. So I plow ahead, clearing my throat and diving right into my bit.

My best friend, Lisa Schwartz, puts her fingers to her lips and gives a huge whistle as I begin my routine. "Yeah, girl!" She's almost as unknown as I am in the comic world, which is why we make a good team. "You're sexy!"

Besides Lisa, the only other sane person is the bartender, who is being paid to watch me. Then there is Crazy Phil—his words, not mine. He lives next to the mailbox out front, somewhere between the curb and the front door. He's my number one fan, aside from Lisa.

Ten minutes later, the light at the back of the room flicks on and off, signaling my time on stage is coming to an end. I close with my most practiced joke, wave to the empty room, and then hand over the microphone to the bartender who doubles as MC.

"Nice job, Andi," says Rick the bartender. "You're getting there."

"That's the same thing you tell me every week."

"It's true," he says. "But I'll stop saying it if you want."

Lisa, bless her heart, leaps up from the front row and runs to squeeze me as if I've just performed at the Laugh House. "You're damn right, Rich! Pretty soon you'll be paying *her* to play this bar."

I roll my eyes. They're lying, but they know how to make me feel like a Snuggie inside—all warm and fuzzy and Cheetah-print.

I accept a vodka soda from Rick. "You guys are sweet, but I'm going to be working for my dad until I retire."

"That's not so bad." Lisa grins. "At least you get free pizza."

"And a show," I say, and then slowly, deliciously, I reveal my latest adventure to Lisa. I tell her all the gory details of the sexfest I witnessed, and I don't leave out anything except for the fact that my car almost broke down when I tried to make a quick getaway.

Lisa laughs at my descriptions, though I still haven't dropped the biggest bomb of all on her. I haven't revealed the mystery man behind the door.

"Show up with another pizza tomorrow wearing nothing but a trench coat," Lisa says thoughtfully. "See if he'll give you the same service. It's been a while for you, and you don't want a dusty vagina."

"My vagina's not dusty."

"You've gotta keep that shit active, or else it gets wrinkly!"

"You're disgusting, and anyway, this guy would never be seen with someone like me."

"What do you mean? Don't say stupid stuff like that. You're gorgeous, and you're funny, and you totally deserve to be with anyone you want," Lisa says. "Sure, you're crazy, but so am I."

The real kicker is that she believes it; I can tell in her eyes, and this is why I love her. I propose to her right then and there.

"Sorry," she says with a wink. "I'm not your type. It's not you, girlfriend, it's me."

"Well, even if he *would* consider helping keep my vagina from getting dusty, he's obviously got a girlfriend."

"Yeah, that's annoying." Her eyes brighten. "Or…maybe it was a one-night stand! That could work for you. You're not exactly Miss Spontaneous when it comes to men, and it'd be good for you. If he's into one-night flings, see if you can sign yourself up. Consider it your MBA in sex. Very educational."

"Lisa—"

"Well, I'm just saying he has to be super rich or super hot—otherwise, if I were the girl, I'd have waited for the pizza. I need my energy before I get busy."

"He's *both*."

She raises an eyebrow. "You're not telling me something."

I pull her close and drop my voice to a whisper. "Does the name Ryan Pierce mean anything to you?"

"Shut the fucking front door."

"Yah. I'm positive."

"How positive?" Lisa sucks in a breath. "Let me dream about this moment for a second."

"Lisa—"

"Hold on, bitch! I'm dreaming."

I fall silent as she dreams.

Finally, she sighs. "Dang, I wish I had been there. I would've grabbed him."

"This is why my dad refuses to hire you."

Lisa scrunches up her face. "I suppose. So what's your plan?"

"What do you mean, *plan*?"

"I mean, when are you going to see him again?"

"I'm not." I shrug. "I mean, maybe on TV, and I do collect

magazines with his face on them, but he'll never order from Peretti's again after what happened tonight. I have a sneaking suspicion he knows I caught the end of the show."

"I'm torn between embarrassment for you and envy of you."

"Me too, which is why I forgot to collect payment from him, and now I owe my dad money."

"Go back!" Lisa's eyes widen. "This is your opportunity! Show up and ask him for the money he owes you."

"No, that's embarrassing!"

"I'll do it, then, and I'll give him two options. How's this?" Lisa takes a step back and gives some serious hip swagger. "Hello, Mr. Pierce. You have two options: either give me the pizza money, or take me inside and ravage me on your kitchen table. If you choose option two, the pie's on me."

"Yeah, all right. Go ahead." I wave for her to go outside first. "I've gotta run. Thanks for coming out tonight. I'll see you tomorrow."

"I still say you go collect from Ryan."

"If I listened to all of your advice, I'd be in jail."

"Well, I'd be in jail with you."

"That's why we're best friends."

Chapter 5

Andi

I throw my car into park and hustle into Peretti's just before two a.m. I skid through the door seconds before the cleaners lock the place up.

"Here's your money, Dad." I don't meet Angela's eyes. She's scrubbing a pan in the industrial sink and shooting daggers at me. "From my last delivery."

"You're lucky." My dad looks up. He's sitting at one of the small diner tables counting out the day's tips, blatantly ignoring the cash in my hand. "Turns out we have an honest customer."

"What are you talking about?" I tuck the crumpled bills back into my pocket before my dad can change his mind. I pulled them from my secret stash in the Toyota's trunk where I keep cash for emergency scenarios, like when a hot man opens the door in a towel and turns my brain synapses into fireworks.

"I got a phone call an hour ago from a guy who said he ordered a smiley face pizza. Said the delivery girl was very professional and delivered an excellent pizza, but that he forgot to pay. So, he gave me his credit card over the phone and took care of the bill."

"Oh, uh…" I clear my throat. "That was really nice of him."

My dad pushes his glasses higher on his nose. He peers over the sheet of paper where he's tallied the sales by hand. He believes

21

computers are evil and will rise up and kill us. Our tax guy is never impressed by this belief. Last Christmas, Angela and I invested in a laptop for him, hooked it up, showed him how to use it, and…he now uses it as a shelf for his lunch box.

I turn to leave. "That's nice. See you tomorrow."

"Andi, wait." My dad stands. He sighs, counting out a few bills from the pile on his desk. "This is for you."

"What?" I gape at the stack of twenties in my hand. There are at least five of them here. I'm not particularly great at math, but I can calculate this one. "A hundred-dollar tip?"

"Apparently your friend is generous. He left a two-hundred-dollar tip, but I'm keeping half as a penalty because you forgot to collect payment." My dad crosses his arms. He'd look sort of cute, his face a little wrinkled, round glasses that Santa might wear perched on his nose, but right now he's wearing a frown and looks grumpy. "And because you ditched work twenty minutes early for your show."

"Thanks, Dad!" I don't care about him keeping half the tip. This hundred bucks is more than I'm used to walking away with on any given night, let alone a single delivery. I'm still staring at it as I head toward the door. I can buy coffee for weeks and weeks with this.

"Andi," he calls after me. "What'd you do for him? Did you get naked? I told you not to do that."

"Dad, I have never gotten naked in front of a customer."

I don't add that this statement would have changed in the instance of Ryan Pierce inviting me inside—the fantasy in Lisa's brain wasn't an unpleasant one. I also didn't add that *Ryan* had been naked underneath that towel, which was the reason for my lapse in judgment in the first place.

My father leans in, his eyes suspicious. "I've never seen a two-hundred-dollar tip for a single pizza, and I've been in the business for a long time."

"The smiley face must have impressed his girlfriend."

My dad doesn't look convinced, but he sits back down and resumes counting bills. He's a bottom-line sorta guy, so as long as I'm not breaking the law or taking my clothes off, he doesn't ask many questions.

Chapter 6

Andi

"How?" Angela's hair is done up in two Mickey Mouse-style buns, and I think she's sprayed glitter on her head because I inhale a whiff of dust when I lean close. "Another smiley face pizza? This is the second one in two weeks."

A week has passed since my run-in with Ryan Pierce, and the memory is still hot in my mind, along with my embarrassment. "We've got to take that off the menu."

"Agreed. Too much rainbow-farting-unicorn bullshit," Angela mutters. Then she comprehends my words. "You think it's Ryan Pierce...*again*? Your dad took the call and didn't get a name."

I shrug, remembering the sounds of passion I'd nearly interrupted last week. "Maybe he goes through a girl every few days, and this is his routine."

"I hope so," my dad calls from across the room. "He's good for business. Throw in a free side of breadsticks and a soda, understood? Whatever this man wants, he gets."

"Loud and clear," Angela mumbles.

"Apparently my dad can be bought for a two-hundred-dollar tip," I say, shooting her an apologetic look. "Sorry."

"Don't be sorry, I'm just disappointed you get all the action."

"There *was* no action—not for me, I mean."

"All I'm saying is that if Ryan Pierce wanted me, I'd lay myself out for him," Angela says. "Dinner on the house."

The phone rings, and I grab it. "Hello?"

"Hey, is this Andi?" The smooth, masculine voice says my name like a song, and my ovaries explode instantly. "This is Ryan calling about the pizza. I forgot to ask—"

"Hi, Ryan," I interrupt, loud enough for everyone to hear. "We're just popping your pizza in the oven. We'll send free breadsticks and drinks, whatever you'd like. Sorry for the delay."

"No, don't worry—"

I can't stop interrupting him. My mouth continues to speak. "How about some extra cheese?" I volunteer. "I love double cheese."

I don't know why I tell him this, but it seems to work because after a moment of silence, he makes a noise of agreement. "Extra cheese?"

"I'll give you a hundred Parmesan packets."

"Three would be fine."

"Three it is." I hang up, and then I pound my head into the table. I don't even know why he actually called. "I *choked*," I whine to Angela. "I don't know what's happening to me."

I continue to moan to Angela as she makes the pizza, begging her to take the delivery.

"Do it yourself, Andi," my dad says. "For some reason, he seems to like you. No man leaves a two-hundred-dollar tip because they had a bad experience."

Maybe Ryan is buying my silence, I think to myself. He is famous, after all. His face is plastered on television, in the papers…maybe he doesn't want word getting out about him banging in front of the delivery girl. Then again, I'm not sure that's anything to be ashamed of, especially the way his partner was moaning.

"Fine, Dad, but I get to keep the full tip this time."

"Mr. Peretti to you," he replies. "You're at work, Andi. Act professional."

"Fine, Mr. Peretti."

"Is that sarcasm?"

I grab the pizza from Angela and stomp out the front door. "Bye, *Dad*," I say. "I'm never sarcastic."

"Andi!" My dad's warning hits the door as I rush to the car. "That sounds a helluva lot like sarcasm to me!"

Despite my complaints about delivering the pizza, somewhere in my stomach, tiny little butterflies begin to stretch their wings. I hate to admit it, but I'm excited to see Ryan again, which is ridiculous since he was bumping lovelies with another woman last time.

My phone rings before I'm even out of the driveway. "Hurry back, Andi. You're the only delivery girl scheduled for tonight. No dangling around."

"Dawdling."

"Are you being sarcastic with me?"

"No," I say. "It's dawdling, not dangling."

"Whatever it is, don't do it."

No problem. I don't have a show tonight, and I could use a cash infusion. Scratch that—I *might* have a show tonight, but only if Ryan is putting on act II of *his* performance.

I drive across the city, and traffic is lighter than normal—either that, or the thoughts of Ryan opening the door in nothing but that towel distract me for the entire journey. I arrive in no time at all, and by the time I park, my girl parts are tingling like a pack of Pop Rocks.

I flip the mirror down as I turn onto Ryan's street and check out my appearance. The sight of my face shocks me straight back to reality. In my fantasies, I'm not wearing my red Peretti's Pizza polo shirt. *Nobody* looks irresistible in a Peretti's Pizza shirt, not even

Angela, and she has a rack a Playboy Bunny would envy.

Maybe I have an extra tank top in my back seat. I often keep a black one there because it's simple to throw on with jeans and I can wear it from work to a show. Practical Andi. I fumble around in the back seat one-handed after easing my car to a stop, all the while dreaming of Ryan pulling one strap down, and then the next, until—*shit!*

My car lurches forward, and not on purpose.

Crap, crap, crap. I'm so flustered from my daydreams that I forgot to put the vehicle into park. I climb out to assess the damage; luckily, it appears I've only run into the curb, and not the beautiful black Ferrari three feet ahead of me. My front bumper has fallen off, but this is okay. The car is old and ready to disintegrate.

I slide back into my front seat and quickly squish into the tank top. I'm no Angelina Jolie in *Tomb Raider*, but anything is better than the collar. *Better*, I think, glancing in the mirror.

Though not quite good enough.

As my spirits sink, I briefly debate driving away to Mexico, just so I don't have to face Ryan. My life suddenly feels a little bit sad. I'm bringing smiley face pizzas to the most famous hockey player in the league, and here I am scrubbing sauce off my black tank top.

The more I think about it, the more this idea makes sense. I have a car without a front bumper, a piping hot pizza, and four dollars and sixty-eight cents in my cup holder. I hear Mexico is less expensive than Los Angeles, so all systems are a go.

I get out of the car, carrying the pizza, and then the worst happens.

My car scoots forward again. It's in park, but apparently the brakes are tired. The whole thing just sort of rolls a few inches down the hill and bumps into the back of the Ferrari.

Mexico it is.

Then my damn conscience kicks in, and I sigh. I will offer to pay for any damage, and I will be indebted to Ryan Pierce forever—I suppose there are worse things in life. Making my way toward the house, I find myself desperately hoping Ryan is not having wild sex with his girlfriend. I can handle him having sex and I can handle apologizing for the dent, but I can't do both at once.

Chapter 7

Andi

There are no screams, yelps, meows, or any noises of that nature coming out of Ryan's house. I hold my hand poised above the door to knock and blink, hardly able to believe my luck.

I use this moment of peaceful quiet to run through my speech.

Hi Ryan, I'm sorry, but I was fantasizing about you while driving here. It's a compliment, really. In fact, I was so distracted, I forgot to brake and bumped into your car. Anyway, here's your pizza! Don't worry, I threw in some extra breadsticks and cheese.

The door opens mid-conversation with myself. I realize I haven't knocked, and this is embarrassing. Instead of my well-rehearsed speech, I'm now speechless. Somehow, my mouth decides to squeak. I can't explain it.

"Ryan?" I extend the box. "Pizza."

"Andi?" He raises one of those dark eyebrows up to where his curling locks flop over his forehead. Instead of a bare torso and a towel, this time he wears a gray sweater. It looks so soft that I almost reach out and touch it. The wool top flows into a flannel pair of pants, and...*oh, boy.* There it is: the very subtle outline of his manhood. I want it. All of it.

"It's Andi, right?" he asks again. He peeks in the little brown baggie on top. "Thanks for the Parmesan."

By the time I look up, my face has turned Peretti Pizza shirt red. I nod and go mute. It's taking all my willpower not to look at his personal hockey stick.

"Here you go." He hands over a wad of bills. "Hope this covers it."

The money doesn't register, which is saying a lot. I like money, I really do, and I'm sure he left another big tip, but you know what's even bigger? The thing in his pants. *Wowzers.*

"I hope you enjoy your pizza," I say, realizing far too late that I'm speaking to his crotch. I force my eyes up to his face and cough. "Thanks for ordering with Peretti's. We'll see you next time."

Ryan's face now brightens with a devilish grin as I peek upward, his lips looking so soft and primed for kissing. "I sure hope so. The pizza last week was fantastic."

I should leave now. He's waiting for me to leave but, for some reason, I stay. Even worse? My eyelid goes ahead and winks all on its own.

"It's good to see you again," I say, praying my eye lays off on the winking thing. My brain has nothing to do with it, but for some reason, my face—more specifically my eye—feels like flirting with Ryan Pierce. *The Ryan Pierce.* "I thought you'd ordered just to see me again."

He tips that beautiful face of his back and laughs, a real laugh that has me grinning along with him. Then he leans against the door, and one scan of his torso tells me there are rock solid abs underneath that sweater. "I was hoping you'd show up, and in case you were wondering, I got your name from the receipt last time."

"Oh, I thought you'd stalked me."

"Unfortunately, that's not my area of expertise."

The reminder of him paying last week registers, and I recall his generous tip. "You tipped far too much last week," I say. "It was my mistake forgetting to collect payment. Here, this one's on me." I thrust the cash back into his hand, as if this makes everything better. "Please."

He reaches out, a large hand closing around mine. A *zing* of electricity shoots through me, even more exciting than the pile of bills in my hands. "You're worth every penny."

"Oh."

Then his face goes slack. "Christ, that sounds—I'm sorry, Andi. I didn't mean it like that."

I wave a hand. "So why the smiley face on the pizza? Seems... unusual."

"To annoy my brother," he says. "My mom started the tradition when we were kids. This is my brother's house," he adds. "Although the woman taking orders at your restaurant didn't seem very excited about it, so I promise to go for the regular sausage next time."

"That's just Angela. She thinks smiley face pizzas are too much rainbow-farting-unicorns bullshit."

Now Ryan *really* laughs. He sets the pizza on a table just inside the door, his eyes dancing when he faces me again. "And what do you think?"

"I thought you were using it to get laid." I shrug. "Guess I was wrong."

"Why would you think that?"

I raise an eyebrow. "No comment. In fact, I should be leaving now."

I make it halfway down the stairs before he calls after me.

"So, Andi," he says, and I look over my shoulder at him. "Would you like to come inside and have a bite of pizza with me?"

I turn around, halfway down the front lawn. "Me?"

"No, the other Andi."

I frown at him. "You tipped me in cash. If I come inside, that's basically prostitution."

"I wasn't trying to hook up with you. I just think you're funny, and otherwise, I'll be eating alone."

"Oh." I stand still, trying to figure out if this is a good development, or a very, very, bad thing. I mean, I want to be a comic, so funny is good, right? But at the same time, it feels a little bit like I've been insta-friend-zoned.

I'm still puzzling on what he means when a figure appears in the doorway behind Ryan. It's a woman, and she's holding a sheaf of papers in one hand and high-end shopping bags in the other. Her hair is a gorgeous chestnut brown, long and wavy and perky. I wonder if it's the mystery woman from last week, or maybe a new one?

She looks up and smiles at me. "Hi."

I give a dumb-looking finger wave as she turns to Ryan, quickly kisses him on the cheek, and then hurtles her lithe frame down the steps. Her yoga pants show off a nice, toned ass, and I remember that I *really* need to do more squats, stat.

"I won't be home tonight, flying out of town. Back tomorrow evening," she calls over her shoulder. "Behave!"

Ryan calls a goodbye after her. He waits for her to flounce out of the gate—yes, she flounces—and then turns to me. "Where did we land on the subject of you coming in for a bite to eat?"

I shake my head. "Listen, Ryan. You seem fun, and I think I like you as a person, which is why I hope you'll understand when I tell you that…I accidentally ran my car into yours."

"What?"

"So as for the bite to eat, it's probably best if we skip it, especially with your girlfriend just leaving."

I want to hit myself in the face. I'm using the oldest trick in the playbook in an attempt to find out if Ryan's single, and in the process, I admitted to crashing his car. Thankfully, he blows by the whole car issue and focuses on the brunette.

A complicated expression crosses his face. "That's Lilia."

"Lilia," I mumble. "Of course."

"My *brother's* fiancée," he says. "This is his house. I'm just staying here for a couple of weeks."

I gulp for oxygen, feeling like Nemo out of water. Then I step backward and realize I am officially the world's worst delivery girl. I'm prying into his personal relationships, a topic I have absolutely no business prying into.

"Hey, where are you going?" Before I can fall off the front steps, Ryan reaches out. His fingers loop around my wrist and it feels like I've been burned—burned by the most intense, sexy fire imaginable. "You never explained what you meant about the car crash."

"Car crash?" I feign ignorance. He leans his cozy, sweatpants-clad figure out the door, and I can see his muscles straining under the material. It's distracting. "Sorry?"

"Are you okay?" His eyes darken with concern.

"Here," I blurt out, throwing a few twenties at his hands as I turn around. "I'll leave my insurance information on your windshield."

Ryan watches me leave. He appears bewildered, and I can't blame him. I am responsible for bamboozling Ryan Pierce.

I scribble the name of our insurance company as fast as possible and stick it on the windshield of the slightly dented Ferrari. I climb back into my car and roar away from Ryan's estate as fast as I can. *Mexico, here I come.*

Before I round the corner, I catch a glimpse of Ryan emerging onto the street. In my rearview mirror, I watch him examine the trophy I left behind—my bumper.

Chapter 8

Ryan

That woman is a walking disaster.

If I were smart, I'd call the insurance company and have them sort out the details, figure out what it'll cost to repair the damages from her shitmobile bowling into my Ferrari, but somehow, I can't manage to do that. It's clear she doesn't have a lot of money, and it's my fault she was here in the first place.

Anyway, it's not a *huge* dent.

Plus, it's a rental. My idiot brother lined it up, thinking I'd want a Ferrari. I didn't. I *don't*. It deserves the fucking dent.

I haul her bumper off to the side of the road. I debate calling Peretti's to let them know I have a piece of Andi's car, but somehow, I expect that might not go over well if it's a company vehicle. I figure I'll give the bumper a nice little home on Lawrence's street until I can order another pizza. I have to give it a few days before I call Peretti's again, otherwise I'll be in the stage-five-clinger zone.

Once I put a tarp over the top to keep the thing all warm and fuzzy, I head inside and retrieve the pizza from the front entryway. I throw it straight into the refrigerator without taking so much as a whiff. It'll be gone the second Lawrence and Lilia get home, but I don't care—I wasn't even hungry to start with.

I just ate a massive lunch. What I'd *really* wanted was to see her again.

Andi.

The name fits her. It's a normal enough name, but it's also a little bit feisty, somewhat bouncy—just like her boobs. Now, I know that's not the classiest thing I could say, but it's impressive when a girl can fill out a stupid red polo shirt like she can, and they were even more noticeable in the tank top she was wearing today. I'm allowed to comment on her chest—it's *that* fantastic.

Also, she's funny. Half the time I'm not sure whether it's intentional or not, but the whole thing works for her. I *want* to get to know her better, and not only her boobs—her face too, and her personality, I'm just not sure how to get there. At the moment, the only thing I can think of is ordering more pizzas.

See, I'm only in town for a few more weeks, just until we get this business sorted out with the Ice Queen, and I'm not looking for anything long term. I'm not even looking for anything short term. I'm looking for one night, maybe—two tops.

Andi seems like the sort of girl who doesn't have time for bullshit. She probably considers a one-night stand bullshit, and that's completely fair. I want a no-strings-attached, fantastic night with Andi, and for once, I'm not sure how to get it.

Don't get me wrong, I'd make sure it was fantastic for her, too—I'm not a pig. I just don't have time for a relationship. I'm also honest and up front, so I'm not going to ask for something she's not willing to give.

But even so… I'm beginning to wonder whether it's rude to ask a woman if she's up for a roll in the hay and a few orgasms? I intend to make it worth her while.

It makes everything more difficult that I didn't have the balls to ask for her phone number while she was right in front of me—

although, I really do think it has less to do with my balls than the fact that she distracted me with the news about my car, and that she glanced at my crotch, blushed, and then sent my mind spiraling toward dirty places.

Plus, it just feels like I'm being a perv if I ask for her number while she's holding a pizza. She must get hit on all the time as a delivery girl. With a chest like hers and a smile that makes me want to hold her, take her inside, and never let her leave, it's a no-brainer—she probably has dates lined up every night of the week.

To add proof to my theory, she *did* already turn me down once. I asked her to come inside for a slice of pizza, and while most girls would've dropped the pizza and taken off their clothes right there, she ran away so fast she left her bumper behind.

Now, I'm not trying to be cocky here, but when a young, single hockey player is having a great season and looking to sign the deal of the year, bunnies come running. I can't help it; it's a fact of life.

But I don't want a bunny. I don't get any satisfaction out of sleeping with a bunny, even if I've fallen victim to their charms once or twice. I prefer a girl with her head on her shoulders. Andi's head might be a little awkward, judging by the things that come out of her mouth, but I can tell she's a nice girl.

I'm pacing around my kitchen like an angsty teenager. Andi persists in my mind, no matter how hard I try to get her out. It's not until I glance at my watch that I'm startled into action.

Exhaling a less-than-enthusiastic sigh, I head upstairs to get ready for my night out with the Blonde Bitch. We're going to some hoity-toity restaurant in The Hills and then to some show at the Pantages to "talk" and "get to know each other."

I have no clue why she cares about my personality—if I'm good enough on the rink, I'm good enough to be signed—but Lawrence set this up as a favor. As much as I sometimes can't stand my brother, he's gone out on a limb for me, and I won't let him down.

As such, it's time to shower, shave, and hit the road.

And try not to think about Andi. Though she left a temporary dent in my bumper, she left a permanent impression on my mind.

Chapter 9

Andi

It's been another week, and I've heard exactly nothing from Ryan Pierce. I suppose crashing into a man's car will have that effect on a relationship—not that what Ryan and I have between us is a relationship. It's nothing at all, really.

Although, I did answer the phone once this week for Angela, and I thought I heard his voice. I hung up immediately. It might not be mature, but it was for the best. Our insurance companies can work things out without me getting involved.

In fact, it is best for the city as a whole if I cut off all contact with Ryan Pierce. I nearly totaled one car after a quick glimpse of his abs; if I saw Ryan naked, all of Los Angeles would be in flames. It's safer if we don't have contact.

In other news, it has been a promising week for the comedy business! I've had gigs more nights than not. I performed at seedy clubs and dark venues where it was probably best my car lacked a bumper, but at least it was something.

I even picked up a part in a movie—a low-budget movie, but the part paid a hundred bucks for the day and offered free food. I went for the food.

"Andi, quit talking to yourself in the mirror!" My dad pounds on the bathroom door at Peretti's. "We've got an order for you."

I'm not talking to myself; I'm on the phone with the insurance company, speak of the devil. Surprisingly, they'd heard nothing about a car crash between my old clunker and an uber-fancy Ferrari.

I pestered the insurance lady so much she finally huffed off the phone and said she'd review her records. It's not that I *want* to pay for an expensive fix on a Ferrari, but I'd rather go in debt over it than have my dad find out.

"I'm coming!" I yell, whispering to the insurance woman that she'll be hearing from me soon. "One second, I'm waxing my face."

My dad makes a disgusted noise in his throat and yells at me about improper use of company time. I nod along in the mirror and take a look at my thighs. They might be a little bit skinnier because, for the past week, I've been parking the car around the block and running to and from our building every time I have a delivery. I haven't figured out what to tell my dad about the missing bumper.

My dad's footsteps march away, and I quickly hit redial. "Hello, Amanda, it's me again..." I pause as Amanda the insurance lady transfers me at *hello.*

"Ma'am, as I've explained every day for the past week, I will call as soon as I hear something," Tom says. Tom is the exasperated operator I've talked to every *other* day this week. Tom and I are friends.

"Are you sure? Remember what I told you yesterday—"

"I *remember,* Andi. I have your name and your number memorized, unfortunately. I know that in the event of a claim, I should *not* call Mr. Peretti, who is listed on the account. Is there anything else I can help you with?"

"Good, yes. Very good." I nod to myself. "Thanks Tommy."

"It's Tom. We're not friends, Andi. I've gone over this with you."

"Got it."

"Goodbye, Andi."

"Bye, Tom."

My father pounds on the door. "I don't care if you have a mustache, I hope you clocked out for this, Andi!"

I close my phone and slide out from behind the door. "Dad, we've talked about this. When I'm in the bathroom, you have to leave me alone."

My dad's thick black hair stands up like a miniature afro. "I would, except you're missing a very important call. Until you graduate, you've gotta listen to me."

I roll my eyes to the ceiling. I am about to start my last semester of school. I'll graduate this winter, one semester early, with my degree in accounting. My dad reminds me quite often that if I want to work for the family business and live at home while trying to get a foothold in the comedy industry, I need to be in school. Once I get my degree, I can "try that comic thing" with his blessing. If it doesn't work, I can be an accountant.

"Delivery, Andi!" Angela saves me from this conversation. "You're gonna love this one."

I worm around my dad and lean my arms against the counter. "Cool, where to?"

"Los Feliz."

I shake my head. "Oh, no. No, no, nope."

Angela gives a fake pout, and then she lifts up a pizza. It has a smiley face. "Say hello to your new lover boy."

"I'm sick." I fake a cough. "Can you please, please go for me?"

My dad shakes his head. "Ryan asked for you. Put a smile on your pretty face and deliver the pizza."

"I don't have a pretty face," I moan. "And how do you know his name?"

"Then find one, somewhere," my dad says. "Borrow Angela's. Smiles wants his pizza."

My dad has taken to calling Ryan "Smiles". Earlier this week, when Ryan hadn't called in for a few days, Papa Peretti cornered me and asked if I'd done anything to upset our number one customer. I didn't really lie, I just...dodged the question.

"Gotta go, Dad!" I lean against the counter and try one last attempt to persuade Angela. "Please, please, can you make this one delivery for me?"

"You know I don't do deliveries," she says. "Plus, I've got three pizzas waiting in the oven. No offense, but if I leave you in charge of them, this place will be burned down by the time I get back."

"That might be true, but at least we could collect insurance money."

She shrugs. "It won't be so bad. Drop it on the front steps and play ding-dong ditch. Say it's a free pizza. He's tipped enough for ten free pizzas."

I nod, thinking maybe she has a point. "Yeah, all right. I think I can do that."

"But if they're having sex, don't ring the doorbell. That's a real mood killer," Angela says with a serious expression. "That sort of *ding dong* ain't welcome in the heat of the moment."

"Lovely. Your visuals are really out of this world."

"And if he opens the door in his undies again, take a picture."

"No, that's creepy."

Angela gives me a skeptical expression. "Right, and hiding in his bushes *isn't.*"

"What am I supposed to do, whip out my phone, snap a photo, and say *gotcha?*"

"God, you need to learn how to be sneaky."

"I'm not a creep! I don't need these skills."

"Oh, you're a creep, you're just a bad one." Angela shoves the pizza toward my chest. "Now *go* before your dad has an aneurysm."

I grumble and slink out of the store, beginning my half-mile jaunt to the car. I look longingly at the empty company parking space. Maybe I should talk to Ryan about the car. Maybe we could make some sort of deal where I could clean his toilet or rake his leaves for the next three years in order to work off the damage.

There could be worse things in life. I might catch another glimpse of his abs.

Silver lining, folks.

Chapter 10

Andi

"What are you doing?" Ryan opens the door to his brother's home.

I'm bent over, ass in the air as I arrange the perfect smiley face on the pizza, just how Ryan likes it. I was *also* preparing to ding-dong ditch my dad's star client, but I've been caught in the act, which defeats the whole *ditching* part.

The note I was writing flaps in the breeze and draws both of our gazes to it. As Ryan's eyes light with curiosity, I find myself praying an eagle will swoop down and carry it away for me.

"Ryan!" I stand, stretch, and pretend not to be embarrassed. Not that I'm counting, but this is the third time he's opened the door to find me in a strange position. "How's it going?"

He leans against the door, this time dressed in washed-out jeans and a half-zip sweater, the kind with soft fabric, a half-collar, and a whole pile of sexiness. He looks relaxed and so freaking sexy I almost squash the pizza as I take a step backward.

"Why's the pizza on the ground?" His eyes are still focused on the note and, by the time he looks up, understanding has dawned in his eyes. "You were going to ring the doorbell and leave."

"Not exactly."

"You were going to ding-dong ditch me." Ryan steps over the

pizza and moves close enough that I can smell his cologne. "Why?"

It's delicious, like a pan of warm-baked brownies, and I take a deep inhale. "I would never do something like that."

"Right."

"I was trying to put the extra Parmesan cheese packets in the box like you asked. Angela forgot, and we at Peretti's like to deliver top-notch service."

His eyes turn all sparkly, as if he's amused. The smile curving his lips upward makes my insides tingle. The thought that I made Ryan Pierce smile is like getting all I ever wanted for Christmas. It's incredible the way he's looking at me like I'm someone important, someone he might like to be friends with, and I want to say more funny things just to keep that grin on his face.

"Where can I leave a review?" he asks. "Ten stars on a scale of one to five. You're perfect."

I'm melting inside like one of those lava cakes. He's standing barely a foot away from me, hands shoved into his pockets. That sweater is calling my name; it wants my arms inside, wrapped around Ryan's tapered waist, my head on his chest, that gorgeous smile pressed against my forehead.

"It's nothing." I wave a hand, feeling my cheeks redden. "I'm going to head out now. I didn't mean to interrupt."

"I have to pay you."

"Oh, no. This one's on me. You've over-tipped me so much I owe *you* a pizza." I thumb over my shoulder. "Anyway, I didn't mean to interrupt, so I'm going to head out, and I'll—"

"Interrupt *what*?" Laughing, Ryan reaches for my arm. His fingers clasp around my wrist before I've made it off the steps. "I just ate, Andi. I ordered the pizza so I could talk to you. You're not interrupting anything."

This is the closest thing I've heard to a pickup line in almost a year, and it quite literally sends shivers down my spine.

Ryan's looking concerned since I'm shivering in the middle of summer in Los Angeles, but he must be used to my strangeness by now because he lets it go and turns his attention back to the pizza.

It's now that I realize those damn eagles never swooped in to steal the note I'd been writing. He reaches over to grasp it. I see it happening, but I'm too late to stop anything. I make an attempt to lunge for it, miss wildly, and pretend to tuck hair behind my ear as he straightens, paper in hand.

"What's this?" he asks.

I make a weak grab for it. "Please don't read that."

"But you've written my name on it. You were leaving this for me, right?" Ryan's eyes twinkle as he pulls the note closer to his face.

I make a second feeble lunge for the note, but Ryan dodges, his athleticism obvious even in the simplest of movements. While Ryan dodges, however, my hand continues its trajectory toward his stomach where, instead of retrieving the piece of paper, I cop a feel of his abs—and what a damn good feel it is.

"Sorry," I say, retracting my hand like I've been burned. "I was going for the—"

"Is this a breakup note?" Ryan's eyebrows shoot up, a grin blossoming across his face. "Andi Peretti, are you breaking up with me?"

"No." I give up reaching for the note and stare at my toes. "I didn't mean it."

"But Andi…" That sexy smile peeks across Ryan's lips as he steps forward, his breath hot in my hair. "How can we break up if we've never consummated our relationship?"

"Well, uh…" I step back. "It's sort of a breakup note. I'm breaking up with you…as your delivery girl."

Ryan reads the note once more, this time aloud.

"Dear Ryan, These last few weeks have been really, *really* fun, but I don't think I can see you any longer. I've interrupted your sex life, crashed your car, and now I've ding-dong ditched you. I'm the world's worst delivery girl. Please consider ordering from another pizza place. Sincerely, Andi."

"I hate to point fingers," I say once he's finished, "but if you hadn't answered the door in your towel, none of this would have happened."

"How is that related to anything?"

"Forget about it."

Ryan steps forward. "And what is this about my sex life?"

"The other night! Well, a few weeks ago now. The first time I delivered your pizza…"

He blinks. "That's impossible."

I cough. "Um, I'm pretty sure the sounds I heard weren't in my imagination. Unless—" I clap a hand over my mouth. "Was it a movie?"

Ryan looks more confused than ever. "What are you talking about?"

"Wait a second, it couldn't have been a movie." I gesture toward his front window. "I saw shapes and…parts."

He thinks for a long minute and then finally, he smiles. It's more of a smirk than a smile really, and he laughs. "Oh, shit. I'm sorry."

"Don't be."

"That wasn't me. It was my brother and his fiancée."

"Lilia," I fill in. "We've met."

"Ah," he says. "Well, yes. What can I say? They're in love, and it is their place. I'm just crashing here on business. I *am* sorry you had to see that, however."

"There's one question I still need answered."

"Okay, shoot."

"If they were the ones having sex, why were you naked too?"

He runs a hand through his shaggy mess of hair. "I was hardly naked!"

"You had a towel around my waist."

"*My* waist," he says, calling me out on my Freudian slip. "I had a towel around *my* waist."

"Yeah, well…" My face is heating. "You didn't have anything on underneath."

"You looked?"

"No, but—"

"It's okay, I looked too." He winks at me, and I forget my train of thought. Then he speaks again, and I snap back to attention. "And I liked what I saw."

I swallow. "What did you see?"

"You, Andi. You are goddamn sexy."

I'm flustered. Hot and bothered doesn't even begin to describe it, so I do my favorite thing and change the subject. "You never answered my question, Mr. Pierce!"

"What question?" His eyes are dark and hooded, as if he's thinking dirty thoughts in that beautiful head of his. "I'm distracted."

"Why you opened the door next to naked!"

"I was in the shower and didn't realize you'd get here so quickly. I hopped out expecting some pimply-faced kid."

I grin at his honesty then change the subject again. "I'm sorry about your car."

"Don't apologize." Ryan shifts in the doorway, leaning closer to me. "It's already fixed. I have a buddy who gave me a great rate."

"I want to pay for it," I say. "Maybe I can just pay out of pocket. Or, if you need something—you know, a housekeeper or whatever—I can work off the payment. I'm in school now, so cash is tight."

"Nope, we're all good." Ryan takes a glance at the note in his hands. "So long as you agree that this breaking up business is bullshit."

"Bullshit," I offer with a nod.

"I don't want to see other delivery girls," Ryan says. "I'd like to be exclusive with you, Andi Peretti."

I clear my throat and bob my head again. It's safer to remain silent, seeing how my mouth has been doing nothing but getting me into trouble.

"Come inside for a slice," Ryan says easily. "It's just *pizza*, I promise."

"No, I...can't. I have other deliveries."

"I'll take care of that."

"You're going to deliver my other pizzas?"

"I have a different idea." Ryan raises an eyebrow. "I'll pay your dad for all the deliveries you need to make tonight. Will that keep him happy?"

I tilt my head to the side, trying to decide if he's drunk. He doesn't look it, smell it, or act like it, so I conclude he's sober. "I can't let you do that."

"I'll take that as a *yes*." Ryan reaches out and grabs my hand. "Will you come inside for a coffee? My brother's housekeeper is home, so we won't be alone. I promise I won't try anything on you. I'm just new out here, and I like your company."

I bite my lip. It's tempting—*very* tempting—but I can't decide yet, so I let my mouth babble away. "Hey, how did you know I was outside the house? I didn't even knock when I showed up today."

"I was waiting for you."

"Me?" I squeaked.

"I mean it, Andi! Your visits are the most eventful parts of my day."

Well, that does it. I'm a puddle. I don't even know what he means by *eventful,* but the fact that he was waiting for me to arrive with those puppy dog brown eyes of his makes me weak. So, I agree, somewhat overenthusiastically.

"I think I'm in love with you—" The words slip out, and before I can rein them in, they're out there, sitting right there in the open.

Ryan's eyebrows shoot up so high they almost disappear into his hairline.

I have to do something, so I stutter. "Y-your *abs.* Love th-the abs." This is not much better, but I've already failed enough today, so I leave it at that. No sense digging my hole any deeper.

Then, Ryan does something I don't expect. "Well, if that's the case, then here. Hopefully this will make your decision easier."

I'm confused as he reaches for the bottom of his sweater. He lifts the edge, exposing the slightest hint of skin there. Though I can't see much of him at all, what I can see is solid—hard, defined skin completely and utterly ready for kissing.

"What are you doing?" I ask, still staring.

"My abs would like to invite you inside for a coffee."

He lets his abs sit on display for a solid thirty seconds. I hate to admit that during those thirty seconds, I look, and I look, and I look some more. When he drops his sweater again, I clear my throat and meet his gaze.

"Do you flash all your delivery girls?" I ask, and luckily, this breaks the tension.

Ryan laughs a deep, genuine laugh that makes his chocolate eyes dance. He adjusts his shirt. "You're the first, Andi. I'm doing whatever I can to get five minutes with you. I'd beg, but that wouldn't be very manly of me."

If anyone else had shown me their abs and invited me inside, I'd have called them a cocky bastard and hightailed it out of there. However, the way Ryan's eyes glimmer with life, fill with amusement, dare me to say *yes,* I can't help it. I snort.

"Fine," I agree. "You've worn me down. I'd love a coffee."

"I'm glad we've made up," Ryan says, pulling me into the house, his hand wrapping around my lower back. "I don't know how I'd survive if you broke up with me."

"Eat a salad?"

He frowns. "Don't joke about such things."

***

Andi

> Me: Angela, can you cover for me? I had something come up and won't be able to make it back for my next delivery.
>
> Angela: Ooh, let me guess. *What is...*
>
> Me: You watch too much Jeopardy.
>
> Angela: *What is...* Ryan's penis?!
>
> Me: Please cover?!
>
> Angela: On it.
>
> Me: Thank you, I love you times a million. xoxoxox<3<3<3<3
>
> Angela: Enjoy his hockey stick.

She sends an eggplant emoji. It's obvious what she's insinuating with that poor fat eggplant, so I turn off my screen before Ryan can see the messages. Then I follow him into his brother's home.

Ryan's busy giving me a moment of privacy as I finish sexting with Angela and her eggplants. When I look up and smile, he closes the door behind me.

I step farther into the entryway and take special care to brush against the front of Ryan's sweater. He smells edible—shower gel mixed with the scent of the pizza on the nearby table. He smells so great, I wouldn't mind sniffing him, but I refrain, because that's weird.

I look up and admire the vaulted ceilings, which make the entryway feel a little like a museum. "Nice place," I say, but it feels like I've called the Louvre *pretty good*.

Ryan shrugs, unimpressed. "It's my brother's taste."

Past his shoulder, stainless steel appliances glimmer down the hall. Over the scent of pizza, I smell flowers, which is different than my house. Our house *always* smells like food—my sister is usually baking one cake or another, though sometimes she'll try her hand at cookies. She gets it from my mom. My mom loved desserts.

"The place smells fabulous."

"I've never figured out how it smells that way. I'm guessing it's some cleaning shit Marissa uses."

"And Marissa is…"

"The housekeeper."

"Right." I finger the flowers on the entryway table. "Beautiful."

"I suppose." Ryan looks at the flowers. "I don't know why she stocks them since my brother and Lilia are hardly ever here. They travel all the time."

"I think they're a nice touch." I pause awkwardly, looking down at my feet, wondering if this is the sort of home where I should take my shoes off and bathe them in frankincense before walking around.

My jeans and collared shirt feel wildly out of place, despite Ryan's jeans and sweater. He looks like Zeus on Zeus's day off, while I look like…well, a pizza delivery girl.

"Wine?"

Ryan gestures for me to follow him into the kitchen before I even have a chance to say yes or no. *I'm just here for a slice of pizza*, I remind myself.

"This escalated quickly," I say with a smirk. "What happened to coffee?"

I decide this is a shoes-off sort of place and slide my feet out of my sneakers. I stare at my socks, wondering if they need to go too.

"Leave your socks on," Ryan says, reading my thoughts. "Don't think so hard. Whatever goes at your home goes here, too. Now come into the kitchen and please, *relax*."

Damn, I like a man taking charge—especially when that man fills those jeans out the way he does, and…*oh, God*. I'm staring at Ryan's ass again, and he catches me in the act.

"Would you like to touch it?" Ryan doesn't look at me as he selects an ancient-looking bottle of wine from the rack above the counter. "Be my guest."

"Touch *it*?" I step forward, reach for the bottle, and poke my finger at it.

"I meant my ass." He turns, catching me in his arms. We're in an awkward sort of hug, and I can't quite meet his eyes because I don't have a good answer. "I caught you staring."

I cross my arms, determined to look confident, even if I feel like a trembling leaf inside. "I saw you checking out my rack earlier. Fair is fair. You look at my boobs, I look at your ass. I'm all about equality."

"Me too." Ryan sets the bottle of wine on the counter, takes out two glasses, and sets them down, but he doesn't pour the drinks—not yet. Instead he puts his hands on my hips and guides me back, pressing me gently until my rear end hits the countertop.

My breath catches in my throat, and all of a sudden the world crashes around me. Here I am, Andi Peretti, standing in the kitchen of Ryan Pierce, and his hands are in the vicinity of my vagina. *No. Shit.*

I find my voice as he holds me against the counter and ask, "What are you doing?"

His fingers dig lightly, deliciously into my flesh, the slight prick of his nails making my stomach twist into knots.

"If we're both about equality…" Ryan steps back, holding his hands out in a gesture for me to stand still. His eyes catch mine, those dark eyes killer against my willpower. "Then I need to make things equal. You checked me out, I get to check you out. Fair is fair."

"But—"

"Andi." Ryan's voice rumbles in a pleasingly low octave, his smoldering eyes sending my body bursting into flames.

I've never been looked at the way Ryan looks at me—with an appreciative eye. Sure, his gaze lingers on my chest, but also my face, my curves, and most importantly, my eyes. Though I have a feeling he was teasing with the whole *equality* speech, when his gaze meets mine, it's not filled with laughter.

There's a longing expression there, almost as if he's hungry. It's then that I look over my shoulder and see the pizza on the counter. My sail of excitement deflates a bit. "Would you like a slice?"

He looks startled by my voice. "Not of pizza."

My sail goes right back up. "Interesting."

The way he laughs is happy, reflecting the bright smile in his eyes. It's more intimate than before, and I can't help it—I can feel myself fluttering toward him like a moth to a flame.

"Thanks for coming inside." Ryan pours two glasses of wine. "There's not much to do out here when you don't know anyone."

"What *are* you doing out here?" I ask. "You mentioned business?"

He hesitates.

I wave a hand. "You don't have to answer, I'm being nosy."

"You're not being nosy." He brings a glass of wine to his mouth, and in doing so, brushes against my arm. "I'm out here in talks with a new agent. My brother has always been my agent, and he's great, but it might be time for something bigger. Jocelyn Jones mean anything to you?"

I suck in a breath. "She's big. Well, big-time, I mean."

"That's what I'm hoping," he says. "We've met a few times, and she's *getting to know me*, whatever that means."

I give him a blank stare. "You know what that means."

His eyes crinkle as if he's truly clueless. "Do I?"

It's my turn to hesitate. I don't follow much hockey—except for the pretty faces, of course—but even *I've* heard of Jocelyn. She's the Ice Queen slash Blonde Bitch, depending on whether she loves or hates a person.

Regardless, she's rich, stunningly gorgeous, and usually dating someone with a famous face. "She's dated hockey players before," I say. "You haven't considered that she might be trying to hit on you?"

"Jocelyn?" His forehead crinkles. "No. We've already talked about that—well, not about *us*." He clears his throat. "One of the conditions of me signing with her is that I can't *have* a love life."

"Sorry, but that's insane."

He shrugs. "I understand her point. Ricky Anderle signed with her a few years back, fell in love, and ditched her midseason to move to South America. He was destined for big things.

"But love distracted him."

"Guess you could say that. She got burned pretty bad, so now she makes a big stink about signing young players in new relationships."

"But you're not in a relationship," I say. "So what's the problem?"

"There's no problem, but it's a tough career," he says. "She's right in saying that I *do* need to be focused on the game, especially at this point in my career."

"I mean, I don't like hockey but your face is familiar, so I think that means you're doing okay."

"Don't like hockey, huh?"

"I'm from LA! The closest I get to snow is the fake crap at The Grove during Christmas."

He laughs. "Well, I'm at a point where my career can go either way. If I focus and do well, the sky's the limit. Or, I could screw up big time and blow everything and I'll be working at Starbucks tomorrow. Not..." He stutters and backtracks. "N-not that there's anything wrong with the food services industry."

"Don't worry, I work in the food industry, and I wouldn't recommend it. For me, it's temporary. I'm in school now, studying to be an accountant."

He looks surprised. "Really? I would've pegged you for something... different."

"I hope that's a compliment," I say. "Because I don't *want* to be an accountant, but my dad was adamant that I finish school before doing anything else."

"What is it you love, Andi?" The way he asks the question tells me he's found his passion, knows exactly what he's talking about. His eyes light up when he talks about hockey, and the way he emphasizes the word *love* says it all. "If you could do anything, what would it be?"

"I like to make people laugh," I say, surprising myself with the honesty. "I'm working to become a comedienne."

"Now that makes more sense," he says. "You'll be great at it."

I blink and look down, surprised at how much his simple vote of confidence means to me. All my life I've been told that it's impossible to make anything of myself in the entertainment industry, especially in such a male-dominated field.

Even my dad, who tries his best to show his love in his own weird ways, has explained in no uncertain terms that he feels strongly that I need to get a degree *just in case.*

I understand his point and am doing as he suggested, but the underlying message is also there: you won't succeed in doing what you love, Andi, so find something that pays the bills.

"Hey, I get it," he says. "Nobody's supposed to make money playing hockey either, but look at me. I did it and believe me, if I can do it, you can do it."

"But I don't want to play hockey," I say with a small smile. "I want to be a stand-up comic."

He grins. "When did you know that's what you wanted for a career?"

"It's hard to describe," I say. "I sort of feel like I was born to do it. It was never really a choice—I didn't *decide* on anything. Once I uncovered what I loved to do, it was simple. For a while, it was just hiding underneath what everyone else *told* me to do."

He nods, and it's clear he can sympathize. "I'll always remember the first time I strapped on skates. It's magical finding something like that, something to love in all of its purity."

"I don't know how pure comedy is," I say on a laugh. "But I know what you mean. You're skilled with words, Mr. Pierce."

"That's not the only thing I'm skilled with."

I eye him as I reach for a glass of the deep red wine. "Is that right?"

"I meant my hockey stick."

"Sure you did."

"On the ice." Ryan takes a sip from his cup. He glances at mine, which is mysteriously half-empty after just a few sips. He refills it. "You didn't say when you decided to become a comic."

"When I was five, my grandpa died," I say, my fingers tapping the glass as I stall. "I was just old enough to remember how much I loved him, just old enough to feel the hurt when I started to realize he'd never come back."

Ryan reaches out, squeezes my hand in his. "I'm sorry."

I shake my head. "At the funeral, we were all sitting around the table, and my mother…it was the first time I'd seen her cry like that, all shaky, as if her entire soul was sad."

Ryan rubs small circles with his thumb against the skin on the back of my hand. "Andi, I'm so sorry."

"No, it's okay, really. I remember that day. At the dinner table after the ceremony, I made a joke, something about Grandpa being proud we'd included hot dogs at his wake, and everyone laughed, even my mother."

I blow out the breath of air I was holding, shocking myself at how tightly the story has wound my stomach into knots. It still hurts to remember, even though years have passed. Ryan's touch on mine helps, however, and I continue.

"I never forgot the sound of her laughter that day, or the way it felt to see my family's eyes light up when nothing else could make them smile."

I pause for a breath, Ryan's hands tight against mine.

"You'll succeed, Andi," Ryan says. "I might barely know you, but I've just got this feeling."

"How can you say that?"

"You're too stubborn to fail," he says with a grin. "I know because I am too."

My chuckle is a little hollow. Somehow, Ryan has opened a vein in me, and I'm not done bleeding. "I sort of forgot about my dream for a long time. I was good at math in school, all my teachers told me to be an analyst, blah, blah, blah…"

"What happened?"

"A few years ago my mom died, and it was hard. So hard. She was my best friend."

He pulls me into a hug as I swallow past the lump in my throat. I try not to cry—I've cried plenty over her absence—but it happens anyway, just a few tears that hardly make an imprint on his shirt.

When I pull back, I brush a hand over my eyes and sniffle. "Look at me. Bet you didn't think your delivery girl would end up crying on your kitchen counter today, did you?"

"No," he says, lips quirking upward. "How could I have known I'd be so lucky?"

"Anyway, that's my story," I say, grateful he's taking everything in stride. "After she died, I sank into a dark place for quite some time. I hated it, every second of it."

"But you pulled yourself out."

"It took a while, but when I finally began to drag myself out of the funk, I vowed to find the light in all the dark places. Ever since, I've been taking classes, performing at every bar and club I can get in to, you name it, and for all my efforts, I've made a whopping ten dollars. So, it looks like accounting will be the way to go."

"Hey," he says, brushing a hand over my cheek where I've missed a tear. "You're not allowed to talk like that. If I barely know you and I'm saying you can do this, you'd better believe it's true. I'm not lying, Andi. The passion's there. The hard work is there. Keep going with it, and you'll succeed."

The ghost of a smile I'm wearing is a mask, hiding the bubble of warmth deep in my soul so that Ryan will never know how much his encouragement means to me.

"My only request is that you believe in yourself," he says with a shake of his head. "Because nobody's going to do it for you. Nobody put a puck in my hand and worked me for hours a day, but I wanted it bad enough, and I know you do too. Have confidence. You're beautiful, smart, and funny. You can do it."

When a man as hot as Ryan is saying things like that, it's enough to send a girl into a coma. However, I hold on to reality and focus on those gorgeous brown eyes of his, that shaggy dark hair drooping onto his forehead. "Thank you for saying all of those things."

He turns away slightly, as if unsure, so I reach up and put a hand on his arm. His bicep is *insane*, but I ignore that for now and focus on his face.

"Really," I tell him. "I can't tell you how much it means to me."

"Would you like to move somewhere more comfortable?" Ryan asks. "Where we can continue chatting?"

"The bed?"

He raises his eyebrows. "I was going to say the sitting room, but I'm open to suggestions."

I blush furiously. "Sitting room is great."

I leave my empty wine glass on the counter—I have to drive home, after all—and follow him into a luxurious space that belongs in a historic mansion somewhere.

The living area is tucked cozily in the corner on the first floor, the furniture newer and squishier. Unlike the entryway and the kitchen, this room looks lived in and welcoming, warm and recently used. A fire roars in the hearth, even though the temperature has hardly dropped below fifty degrees outside.

I raise my eyebrow at the fire. "You do realize we're in Los Angeles right?"

"Reminds me of home." He grins, and I remember that he's not from the land of sunshine.

"Minnesota?" I ask, as if I don't already know. I *do* know—it's listed in the article next to my bed.

"Yes," he says. "I still live there full time and play for the Minnesota Stars."

"Why are you looking to move?"

"Bigger budget, bigger chance at the playoffs," he says. "I'm not going to be able to play for the rest of my life, so I have to make the most of this career while I'm able."

"If you play out here, won't you miss your home?"

"I'm not looking at this as a permanent move." He looks at me out of the corner of his eye. "I really love Minnesota. Any move away from there is for the short term."

"I see."

"I always figured I'd end up back in the Cities once I…well, after my career. There's nothing like skating on the lakes during those winter months. The magic of that first snow, the first ice of the season." A longing expression comes into his eyes and he smacks his lips. "It's really something else."

"You miss the snow?"

"I miss home," he says, and something about the way he says *home* makes me long for a place to call home in that way.

I have a home, and I have Angela and my dad and my sisters, but one sister lives in New York, the other San Fran, and the youngest is off for a semester in Spain. The latter is the one who bakes, and our house has *not* been smelling like cookies recently. My brother's in college in California, but we rarely see him these days unless it's Christmas.

Ever since my mom passed away, my family has sort of drifted apart. Home doesn't mean as much anymore. Without my mom holding our family together, we've blown like dandelion seeds around the world. We love each other, of course, but things are different now.

I swallow, figuring it best to change the subject. A book is flipped upside down on the end table, as if someone has just been reading it. I run my fingers over the cover. "You read?"

"I dabble," he says. "You sound surprised. I did go to college, believe it or not."

"I'm sorry, I didn't mean it like that. I'm surprised you have the *time* to read."

Ryan laughs. "Before you assume things about me, I have to make a confession."

He sounds serious, his face turning stony. I lean forward. "What is it?"

He stares back, his lips a thin line. "I've never read *Gone with the Wind*, or Hemmingway."

I fake gasp. "No."

"Yes," he says. "If that's a deal breaker, then you can leave."

"Here is the twenty-million-dollar question," I say. "Are you reading this book right now?"

I rap my knuckles against the novel before us. It's *Harry Potter*, and I've read it exactly one million and ten times.

He turns to me, that serious expression taking over again. "I solemnly swear I am up to no good."

My jaw drops. I have to shut it using my hands. "Will you marry me?"

"Yes."

I take a gulp of air because I have no clue what else to do when Ryan Pierce accepts a marriage proposal I meant in jest. "That's cool."

"Shall we pick a date?"

"Ryan…" I awkwardly shift in my seat, not sure quite where to go from here. "I was joking."

"I know, but it gave me an idea."

"Oh, this sounds like a horrible idea."

"Lilia, my brother's fiancée—you met her," he says without waiting for confirmation. "Their wedding is in two months."

"That's great," I say.

"Come with me."

"What?"

"Come with me to the wedding, as a friend."

I shake my head. "I just met you. I don't understand."

"Yes, we just met, but it is perfect timing. My mother threatened to find me a date if I don't find my own, and she'd pick Chelsea Heimlin, and there is *no way* I'll survive an evening with Chelsea."

"Why me?"

"Because you are perfect," he says, and my heart flutters. "You are beautiful and hilarious and down to earth. I'm just asking you to come as a friend. Most girls would misconstrue that or say yes in hopes that we'd turn it into something more."

"But—"

"I know Nick Bennett."

My jaw drops. "You know Nick Bennett?"

Nick Bennett is the legendary talent agent from one of the largest agencies in Hollywood. He's known for handling most of the household-name comedy talent. If I saw him in person, I might fall to the floor.

"My brother has all these connections because of his job," Ryan says. "What do you say I get you a meeting with Nick and in return, you play my girlfriend for one weekend? I won't make a move on you if you don't want me to."

"Oh, I couldn't."

"Why not?"

"I hardly know you!"

"We've been exchanging pizzas and money for weeks now," he says, concern in his gaze. "I feel like I know you better than my best friends."

I laugh because his eyes are alight with mischief, and his smile is contagious. "That's ridiculous. You don't have to get me a meeting with Nick—you didn't let me pay to fix your car, so I already owe you for that."

"Does that mean yes?"

I rest my fingers on my lips, thinking.

"Fly out for two days," he says. "I'll pay for everything and I'll get you a private hotel room so you don't have to stay with me. Come on, Andi. It will be fun. Please?"

I don't know what makes me say yes, but I find myself nodding my head a second later. "Wait," I say, sort of changing my mind. "It's two months away? What if we're not even talking by then? A lot could happen to our delivery girl, pizza order-er relationship by then."

"Give me two months to *date* you," he says. "We'll hang out and get to know each other. If you still like me by then, you'll come with me to the wedding. If not, well, no harm done. Hopefully we can have some fun in the meantime."

"*Date?*"

"Look, Andi, I'm going to be honest. I already mentioned this business with Jocelyn Jones—if I want to get signed with her, I have to keep my love life squeaky clean. No relationships, no public hookups, no drama. She's like a skittish horse at the first signs of drama."

His meaning starts to sink in. "I understand. I'm the easy option. Hang out with me as a cover, and then when it's crunch time, we go our own separate ways."

"No," he says. "You're not the *easy* option, you're the *best* option because I actually like you, a lot. I can *talk* to you. Do you know how hard it is to carry on a conversation with a puck bunny?"

"I've never tried," I say dryly. "Though I imagine it's riveting."

He laughs. "Look, I understand if you don't want to. I'll still get you that meeting with Nick. I didn't mean to make it sound like an ultimatum, and you deserve a meeting."

"Ryan—"

"I was just thinking it would be great all around. It'd make my mom happy if I didn't show up alone, Jocelyn would be pleased that I don't have any relationship drama to speak of, and most importantly, I'd be happy because I'd get to hang out with you."

This is not where I thought today would go. It's been a rollercoaster for sure, but this makes more sense than anything else. It makes more sense than him *actually* being interested in me.

I should've known he wouldn't want anything more from me than a friendship. I am good at being the friend, just not so good at being the *girlfriend*.

But then Lisa and Angela's words enter my mind—Lisa telling me I never take risks on guys, that my vagina is getting dusty—and I decide that enough is enough. I don't want a dusty vagina any longer; I want to have a great time with Ryan Pierce.

"You know what?" I say, new energy in my voice. "I'm not in a place to have a relationship either. I'm graduating school soon, and then I have to focus on my career. I suppose it wouldn't hurt to have some fun in the meantime."

"Just fun," he says. "No strings attached."

I'm not sure if that means sex or not, but I figure we'll play things by ear. "Just friends?" I confirm. "We're not agreeing to hook up?"

"Just friends. I won't make a move unless you kiss me first," he says with a wink. "I don't want to screw this up."

"Fine," I agree. "With one exception: you don't have to *date* me. That'll just make things complicated. Let's just hang out as friends. I already owe you enough for the car ordeal, so if I go with you to the wedding, will you consider things even?"

"They already were, sweetheart," he says. "But yes, let's consider it even."

I stand up and extend my hand for a shake.

He surprises me by extending his hand, clasping it around mine, and bringing the whole thing to his lips. "Even if I don't *have* to date you, Andi Peretti, I'm going to date you these next two months, harder than anyone has ever dated you before."

Despite all my best intentions, little butterflies bang about in my stomach. "Oh, boy," I say. "What a ride this will be."

"It'll be a ride—" Ryan is interrupted by a beep from my phone.

I excuse myself and open the message. It's an urgent note from Lisa.

> Lisa: Get your ass to Laugh House. I just booked a last minute gig and it's paid!!!! Hurry. I will literally die if nobody is in those seats when I go on. Twenty minutes.

Chapter 11

Ryan

Something's wrong.

Here I am thinking that we've finally turned a corner and…*shit*. That look on her face as she's reading her texts is not good. She's about to pull out from this agreement, and I was just starting to feel excited about it all—the possibility of Andi being mine, even if only for a short time, and only for pretend.

I should never have roped her into this thing with the wedding. I'm such a selfish bastard. And what the hell was I thinking bringing up Nick Bennett? Am I that big of an asshole, trying to name drop like some clown?

The thing is—well, I can't explain it. There's a part of me that wants to be next to Andi more than anything, and I'm not above pulling a few names out of my pocket to make that happen. I need to prove to her that I'm not the same sort of asshole she usually spends time with, judging by the way she's acting surprised at the simplest things I do for her.

I saw the way she was uncomfortable in the kitchen, and it annoyed me. To think that someone wouldn't see Andi for who she is—smart, funny, a great girl. I knew already that she'd see straight through any one-night stand bullshit I pulled on her, which was why I wasn't going to try that route.

Andi isn't a bunny. If she were a puck bunny, I could've already had her shirt off and my hand down her pants, but that's not the case. I'm not interested in bunnies anymore. I'm interested in Andi.

Now, I need more time with her to show her that. The ten minutes a week we spend awkwardly exchanging pizzas isn't enough, and now I went and ruined even that. Something's clearly wrong judging by her face. She's still looking at her phone like somebody died.

Or maybe she's come to her senses and realized my intentions, that I don't *want* to be friends with her, that I want to make her mine, to take the piece of Andi that she showed me earlier—the strong, aching piece tinged with sadness—and make her forget all the bad. I want to bring her only the good, and I want to hear her laugh more than anything in this universe.

"Andi, is everything okay?" I ask. She looks frigging amazing in that collared shirt. I try not to focus on her boobs and keep my eyes looking at her face, but it's hard. *I'm* hard. I want her—*why can I not focus on her words?* I clear my throat and try again. "What's wrong?"

"It's nothing," she says quickly. "Nothing bad, but I have to go."

"Did something happen?" I wonder if it's me. "Did I say something?"

"No, no, nothing like that," she says, her eyebrows crinkling. "It's just my friend…"

Even her eyebrows are sexy. *What the hell is wrong with me?* I accidentally tuned out, and now she's talking about something else.

"…booked a show, and we have this stupid promise." She looks sheepish. "Lisa and I have been friends forever, and we made a promise that we'd always go to each other's shows. It sucks to be alone, so we promised to never let that happen to one another."

"I don't think that's stupid at all."

"You don't?"

"No, I think it's nice of you. You're a good friend."

"Sometimes being a good friend sucks." She gives me a sly sort of look, and I realize she's hinting at not wanting to go. "I hate to leave, but Lisa booked a show and I have to show up. The pact, you know."

She stands up and wobbles as she takes a few steps.

"You're in no shape to drive," I say. "Let me take you."

"Don't be silly, it's across town. I've only had a glass of wine. Or, I can Uber."

"*I've* only had half a glass, and I weigh over two hundred pounds. I also ate a foot-long sub before you showed up, so there's no way I'm even the slightest bit tipsy."

She faces me. "Why would you do that?"

"Do what?"

"Eat a foot-long! I was bringing you a pizza!"

"Oh, uh—"

"I'm kidding." She grins. "I'll call an Uber."

"No." I stand and rest my hand on her arm. Christ, her skin is soft. I want to touch her everywhere, and dammit—if driving across town to some seedy comedy club is what it'll take to get there, I can't jump on board fast enough. "I want to go with you."

"It's a dirty, underground comedy club. It's probably gonna be me, you, Lisa, and Phil."

"Who's Phil?"

"The homeless guy who lives by the mailbox."

My smile grows bigger. "Perfect. My kinda place."

"Really?"

"I prefer the *out of the way* sort of places."

I don't tell her that otherwise, I have people in my face all the time asking for autographs. I love fans, don't get me wrong, but sometimes I crave a little privacy.

"Ah, the problems of the rich and famous." She winks, not fooled by my chivalry. "Well then, I will take you up on your offer of a ride, but"—she points at me—"this isn't a real date."

"It's not even a fake date," I say, raising my hands in surrender. "I'm just giving you a ride like any good Samaritan would do."

She laughs, and I can barely restrain my tortured groan. I may want to sleep with her more than I want to breathe, but I can be patient. I can feel when a girl is different, special—at least I think I can. It's never happened before, not like this where my heart almost beats out of my rib cage every time she smiles.

"You don't have to finish that," I say as she reaches for my now discarded glass of wine.

I don't want to be responsible for getting her too drunk on our first semi-date, even if it's only a fake one. Not only is it just not a good idea to get drunk, it's more than that.

Whenever she kisses me for the first time—and she *will* kiss me eventually—I want her to remember every damn second of it, and I want her to come back for more.

"Oh, yes I do." She reaches out a hand, rests it on my chest. "The bar where we're going has a two-drink minimum. I order two diet Cokes instead of booze because it's cheaper, so I'll just drink this wine now, and we'll be good to go. Plus, I've got a designated driver."

She dances her fingers up my chest, and I'm turned on by her touch.

"Are you ready?" I ask, my voice husky. If we don't get out of here soon, I'll be throwing her onto the bed and pulling off that stupid collared shirt. I grab her hands. "Move it, or we're never leaving."

Chapter 12

Andi

"This is the place?" Ryan somehow makes his way around his brother's BMW before I can open the door. He guides me out slowly, and I apologize for the fiftieth time that his car is too busy getting fixed to be driven.

"Relax," he says. "It's nothing."

"I shouldn't have brought you here." I lean against the car and stare at the somewhat dilapidated building ahead of us. "This is no place for *Ryan Pierce*. If you leave now, I can Uber back. Plus, I'll still deliver your pizzas."

"I'd hope so. Rumor on the street is that I tip pretty well for good service." Ryan moves his hand so that his fingers are low on my back, teasing me with a hint of skin-on-skin contact between my cropped tank and my jeans. "Let's grab seats, show starts in three minutes."

I traded in my Peretti's collared shirt for a black stretchy tank top and a fake-leather jacket slung across my shoulders, retrieved from the stash I keep in my car. I can't help the slight cheesy-pizza scent radiating from my work jeans, but I look decent enough to get inside the Laugh House. With a bit of added mascara and a swipe of lip gloss, hell, this is *almost* a date.

The Laugh House is a middle-of-the-road place. The only time a famous face might be seen around here is if they're testing out new material before hitting the big stages. Even so, it is a way bigger deal than the clubs Lisa and I normally play.

How can I tell it's a big deal? Because there are people here. Real, live people mingling about the bar, waiting in line to get into the club. I often come here to watch classmates who have gotten their medium break into the industry, so I know Bruce, the bouncer. He works here mostly to get some free stage time, moonlighting as a comedian when his ex-wife has the kids for the weekend.

"Hey, Andi." Bruce pulls me in, kisses both of my cheeks, and then rakes his gaze over Ryan. "Sweet gig for Lisa, huh? What a turnout. I'm happy for her."

"I can't wait to see her up there," I gush. "She's going to have a cow when she sees a crowd this size."

Ryan hasn't once moved his hand from my lower back, a choice I decide to appreciate. Bruce, however, is protective of his fellow comics and growls at Ryan for ID.

"Come on, Bruce," I say. "He's with me. Lighten up."

"It's fine." Ryan hands over his ID with a smile. "I don't mind."

I glance with suspicion at Ryan—he looks positively giddy. That's when I realize he probably never gets asked for his ID because people *recognize* him. This is exciting for him, I think, in a strange way.

Bruce grunts a moody *move along*.

"Nice guy," Ryan murmurs, squeezing me tight as we slip through the doors. "A friend of yours?"

"Yeah, he's a softy inside. He just watches out for the regulars." I smile. "So, can I buy you a soda? I don't have enough cash on me for anything more."

Ryan opens his mouth to respond, but I interrupt him first.

"Wait!" I yank out the cash from the pizza delivery. "I have your tip. Would you like a glass of wine? Let's go all out tonight."

"I'll take a beer. Driving," he says as an explanation. "And I have to head back to Minnesota next week for some preseason training."

"Minnesota?"

He shrugs. "Until the deal's done out here, I'm still with the Stars. My duties are still to my team there."

Ryan seems bothered by something, but I can't quite put my finger on *what*. Before I can beat him to it, he orders a beer for him and a glass of wine for me and pays in cash. Then he selects a table near the front and pulls a chair out, gesturing for me to slip into it.

His whole gentleman act is dangerous.

I could get used to this, and that's the last thought I need to be having right after agreeing to be his *friend-date* to his brother's wedding. I mean, he basically told me that the only reason he trusts himself to behave is because he doesn't want to have sex with me.

Which is unfortunate, because I'm thinking that adding a one-night stand into the mix of this whole fake-girlfriend thing might've sweetened the pot. We'll see. Maybe he's open to negotiation.

"Why do I feel like you've never been with a man who deserves you?" Ryan leans over, his breath tickling my ear. "You act as if I shouldn't be doing this—opening doors, buying you drinks, driving you around town."

"I just..." I pause, flustered. "I'm not used to it."

"Then you've been doing it all wrong."

I look down at my drink. It's a reflex, not because I want pity. I just don't have anything else to say. That's why I'm still single, I suppose—I've never met a man who makes me feel good enough—not until Ryan.

"Hey." He reaches out, tilts my chin up. "You just didn't know what you were missing. Now you know. Andi, you deserve to have someone open your door and buy you a drink. Don't settle for the assholes that can't do something as simple as that."

I swallow, nodding along. Usually, I'm a dry-eyed, stoic, laugh-in-the-face-of-sadness type girl, but something about Ryan makes my soul pour out words, share my stories with him. Something about him makes me feel safe.

"That's not everything." Ryan slips his arm around my shoulder, his voice dropping low. "You deserve a man who can kiss you until you forget your name, a man who can take you to bed, satisfy your every need, and then bring you coffee the next morning. You deserve all of that, and so much more."

"Thanks, Ryan, but you don't have to say all this—"

"Nothing I can say will change your mind," he offers. "Except for you. I'm just telling you the truth."

My eyes are really smarting now, and I'm thinking it was pretty stupid to agree to be this man's friend. If I hadn't just agreed to friendship, I might stick my tongue down his throat right now, and I'm pretty certain I wouldn't remember my name when he kissed me back. Sometimes I hate being sensible.

"You're sweet," I start, but he shakes his head for me to quiet.

"I can see the doubt in your eyes, and I don't like it. You've got a lot to offer this world, Andi, and anyone who doesn't see that is an asshat." He pauses for a sip of beer, and then changes subjects slightly. "I'm not saying that *I'm* the man for you, I'm just trying to tell you that there's someone out there who'll treat you well."

I clear my throat, still in slight disbelief that he cares enough to say anything at all. He doesn't *have* to, that's for sure; with the looks he's getting from other women in here, he could have any one of them in bed by midnight—myself included, I'm beginning to realize.

Those dark, soulful eyes of his alternate between alert and sensual, charming and thoughtful. The shaggy mess of hair on his head accents his tanned skin and thick, muscled arms hidden underneath a sweater that's as soft as a minx.

Unfortunately, the only words of his that I can focus on are *I'm not the man for you*—of course.

"Show's starting." Ryan leans back, his eyes focused on the stage. "Do you see your friend yet?"

I shake my head. Lisa's nowhere to be seen. Thankfully, the waiter stops by just then and deposits another glass of red wine. I take a sip. As I sit back, letting the wine sink in and the hot lights warm my skin, I take some time to look around the room.

The space itself isn't big, but it is packed tonight. The comic who canceled last minute has a decent following, and the other comics on the roster were C-listers. We're not talking SNL cast members here; we're talking actors who've had one-liners in movies, recognizable faces who get paid to play gigs, and not the other way around. It is the next step up for Lisa, and I couldn't be more proud.

"I thought you'd never make it!" a voice hisses in my ear. "I was about to order a pizza to the stage just so you'd get here in time. Do you see the *people* sitting there? Real live people! That are here to listen to *me*!" Lisa squeaks as she talks, her breath getting faster and faster as she scans the room.

I grin, kissing her cheek. "You'll do great. Oh, and Lisa, this is Ryan."

Lisa straightens up then, stiff as a telephone pole, and she stares at Ryan…just stares, and stares, and stares. Her mouth opens a little bit, and I raise a hand and manually close her jaw.

"Hi." Ryan extends a hand. "Andi speaks very, very highly of you. Can't wait to see the show."

Lisa shakes his hand up and down with less emotion than most robots. When she speaks, she's looking at Ryan, but I think she's talking to me. "You brought *him*?"

"Yes, as I said, this is my friend Ryan," I repeat.

"You're friends?" She turns to face me. "*I'm* your friend. *He's* the guy you want to bang."

Ryan's eyebrows rise slightly, but he doesn't look all that dismayed by Lisa's huge mouth.

"I didn't say that," I say. "She's drunk on stage fright."

"No," Lisa says, her jaw still open. "You said it yourself. You want to—"

"I didn't say that," I interrupt, my face heating. "Lisa, will you relax? Ryan's here as a favor because we were drinking wine, and he was sober enough to drive."

"You drank wine. With Ryan. Pierce..." She trails off. "You drank Ryan Pierce's wine."

I can't tell if she's more stunned to be meeting the star in person, or if she's shocked I haven't mentioned anything to her about it—which isn't my fault, since it just happened.

I stand up, sensing a flood of questions that may or may not be appropriate for Ryan's ears. Lisa tends to lose her filter when she's surprised, drunk, tired, annoyed, angry—she basically doesn't have a filter, and I don't want to expose Ryan to her brutal honesty just yet.

"I'll be right back. I have to...uh, do something." I flash a brief smile at Ryan before pulling my best friend just outside the doors to the main stage and into a bathroom. "Lisa, get a grip!"

"That's Ryan Pierce," she shoots back.

She's got me there, so I remain quiet.

"How am I just finding out about you drinking wine all up in his house? You've got me all flustered right before my show now," she says, pouting. "You're hazardous to my career."

"Why are *you* flustered?"

"Because Ryan Pierce is in the audience! With my best friend!"

"I'm just getting you ready." I pat her on the shoulder. "You're welcome."

"Ready for what?"

"The spotlight." I pause, softening my tone as I pull her in for a quick hug. "Before you get your undies in a bunch, let me explain that I didn't expect him to be here any more than you did. He ordered a pizza, we talked, drank one glass of wine, and then—"

"You banged your customer?! What will your dad say about that?"

"What? No!" Someone from inside the bathroom stall sucks in a breath, and I lower my voice. "I was *going* to say it led us here, to your show. It happened in like five minutes. And do *not* say anything to my dad about banging customers. It's not true. Ryan does *not* want to have sex with me."

"Bullshit."

"What are you talking about?"

"He looks at you like stuffing on Thanksgiving. He wants to be inside you."

"That doesn't make any sense."

"You know what I mean," she says. "He's got sex eyes for you, and if you send out the right vibes, you'll be getting lucky in no time."

"That's not true. Plus, he's still a customer."

"Damn, what a night. Is your dad hiring? I wanna find myself a Ryan Pierce."

"You're missing the point." I smile though, happy to see her shoulders relaxing, a glimmer of a grin on her lips. "Stop focusing on me. Tonight is about *you.* This is a huge step for your career."

She shrugs. "Maybe."

"Maybe? Seriously! They called *you* tonight when Luke Donahue canceled. Luke Donahue! He just had a line on *Mod Family,* and he played a bit role in *Take Out.* People know Luke's name. You're going places, Lisa. It's finally happening! All these years of hard work are paying off."

She shakes her head. "I'm not ready for it. I thought I was, but all those people—I can't do it! I'm going to trip and fall, or piss my pants—it's inevitable."

"There are going to be more and more people watching you perform. That's just the way it's supposed to go. Be confident. You're sassy. You're bulletproof. You're funny, you're smart, and you're nice, somewhere deep down past all your sarcasm."

She laughs. "You'd have to dig deep to find the niceness."

"But I know it's there, and Ryan is just one of many famous people—athletes, movie stars, politicians, you name it—they will *all* be watching you perform in coming years. So get up there and kill it tonight!"

"I'm terrified."

"Pretend it's just me, Phil, and Bruce," I say. "We'll always be your number one fans. Just don't forget us when you're famous."

She pulls me in for a tight squeeze. I don't miss the way her hands tremble as they clench my back, or the way her voice cracks when she speaks. "What would I do without you?"

"Well, you wouldn't have met Ryan Pierce, that's for sure." I grin, stepping back. "You're welcome for *that*."

"Lisa, you're up next. Six minutes to go." A male head pops into the bathroom. "Finish your business and get out here."

"Bruce, stop sticking your head in the ladies' room," Lisa says.

The woman in the stall gulps another breath.

"And I don't know who you think you're fooling in there, Christine," Lisa calls to the stall. "I can see your shoes and I know you're trying to eavesdrop. Get out here, I need a vodka soda before I go on stage, please."

Our friend, the bartender at the Laugh House, coughs from the toilet. "Coming right up."

We file out of the bathroom, Lisa giving me a nervous glance before heading off into the wings, waiting for her name to be called.

"Everything okay?" Ryan asks.

There's a fresh glass of wine on the table, and I help myself to it. "Fine and dandy. She's going to rock it."

"I know she will."

"But if she bombs, you're still going to whistle like she won the World Series, you hear me?"

"Do you know what sport the World Series is for?" Ryan asks, eyebrow raised.

"Does it matter?"

He throws back his head and laughs, the sound covered by applause for the comedian on stage completing his set. Ryan claps along, both of us hooting and hollering as the MC takes the mic and introduces Lisa. That's when I stand, wave my hands, and do a sort of butt shake dance. Yes, I'm weird. When I finally sit back down, I look over at Ryan to see if he's embarrassed yet.

Instead of focusing on the bright lights, the onstage action, or the waitress asking if he'd like a refill, Ryan's eyes are fixed on me, and they're shining with something that looks like desire.

I guess he didn't mind my dance moves.

Positively boiling inside with happiness, I sit down, grab Ryan's hand, and together, we watch the show.

Chapter 13

Ryan

I'm an idiot.

Friends? I told her I wanted to be *friends*?

I've never seen anyone more alive. Her smile, her laugh, the way she moves her hips when she's whistling for her friend on stage—it's all driving me *insane*.

I need her, even if it's only for a night.

Look, I get it—I'm selfish. I live in Minnesota and she lives in Los Angeles, and long-distance relationships never work, especially in careers like ours. Comedians travel all the time, and so do athletes.

I *should* leave her alone. I *should* tell her I'll go to the wedding with my mom's annoying bimbo-bunny. I *should* quit with the pizza ordering from her dad's place before I get so out of shape I'm kicked off the Stars.

But I can't do it. I already said it—I'm selfish, and I want her.

Maybe not tonight, maybe not tomorrow—I'm patient, you see—but sometime, I need it to happen.

As much as I want her, I think she wants me too. If I can show Andi what sex is supposed to be like, maybe she'll forget about those other assholes who've come before me.

One hot night together would be a win for both of us, right?

Chapter 14

Andi

"You did *ah-mazing*." I grab Lisa at our designated meeting spot outside the club, each of us locking hands around the other's forearms, doing a little girlish dance in the style of Ring Around the Rosie. "You're a star, Lisa!"

"That scared the shit out of me." Lisa's eyes shine like two beams of light, and I can feel the nerves, the exhilaration, the adrenaline sizzling in the air. "I hated it, but I loved it. Damn, I don't know what's happening. I am going crazy! This is *amazing*!"

A shadow moves at my elbow. "You've reminded me how much I like going to comedy shows." Ryan slides one arm over my shoulder, the casualness of his gesture feeling natural. It's nice; I could get used to it.

Before my traitor of a brain wanders to dangerous territories—like wondering if Ryan Pierce might actually enjoy the company of the world's worst delivery girl—I pat Lisa on the shoulder again. "Congratulations. That was an awesome show. You nailed it, really."

"I have to agree." Ryan grins. "So, when's your next show?"

"What?" Lisa blinks up at him.

"Your next show," I say, patting Ryan on the chest, not sure how or why we've become so comfortable so quickly. I turn back to Lisa.

"When is it? We'll be there—or, I mean, I will, and maybe Ryan too, if he wants to come?"

"Of course," he agrees. "That's why I asked."

Lisa opens and shuts her mouth a few times. "That's a good question. Bruce, you got any more openings this week?"

Bruce the bouncer shrugs. "They don't tell me those things."

Lisa can't wipe the shit-eating grin off her face. "It feels different, Andi, when there's more than one person in the audience—different in a good way. And they *laughed*! At things *I* said! Can you freaking believe it?"

Another laugh bubbles up in my giddy friend.

"Of course I can believe it!" I tell her. "They loved you in there. I'll be surprised if you don't get a call to do the show next week. Hell, I'll be surprised if they invite Luke Donahue back at all. I think you might've replaced him."

"You think?" That flash of desperation, the self-doubt that never quite leaves a comedian's soul, appears in her eyes. "Anyway, I'm not gonna worry about it now. A few of the others are grabbing a drink at the bar. You guys wanna come?"

I flick my eyes up to Ryan and wait for his answer.

"I have an early meeting in the morning, so I can't make it," he says, "but Andi, if you want to stay, I'll call a cab and leave you my car, or vice versa."

"Of course, I understand," Lisa says. She releases me from the best-friend pact with a whisper. "*Go with him*. Thanks for coming in the first place."

"We wouldn't have missed it." I stop, clasping a hand over my mouth, wondering where on earth that *we* came from. Praying Ryan didn't notice, I continue quickly. "Your first big show was a success. You should celebrate all night long."

Lisa gives me one last hug and a knowing look, then disappears among the catcalls from her friends waiting at the bar.

I turn to face Ryan. He's wearing a grin the size of a banana.

"Where are *we* going next?" he asks, looping his arm through mine.

"Shut up," I say. "I thought this whole thing was fake, anyway."

"I didn't say I'd *fake* date you," he says. "I have to convince you to spend a weekend—or at least a few hours—with my family. I might as well make it worth your time."

"You're right," I say. "I could use a ride home, then."

"You got it, sweetheart."

Chapter 15

Andi

"This is neither my home, nor your home." I glance out the window after a short drive from the comedy club. We haven't yet entered the ritzy area of Los Feliz, but we also haven't made our way back to my stomping grounds. We are somewhere in between.

"You are accurate, but it is the best coffee shop around." Ryan looks across the center console to where I sit huddled in the passenger's seat. "Fancy a cappuccino?"

I narrow my eyes at him. "Is this another fake date?"

He climbs out of the car, and I beat him to the door this time. He takes my hand anyway and marches me to the front of the cafe. "It feels pretty real to me."

"I thought—"

"I'm kidding," he says. "Your car is at my house, and I assume you want to drive home tonight. You probably need another hour or two before you're good to go. I figure I might as well show you a good cup of coffee."

Of course, I say to myself. All in one sentence he's told me that I'd better find my way home tonight, that he has no intention of this being a real date, and that I'm probably an idiot for thinking this was anything more than an attempt to sober me up.

83

So I do what Andi Peretti does best—I make awkward conversation until the mugs arrive. Thankfully, they give my hands a nice distraction as I play with the spoon and the sugar packets.

Sitting across the table from Ryan Pierce is hard work. He's intimidating because he's so nice, not to mention smoking hot. So, I play with more sugar packets.

"This is the best espresso I've ever tasted." I sip my frothy, foamy, milky cappuccino. The diner is cute, small, and out of the way, so out of the way of normal LA traffic that we're the only customers at this hour, even though it's now two thirty in the morning. I suspect that soon, we might encounter the post-bar-closing rush.

My mind travels back to the way Ryan led me inside, his arm never leaving the small of my back, his fingers brushing the skin between the bottom of my tank and the top of my jeans. He didn't remove his hand when the waitress greeted him by name, or when she showed us to his "usual" table in the corner. Only when I removed my leather jacket and slid into the booth did he move to sit across from me.

"Hang on, you've got some foam right here..." He extends a thumb, hovering it above my lip. "May I?"

"Embarrassing." I swipe at my own lip, saving his fingers from having to remove the bit of froth just hanging out on my upper lip.

I'm an adult—I should be able to control where the food goes when I consume it.

Ryan brings his hand back, looking almost disappointed. Then, he reaches for my cup. "May I?"

"Have a sip? Go ahead." I look over at his cup. "I'd ask for a sip of yours, but I can't handle black coffee. It looks like mud."

Ryan takes a sip of my cappuccino, and when he pulls the cup away from his mouth, his lips are coated in foam.

I laugh at the image, a surprisingly loud sound in the quiet diner.

A waitress looks our way with a frown, but Ryan is oblivious to her. I shift in my seat and try to be oblivious, just like Ryan.

"May I?" I extend my thumb toward his lips, mimicking his actions.

Ryan's hand snakes out and clasps my wrist.

"You may..." His eyes twinkle. "But you can't use your hands."

My mouth goes dry. Then I say the *dumbest* thing that could possibly pop into my mind. "What do you want me to use?"

"For starters, your imagination."

I clear my throat, realizing I almost dropped the ball on flirting with Ryan Pierce. He just gave me another chance, and I'm not about to mess this one up.

"No hands, you say?" I try to be all calm and seductive, but I'm not convinced it's working. "Well, I can't reach you from all the way over there."

"We can fix that." He stands and gestures to the open space on my side of the booth. "May I?"

"I suppose I can make room." I scooch over the smallest bit. "Take a seat."

He sits, the scent of him enough to send my stomach into a rush of nerves. Those brown eyes melt mine as he leans close. "Go on, you can reach me now."

The drop of foam is all but gone by now since he ran his tongue over his lips. Even so, I think he might still want me to kiss him— but this isn't right; we agreed to be friends. Not go on dates.

"Let me give you a hint." Ryan leans toward me, his mouth balanced a hair's breadth from mine.

I find myself drawn toward him, tilting, my lips falling toward his, until—

"More coffee?" the waitress asks loudly.

Ryan, to his credit, doesn't look at all embarrassed. On the other hand, I look like a red hot chili pepper.

"I think I'm good." I push my mug forward and turn to Ryan. "I should head home, now, anyway. You said you have an early morning."

"I don't have an early morning," Ryan says, pulling his credit card out of his wallet and handing it to the waitress. "I just wanted some time alone with you instead of being crammed like sardines into a bar and going hoarse trying to talk over the music."

"Well, I do have class tomorrow," I tell him, trying not to show my surprise. "And I'm fine to drive now, really. I should be going."

"Thanks, Dianne," Ryan says pointedly to the waitress, who is standing there listening to us with unabashed curiosity. "That'll be all."

"Sorry," I say once she's gone. "I don't think she likes me much."

"She's just not used to seeing me here with anyone else. Whenever I'm staying with Lawrence—my brother—I make it a point to come here. Besides my brother and Lilia, I don't know many people, so I tend to come here alone."

"Oh, I'm sorry."

"No, I like it. Sometimes I need to get out of the house—it's not my house, and it's exhausting always being a guest. Sometimes it's a relief to just sit in the corner. Nobody recognizes me here. It was actually Dianne who gave me her copy of *Harry Potter* when she heard I hadn't yet read it."

My heart both warms and constricts at the thought of Ryan sitting here alone, in the corner, with nothing but a book for company. For some reason, the image carries both a sadness and a peacefulness with it.

"Ready?"

While I lose myself in a daydream, Ryan signs the check, leaves a twenty on the table, and stands. "I can bring you home."

"Your home is fine," I say. Then I quickly clarify, "I mean, to my car, which is at your home—or your brother's home, whatever. You know what I mean."

"There's an extra guest bed if you'd like to stay." That arm of his sneaks around my waist and he toys with the end of my shirt. "You're welcome to crash."

His hand, which is moving closer and closer toward my girl parts, is sending contradictory signals from what his mouth is telling me. His mouth is saying I can crash at his place as *one of the guys* while his hand is pretty damn close to getting in my pants. My stomach lights on fire, and I realize that if he tiptoed those fingers a few inches farther down, I wouldn't mind all that much.

Then Dianne, the waitress, gives me a scathing look as we leave the restaurant, and I'm brought back to reality. I'm Andi Peretti, struggling comic and delivery girl, and he's…well, he's Ryan.

"I'm fine to drive," I tell him. "Thank you for the offer, though."

Ryan pauses right outside the diner, holding the door open for me. "I know you're fine to drive." He winks then pulls me close, his arm low on my hip. "But that wasn't the question."

There are those damn mixed signals again. If he doesn't stop, I might just stay over…in his bed…without pants.

Chapter 16

Andi

"Were you born funny?" Ryan asks as we near his house. "Or is it something you've practiced?"

"Funny?" I smile. We've spent most of the ride home chatting about the comedy industry. Whether Ryan is actually curious or just trying to make small talk, I can't quite tell. "Being funny is way harder than it looks."

"I'll bet."

"I've written thousands of words, practiced hundreds of hours of standup, all to whittle my routine down to a ten minute punch that will hopefully make one person laugh."

"I'd love to see your bit."

I shake my head. "I'm too self-conscious."

"You just said you've practiced for hundreds of hours."

"That doesn't mean it gets any easier."

"Sort of like hockey, then."

"What do you mean?" I frown. "Don't you just use that little stick thingy to shoot the little black thingy toward the goal?"

"You think hockey is hitting a little black thing with a stick." He laughs, a sound that warms my heart. "I think being a comedian is saying funny things and making people laugh."

"Point taken," I say, a smile curving up my lips.

"I've practiced for hundreds of hours, skated for decades, dribbled, shot pucks, studied strategy—all of it, for most of my life, and it all comes down to a few minutes, most of the time. Either I choke on the winning goal or I nail it; there's not much of an in between."

"Huh." I sit, still pondering his words. "I've never thought of it like that before, but standup is the same. At the end of the day, when I get in front of the crowd, I either nail it or I bomb completely, all in a few minutes, despite the millions of words I've written to get there."

"It looks easy to everyone else, until they try it."

"Exactly!"

I'd never bonded over my passion with anyone except Lisa. It is so hard for my accounting friends or my business-oriented dad to understand it at all. The hours of preparation, the work that may never amount to anything, the pressure of those moments when it's finally time to perform, the sheer adrenaline of knowing I killed it onstage.

Ryan understands completely. I can feel it, both in his words and in the way he talks about hockey. We might be from different worlds, but we speak the same language.

It's then that Ryan parks his brother's BMW behind my car. I notice he leaves plenty of space. I also notice my bumper sitting on the sidewalk. It's cute; he's put a little blanket over it, almost as if to keep the thing warm.

"Oh," I say. "I'm really sorry about that."

"It's our new art installation," he says. "I like it."

"I bet your brother doesn't."

"I've convinced him to leave it for a while, until we can get you sorted—hopefully with a new car."

"Thank you," I say, and then wait for a long moment. Neither of us moves. "I had a really nice time tonight."

"Are you sure you don't want me to give you a ride home?" Ryan's eyebrows crinkle in concern. "We can figure something out for the morning. I can pick you up before class."

"No, I'm fine. The coffee helped, and it's been almost two hours since my last drink. Thanks, though, I appreciate it."

Ryan leans over the center console, bringing his hand behind my head and pulling me in toward him gently, as if giving me every opportunity to say *no*. I don't, because I'm not insane. Ryan Pierce is about to kiss me, and I'm going to let it happen.

But he doesn't *kiss* me; he merely brushes his lips against my cheek and whispers in my ear. "I'm going to see your standup routine, sooner or later," he says. "Mark my words."

I freeze. "Okay," I say, then get out of the car before I do something stupid and pucker up my lips for a kiss that will *never* come. "Have a great night."

"Andi—"

"I'll talk to you soon!" I'm already halfway out the door as he calls my name. I walk slowly to my car, giving him plenty of time to get my attention in case he has something else to say. He doesn't, apparently.

I climb into my clunker and make my way home on nothing but a prayer. I head straight to Peretti's Pizza, my mind whirling with whatever I got myself into tonight.

Shit, I think, making my way inside the restaurant.

I'm Ryan's fake girlfriend.

A few hours ago, I thought it was the best proposal ever.

But now, I'm not so sure. Being so close to Ryan but not being able to touch him is like being put in a room with an ice cream buffet and being told you can only look, maybe drool a little. Ryan Pierce is my ice cream buffet, and I want him bad.

Chapter 17

Ryan

I let her walk away. I should call her back, press my lips to hers like I know she wants. I can feel it, the electricity between us. Unless I've completely lost my touch, I'm pretty sure Andi wants me too. I thought she wasn't looking for anything physical, but I am beginning to think that's not accurate.

When I leaned in close, her breath hitched in her throat. She inhaled like she wanted something more than a wave goodbye or a ride home. I wanted more, too, but I missed the boat. Now it's too late, and she's halfway home while I'm stuck with a hard-on that won't quit.

So I climb into the shower—again—and take care of myself before getting into bed. I don't have an early meeting tomorrow, but I do have a chat with the Ice Queen at lunch, and lunch is going to come fast—just like I did while thinking about Andi Peretti and her curvy little figure.

On a whim, I pull out my phone and send her a text. It's simple, but I hope it's direct.

> Ryan: Preseason scrimmage in LA next Saturday.
> Come watch, and don't make plans after.

My phone beeps a second later with her response.

Andi: Is this a date?

I wait a few minutes before responding, but only because I can't think of what to say. I know I'm not letting her walk away again. If she comes to my game, watches me play, and lets me take her out to dinner after, I'll do everything in my power to get her back here. Alone. Naked.

I decide not to mince my words and respond quickly.

Ryan: Yes. Clothing is optional.

Chapter 18

Andi

"So, can you get us tickets?" Gio asks, leaning against the pizza counter while Angela fawns over his orange self. "Me and Ang wanna go."

Two weeks have passed since my deal was made with Ryan. I meant to go to his game last Saturday, but I was forced to work last minute by my dad, and one doesn't argue with my dad when he is *hangry*.

Ryan and I tried to hang out afterward, but he'd gotten a minor injury during the game and needed to ice and take care of it. Since then, we've been playing phone tag, and I have to admit the whole thing is fun—really fun.

He texts me horrible jokes to use for stand-up, and I text him back offering awful hockey advice. It sounds stupid, but…it's our thing.

"I can't," I say to Gio, Angela's boy-toy of the week. He's even oranger than she is, and probably spray tans more. I'm getting dizzy with the fumes from the pair of them. "Sorry."

Gio frowns, then reaches across the counter and drags Angela into his arms. He dips her so low her head nearly smacks the floor, and he gives her a sloppy, smoochy kiss. "See you at home, baby. I'm taking you out to dinner then. Screw hockey."

Angela sighs with gusto as Gio leaves. "Isn't he a hunk?"

I make a noncommittal noise in my throat. After catching a glimpse of Ryan in a towel, an orange-faced Ken doll just doesn't compare. "So are you two a *thing* now?"

"A thing?" Angela grins. "I don't know what you'd call it, but he slept over last night."

I shriek, pointing a finger in her face. "I knew it! You turned all lovey-dovey on me. I knew as soon as he called you *baby* that you'd slept with him! I thought you were just hooking up, but is this heading toward relationship territory?"

She bites her lip, throwing a pizza in the oven before turning back to me. "He's really sweet."

"I'm happy for you." I scoot around the counter, giving her a little slap on the rear end. "Get out of here. Go shower. Get ready for the big date."

"I'm supposed to close with you tonight."

"I got it," I say with a wave of my hand. "Go enjoy. Young love, so precious."

"You're sure you can handle it?"

"A few pizzas? No problem. My dad'll be here to cook, and I'll do deliveries if it gets too busy. Don't worry."

"You really are the best." She air-kisses my cheeks and disappears from the restaurant with a finger wave.

I prepare another pizza crust then pull out my phone and text Lisa.

Me: Want an extra twenty bucks plus tips? Need backup for tonight!

Her reply is immediate.

Lisa: I've got two hours. Be there in five.

Two hours later, Lisa and I have made and delivered six pizzas. I give her twenty bucks, she takes home another thirty in tips, and we are both happy. I'm just waving goodbye to her car as my dad arrives, ready to start closing up shop. He sort of comes and goes at the restaurant as he feels like it; I guess that's a perk of being the boss man.

I say hi to my dad but am interrupted by the ring of the restaurant phone line. Papa Peretti answers it and listens with a strange look on his face. I watch while wiping down the counter.

"Twenty?" he says, his voice weak. "Twenty."

My shoulders stiffen. Though I can't be sure, I have a pretty good guess as to who might be on the line.

"No, that's not a problem. She'll be right there." My dad hangs up the phone and gives me another strange expression. "We need twenty smiley face pizzas."

"Dad, we're about to close for the night!" I protest, wishing Angela had picked any night besides this one to go on a date with her new sleepover buddy. "I just let Lisa go. There's no way I can do it all myself."

"Then it's you and me, kiddo."

Kiddo? My dad's tone of voice is actually friendly. "I'll get started on the crusts. You work on the toppings."

We work in silence next to each other, just me and my dad cooking up twenty smiley face pizzas for a man who probably only did this to get my attention. I can't decide if it is cute, or…something else.

I've already agreed to go to the wedding with Ryan, so if this is his doing, I'm not sure why he felt the need to call the restaurant. I thought our relationship had progressed beyond pizzas.

"Why does anyone need twenty pizzas?" I grumble as we work on number twelve.

"I thought maybe you could tell me." My dad raises an eyebrow, glancing curiously at me as I straighten the nose on number ten. "The customer asked for you by name."

"Is that right?" My stomach tightens at the thought. Twenty pizzas—that couldn't be a date. Either it was a joke, or he was having a party.

"You dating my star customer, Andi?"

My head jerks up. "No, of course not. I'm just the delivery girl."

"I have other delivery girls, and none of them have sold so many pizzas to one person, and none of them are requested by name."

"What can I say?" I don't make eye contact. "I'm charming."

My dad snorts. "Right."

I put eyes onto pizza number fourteen. "Why's that so hard to believe?"

"Andi, you're many things—smart, sassy, beautiful—but charming?" He shakes his head. "I hope you know that if he ever makes you feel uncomfortable during these deliveries, you can tell me. I'll take care of things."

"Uncomfortable?" I think back to the way Ryan nearly kissed me in the diner. Uncomfortable? No. Exhilarated? Nervous? Ready for more? Check, check, and check. I try to hide the smile on my face. "No, Dad, it's nothing like that."

My dad stops what he is doing, crosses his arms. "You like this guy."

"No! Dad, just stop, please."

"You're sure? He's not being rude?"

"I'm sure, it's nothing like that." I pause. "He's sort of a friend."

I feel my dad sizing me up in that way only parents can. He's giving me time to see if I will admit to lying, to see if there will be more information between the lines, but I'm as confused as he is about this whole thing, so luckily, there *isn't* any information to hide.

"Well, if that's the case, then get on the road with these." My dad pushes two piles of boxes in my direction, apparently having decided that he believes me enough not to pry. "And if he asks you to marry him, say yes, but it'll cost him a hundred pizzas."

I put a hand on my hip. "You think I'm only worth a hundred pizzas?"

"A thousand?"

I roll my eyes. "I can't believe you're willing to trade me for pizza."

"Hey, you like him, I can tell." He shows me his hands in a sign of surrender. "Admit it, you'd be happy with the trade!"

I take the pizzas in two trips, hop in my car, and hit the road. I don't need to say anything out loud. I'd happily let my dad trade me for a hundred pizzas if Ryan would have me.

I wouldn't even ask for a tip.

Chapter 19

Andi

I park very, very carefully behind Ryan's car when I reach his brother's house, leaving at least ten feet of space between our vehicles, even though my car isn't the only one on the block. In fact, there are at least ten other cars, all of them more expensive than mine, most of them flashy.

I suddenly understand Ryan's need for twenty pizzas. He doesn't want to see *me*.

He's having a party.

I carry as many boxes as I can on the first go round to the front door and, true to form, it opens before I can knock.

"Howdy." The door is flung open, this time by the brunette woman I saw during a previous delivery—Lilia, if I remember correctly. She's pretty in a healthy, radiant sort of way. With an athletic build, form-fitting yoga pants, and an athletic tank top with a hoodie thrown over her shoulders, she looks every bit the picture of a physical therapist, which Ryan informed me is her profession of choice. "You're Andi?"

I raise my eyebrows. "I'm the delivery girl, but yes, I'm also Andi."

She winks then steps out of the entryway. "Come on inside."

I take one step inside the house, pretending I haven't already been here. "This is a beautiful home." I look at the brunette as I speak and she blinks, and then laughs. *She knows.*

"Yes, isn't it?" She glances around appreciatively. "Lawrence did a great job with it. I just moved in. Come along now, take your shoes off."

"I have to get the rest of the pizzas." I gesture to the car. "The order was for twenty pizzas, and I only have about eight here. The rest are on my front seat."

"I'll help you. Oh, I'm Lilia." She extends a hand, helping me set the first eight boxes down on the entry table. She slips on a pair of male sandals four sizes too big for her feet. "I'm Lawrence's fiancée. Come on, let's grab them before they get cold."

"You really don't have to…" I say, but she's already out the front door, and I get the vibe that this isn't a chick to argue with. I sort of like her.

Lilia speaks in a very businesslike and brisk manner, a don't-argue-with-me sort of tone that probably suits her physical therapy work well. I can see her ordering her patients to stretch and bend and move in all sorts of ways their bodies weren't meant to move. I also suddenly remember that it was *her* and her fiancé putting on the show the first night I delivered a pizza here, and I blush.

"You have such nice clothes on," I say, the labels of her expensive yoga pants not slipping past me. "I don't want you to smell like sausage."

"That's what the laundry machine is for." She marches onward, grabs half the pizzas from the car while I grab the other half, and we make our way back up to the front door. "You're the first girl he's ever invited to poker night, for the record."

"What? Who?"

"Ryan!" She eyes me over the pizza boxes. "That's why you're here, isn't it?"

"I wouldn't call delivering pizzas being *invited* over." I give an awkward laugh. "That's like catering a party and saying I'm one of the guests. Don't get me wrong though, we at Peretti's Pizza appreciate the business."

Awesome—now I sound like a pizza robot. I cringe as the words leave my mouth.

"Of course you're invited. We already ate." She gives me a curious sort of smile. "Ryan said he had to buy you the night off so you could come play with us. Apparently your dad is a stickler for you getting your deliveries done?"

A feeling stirs in my stomach, and I can't decide if I'm flattered or mildly annoyed. "Is that right?"

"You're not going to make a big deal out of me telling you this, are you?" She shifts her pizzas. "He was trying to be cute, I think. Please don't be mad at him."

"Oh, no, I'm not mad—"

"Good," she says. "Because he'll never tell you this, but I think he gets lonely out here. He's had to stay a week or two longer than he thought—this business with the agent is running him a little ragged with stress and, well, I think he likes spending time with you."

My heart is now melted. "I enjoy it too," I say quietly.

"Good! That's what I love to hear." She waves me over to the side of the path and lowers her voice. "And there's one other thing you should know. He's not like *them,* the other players. He's from Minnesota, and he acts like it."

"Like what?"

"Well..." She shifts. "He won't tell you any of this, but he's a nice guy, the sort of guy who wants a family someday, and kids, a dog, the big old Christmas cards tradition, you name it. He might *say* he's looking for a one-night stand or nothing but a friendship or whatever, but it's not true. So just be careful, okay?"

"Careful? We're just friends."

"Okay," she says with an unconvinced tone. "I'm just saying that he's going to be my brother-in-law, and I like the guy. I'm watching out for him. We all are."

"Just friends," I say again. "Promise."

She eyes the pizza, but by this time we're already at the door. Stopping once more on the front steps, she lowers her voice and leans close to me. "All I'm saying is you're the first girl I've seen him bring home in a while."

"I'm the *delivery* girl."

"But you're here, aren't you?"

I hesitate. "Lilia, if you don't mind me *asking,* why didn't he just ask me to spend time with him tonight instead of…this." I gesture to the boxes. "He could've just asked."

Her eyes fall on the pizzas. Then she grins. "I knew I liked you," she says. "And I'm happy Ryan's finally found a girl with her head on her shoulders."

"We're just friends."

"Has he taken you to that dinky little diner?" she asks. My astonishment must show, because she continues. "Ryan doesn't take anyone there. It's his special alone place or whatever. He'd kill me if he knew I called it that."

I laugh harder. "It doesn't mean anything, we just wanted coffee."

"Take your shoes off and stay a while," she says, ignoring my arguments. "We all want you to be here. I live here, so I'm inviting you inside."

"I'd love to, but my dad's alone at the pizza place tonight."

She raises her eyebrows. "Have you checked your phone recently?"

"No, why?" I move to get the phone out of my jeans pocket, but my hands are full.

Lilia leads the way inside, relieving me of the pizza boxes.

I look at my phone, and sure enough, there is a text from my dad.

Dad: Andi, is that you? This is your dad.

Me: Dad, you don't have to identify yourself. I have
your number.

My phone pings before I can slide it back into my pocket.

Dad: A very nice man called asking for my permission
to invite you in for a poker night, and then he tipped the
company two hundred bucks. You'll go and you'll play
that poker game, do you understand me?

Me: Dad, are you pimping me out for pizza?

Dad: Don't use that language with me.

Me: I can if it's true!

Dad: None of your other boyfriends have asked me for
permission to take you on a date.

Me: What if I don't want to go?

Dad: You do. I've never seen you so excited for a
delivery. And his sister-in-law will be there. She's a
doctor.

I look up now, scrunching up my eyebrows at Lilia. "Did you talk
to my dad on the phone?"

She nods. "Ryan called to leave a tip, then asked if he could tip
enough to give you the rest of the night off. Your dad had a few
choice words to say to him."

"My dad can be overprotective."

"He just loves you." Lilia smiles. "So Ryan asked him permission
to take you out on a date—a real date—and said that tonight was just

a friend thing. Then I popped on the line, and we got to chatting about physical therapy, and finally he agreed. Your poor dad thinks I'm a nice girl, but boy is he wrong."

She winks and I laugh, but it isn't genuine, because I'm focused on the first part of the statement.

"A real date?" I ask weakly.

"A *real* date," she echoes. "Your dad said it's okay, as long as he picks you up and drops you off before midnight tomorrow. Oh, by the way, you have a date tomorrow."

"Nice of my dad to plan my love life for me." Even though I have a snarky retort for Lilia, part of me shivers with excitement. I've never had a man ask my father permission before he dated me, let alone one as handsome and successful as Ryan. "And remind me how you're involved?"

"I took the phone when your dad asked for references."

I almost faint. "My dad asked Ryan for references?"

"It was cute! So I vouched for Ryan, told your dad I'm marrying Ryan's brother, that I'd stick around tonight to help you as needed. I also had to give your dad my name, phone number, and Social Security number."

"What?!"

"I'm kidding. Your dad just wanted to know you're safe." She grins. "He might seem as if he'll trade you for a stack of pizzas and a hundred-dollar tip, but he'd never. He loves you, I can tell."

My dad has the strangest way of showing affection, but since my mom isn't around anymore, he does his best. With a sigh, I decide to play nice with my dad, even if he's meddling in my love life like his old Sicilian grandmother.

Me: Dad, I'm here with Lilia. She's nice. I'm going to play a game of poker and hang out for a couple hours. I'll be home in a bit.

Dad: Curfew of two a.m.

Me: I'm too old for a curfew.

Dad: You live at home, my rules.

I sigh then look up at Lilia. "I have 'til one thirty. Shall we deliver these pizzas to the boys?"

"We already ate," she says on a laugh. "Let's leave them in the kitchen for a midnight snack. With hockey boys in the room, they'll be gone in a second."

Chapter 20

Ryan

I can't tear my eyes away from the damn door.

I hear them talking in the kitchen—Lilia and Andi—laughing and chatting and going on and on as if I'm not sitting here in my chair, so anxious to see her that I just folded a pair of pocket aces.

But it's worth it, because now she's there, standing in the doorway, red collared shirt and all, looking hot as hell in her tight jeans. Her curvy figure taunts me, breasts straining beneath the slightly-too-small uniform. She offers me a smile, and I wonder if I'm having an aneurysm.

My breath catches in my chest, and that's when I know I'm an idiot. I told her we shouldn't—no, *demanded* we not get involved, and now I can hardly remember how to speak when I'm in the same room as her.

"Hey," I say with a quick smile. I force myself to turn back to the cards and lay a hand down. It's the most difficult thing I've ever done. My eyes don't want to leave her. It's not enough to play these little games together, to have her popping in and out of my life. I want more.

And that terrifies me. After all, I just booked my flight to take me back to Minnesota in two days. I shouldn't have called her over with the pizzas, but I needed to see her one more time before I leave the state. I won't be in Los Angeles again until after my brother's wedding.

Lawrence and Lilia are getting married in the Cities, so these are my last few days to make sure Andi knows how I feel about her, knows I want her to be there, by my side, at Lawrence's wedding. Even better? I want to make it very, very clear that I think this friendship shit is overrated. I want her, in my bed, as soon as possible.

But I suppose it's too late for that. Maybe we're already friends.

"Take a seat," I say with a smile, and she moves hesitantly across the room. "We've got Mo, Brad, Dick—all of them agents. Nicky and Archer play for the LA Lightning," he says, gesturing to a few big, burly dudes who also have shaggy hair. Only the agents are clean cut and dressed in suits. "You already know Lawrence and Lilia."

Andi nods to them all. "I'm Andi," she says with a shy smile. "I'm your delivery girl."

Something about the way she says it is adorable, and the guys break into laughter. She's been welcomed into the gang, and they deal her into the next hand.

Her eyes focus on the cards so thoroughly, I wonder if she even notices my presence. Finally, once it's Brad's turn and he's sitting over there picking his nose, wondering what those numbers are on his cards, I turn to her. "Thanks for coming," I say. "I hope you don't mind that I made you drive over here."

A smile turns her lips up. Then she makes eye contact with me, the blue-green color like Mediterranean water. I can't stop staring at them even when she begins to speak. "I'm happy to be here. Sorry I couldn't be at your game a few weeks ago, I had to work."

I flick over my cards, wondering for the millionth time if she's just saying that. She'd called to apologize about missing the scrimmage, and I don't care about that. I'm just worried that she feels trapped into playing my girlfriend to impress my mother. It would work, too; my mother would adore this girl. Smart, cute, comes from a big family, helps her dad out—she's an angel.

"Can I talk to you for a second?" I ask when she folds. I fold too, even though I'm close to a flush. "In the kitchen."

"Sure," she says, a hint of confusion at the edge of her voice.

Lilia flashes me a smirk as we leave the room, and I'm left wondering what exactly was said between the two women. If Lilia embarrassed me or made Andi uncomfortable, I'm not going to be happy.

"Lilia's great," Andi says as soon as we reach the kitchen. "Really fun to finally meet her, er…face to face."

Now I understand: Andi caught my brother boning his soon-to-be wife and, even though we're all happy they love each other, nobody wants to see that. No wonder she's a little uncomfortable tonight.

"About that," I say. "They're not shy, so don't worry about it. Unfortunately, I've also seen more than I'd like to."

"Oh, no, it's not that." She runs a hand almost nervously over her collarbone. Then all at once she looks up, those brilliant eyes meeting mine. "Why didn't you just call and ask me to come hang out?"

I see the stacks of pizza in the background and feel my stomach sinking. "Christ, I'm sorry, Andi. I didn't even think about the *work* going into these things, I just thought…well, I wasn't thinking. I wanted to see you, and I was trying to be funny. I suck at it, and I'm sorry."

"No, it *is* cute." She steps closer to me. "But you don't *have* to be cute. I like hanging out with you, and we agreed to do this *getting to know each other* thing. Otherwise, it won't be realistic for us to go to a wedding together. I mean, we can't show up to your parents' house and have you wondering if I like coffee or not—everyone would see right through the ruse. If we're pretend dating, we have to know a few things about each other."

"I know you like coffee," I say with a wink. "What else do you like?"

She gives a soft laugh. "All I'm saying is that I expected we'd hang out when I agreed to do this thing. You can save your money—you don't have to order pizzas or tip me or any of that. We're friends."

"Friends," I echo. "Right."

We watch each other in silence for a long moment. Mostly, I use this time to give myself a pep talk. *Don't be a pansy*, I tell myself. *Say how you feel, dickhead.*

"Andi—" I say, finally gathering up the courage.

Right then, Lilia walks into the room.

I love Lilia like a sister, but I want to punt her out of the kitchen in that moment. My hands flex into fists as she bites into a slice of pizza and turns to face us. "What's up, guys?"

I roll my eyes as she gives me a knowing expression, and I'm wondering if Andi said something to her about us, about this friend thing we're trying out. Is Lilia trying to prevent us from getting involved? She *has* to know I left the room—alone—to get Andi by herself, so why is she being the biggest cockblock in the room?

I need to *finally* put my lips on Andi's and kiss her until she forgets all about this stupid friendship idea. I need to show her that I've changed my mind, that I want something different.

That I'm changing the damn rules.

That I want her in my bed.

Now.

Chapter 21

Andi

"I fold." I shake my head. "Crap cards, Nicky. Thanks for nothing."

"About time." Ryan winks at me, and I'm reminded of the moment we shared in the kitchen an hour earlier. "You've been taking our money all night."

I laugh, playing along, but I'm still wondering what he wanted to say while we were alone, if he had wanted, possibly, to tell me what I so desperately wanted to hear. But Lilia, bless her heart, had interrupted, and Ryan and I haven't been able to sneak away since.

I might be the pizza delivery girl, but I also know how to hold my own in a card game, and I took no mercy on these men. I have the most chips out of anyone at the table, and I'm not planning on letting up any time soon.

Lilia sits cuddled next to Lawrence while the agents and hockey players are in various displays of lounging, beers in hand.

"So, I hear we have a wedding coming up," I say to Lilia and Lawrence. "How long have you two been together?"

"Almost three years," Lilia says. "Can you believe it? We met while living in two different states. We lived apart for a while while we both got our careers established, but we always got back together."

"Until I finally put a ring on it and told her I wouldn't tolerate any more nights apart." Lawrence winks. Despite Ryan's assessment of his brother as a dick, any time Lilia is in the room, Lawrence is a big, squishy teddy bear. He looks at me. "I hear you might be coming to the wedding."

Lilia looks up, surprised. Apparently she hasn't heard the news yet.

I glance at Ryan, not sure whether he's told anyone else our plan, or if he's keeping it a complete secret. "Possibly."

Lilia gives Ryan a curious stare. "Really."

"Really." Ryan meets her gaze. Then he glances back to the cards. "My deal?"

"We'd love to have you," Lawrence says. "Ever been to Minnesota before?"

I shake my head. "I've never had a reason to go."

"Well, it's a treat," Lawrence says, and I can't tell if it's sarcasm. "You'll need a week to come down from culture shock when you return to LA—our parents own a farm."

"That sounds like an experience," I agree.

"Enough with the wedding talk," Ryan says. "Pick up your cards and focus."

I look at my hand, wondering if Ryan's upset. He's acting normally otherwise, smiling and laughing and touching my leg now and again, so it's hard to say. I push the thought away, focusing on the game, which ends up paying off big time.

A few rounds later, I've stolen even more of the boys' money. Lilia isn't playing anymore—she's lying with her head in Lawrence's lap, eyes closed, looking all too comfortable.

I'm not even trying to win anymore, but competitiveness is ingrained in me. Working at Peretti's Pizza has given me a good base for card games. My dad taught me poker at a young age. When deliveries were slow, we'd need something to pass the time, and my dad was ruthless.

I've gone home many a night with no tips, but eventually I learned, and now my dad never asks to play anymore. He mostly likes to win.

Unlike my dad, the hockey guys aren't poor sports. They're good sports, which makes the game all the more fun.

"Babe, we should get you in bed. You have a meeting in the morning." Lawrence leans over and plants a kiss on Lilia's cheek. "And if we don't leave right now, I won't have enough money to pay our mortgage next month, since Andi here is sweeping the table."

I laugh then push a stack of chips in Lawrence's direction. "Here, I wouldn't want you to be homeless."

"Oh, he's being a baby." Lilia grins, pushing the chips back. "But I am ready for bed. Goodnight y'all. Behave."

I catch a movement out of the corner of my eye—it's Lilia, Lawrence, and Ryan all exchanging some look I can't quite interpret.

"I'll lock up," Ryan says. "Good night."

Mo stands up, too, waving to the table. "Pleasure playing with you all—except for you, Andi. It was a disaster playing with you. I should be heading out before I lose my cab fare."

I push chips toward him, but he extends a hand and shakes mine.

"You won, fair and square," he says. "But you're not invited back, sorry."

"Andi's got until one thirty this morning," Lilia says as she leaves, the rest of the group trailing after her and Lawrence. "Best get her back on time, Ryan, so her dad doesn't ban us from Peretti's Pizza. Those are damn good pizzas."

With that, she's gone.

Ryan and I look at each other over the stack of chips and cards.

"So, we've got an hour?" Ryan eventually says, his eyes twinkling in the now empty room.

I blink. "Guess so."

"What on earth could we do with an hour?"

I glance around the cozy room, taking in the comfortable ambiance, the sparkle in Ryan's eyes. "How about you tell me what you were going to say in the kitchen before Lilia interrupted."

Footsteps sound as Lilia and Lawrence make their way to the second floor. He waits until they pass, and then gives me a piercing gaze that does things to my heart. "You don't have to go through with this wedding thing," he says. "I've had some time to think about it, and...it's stupid. It's too much to ask of you."

"Oh," I say, not having expected that. I *should* have expected he'd realize this was all a horrible idea—bringing *me*, delivery girl extraordinaire—to a Pierce wedding. "Well, I don't have to come, it's no big—"

"That's not what I meant." His face scrunches up as if all the words have come out wrong. "What I *meant* is that I don't want you to feel pressured into going with me. I'd feel pretty shitty if that were the case."

"It's a little favor. I feel shitty for bumping your car."

"It's just a few bucks," he says. "That was nothing. I'm taking you to a whole new *state*."

A few bucks means two very different things to Ryan and myself. A few bucks to fix Ryan's car was nothing to him, but if he'd made me pay, I'd have been working overtime for a month to pay it off.

"Do you want to come to the wedding with me, Andi?" he asks then. "Forget favors, forget any of it. I like you. I think it'd be fun to go together, and I'll pay for everything. If you want to come as my date, I'd love to have you."

"As your date?"

"Andi." This time, his voice comes out low, husky.

I lean toward him, listening, waiting with bated breath for whatever will follow, and as it turns out, it isn't words. His lips ease toward mine, slowly, gently, until they touch.

Once our lips meet, gentle flies out the window, and it's a tangle of heat, of pent-up desire and passion radiating through my veins.

"I don't want to be your *friend*, Andi."

I can't think, can't speak. All I know is that I want him just as much as he wants me. My fingers wind through his hair and pull tight. I'm loving the feel of his soft locks beneath my fingers.

He groans at the motion then pulls me onto him. It's commanding and fast, and when he positions me on his lap, I can feel him beneath me. He is packing quite the hockey stick. I might be the delivery girl, but he's the one with the package.

His fingernails dig into my hips, and I can't think anymore. I just feel. He grinds against me and as we kiss, grope, my thoughts going black, my desire growing, I let myself be taken completely away— until suddenly, I pull back. I can't do *this*.

I'm about to orgasm from dry humping. This hasn't happened since high school, and I gasp, moving to a half-standing position over him. I can't do this. It's embarrassing. I mean, it's fun, but—no, not the first time, not with Ryan Pierce.

"What's wrong?" His voice is a gravelly road leading me all sorts of places I want to go. "Come to bed with me."

"I have to get going home," I say, cringing as I say it. "Curfew."

The sound he makes is almost animalistic, pained at the idea of stopping.

"I know," I say, and then because it's the only thing I can logically think to do, I sit back down, straddle his lap, and begin the rocking motion again. *Screw curfew*. I'm twenty-three-years old—if I want to wiggle around on Ryan Pierce, I'm going to do it. "Don't stop."

"Andi, no, I've got to get you…"

I imagine he wanted to say the word *home*, but it doesn't make it out because I run a hand on the front of his pants, and he loses all track of what he's saying.

His tongue returns to my mouth with a vengeance, licking, sucking, biting—he's a god with that thing. I swear, that man is about to finish me off while we're both still clothed, thanks to some good old-fashioned making out and a tongue that's MVP in the tonsil-hockey league.

Then his hand comes up to my jeans, groping, caressing through the thick denim there. Even that sends lightning shooting through every one of my atoms, but it's not enough for either of us.

"Get these fuckers off," he says, and I'm pretty sure he's talking about my pants because his hands move to fiddle with the buttons. "*Now.*"

I raise my hands and help him with the buttons. We don't take the time to pull my pants down farther than my thighs. He's got his hand inside them, and that's all that matters. He's about to send me into space like a rocket, and all he's doing is running a hand over the thin, lacy fabric guarding my no-longer dusty vagina.

"You are so wet," he says. "Shit. Damn. Hell."

"Colorful," I say of his vocabulary. "Don't you dare stop, Pierce."

He muffles a half laugh into my neck as he bites at my skin there. If I don't have a hickey, I'll be surprised. Then I surprise myself further because I wind my fingers through the back of his shaggy hair and pull his mouth to my neck.

He creates a light suction, running his tongue along the sensitive skin while his fingers run along the edge of my panties. I squirm with pleasure, with need. His fingers toy with the edge of the lace until one of them dips underneath and I suck in a breath sharp enough to crack a rib.

The moan coming out of my mouth sounds like a bobcat, or a horse, or…something—I can't think. His finger strokes me, toying, teasing, not giving me exactly what I need. His eyes are lit with playful lights.

"Stop teasing me, Pierce," I warn, and then I slide my hips downward.

He laughs, softly. "Say my name."

"Pierce."

"Ryan." He withdraws his finger as punishment, and I'm ready to cry. He meets my eyes, those chocolate chip irises making my insides turn to lava. "Say it," he instructs. "And mean it."

I last as long as I can, but even my stubbornness—which is legendary in the Peretti family—breaks. "Please, Ryan," I whisper. "I need you."

"Not yet," he murmurs back, but before I can argue, he slides his finger past my panties, and I close my eyes with pleasure. From here on out, it's ecstasy as he drives me toward the finish line.

"Let yourself go, Andi."

I do as he says, his name slipping from my lips as I ride a wave of pure pleasure—the longest, tallest, widest wave I've ever been taken on in my life. It engulfs me whole, swallows every thought, crashes my mind into darkness. The tremors don't stop until I'm completely spent, sagging onto his chest, my arms around his neck.

His hands circle my back, his fingers caressing my waist. I could lie here all day on his chest, his soft, warm breaths tickling my neck—until I remember that I'm the only one who's been satisfied at all.

"Oh, my God," I say. "I'm so selfish. Let me…"

He clasps my wrist in his hand as I reach for his pants. "No," he says. "You need to get going. I'll bet your dad is waiting up for you, and I don't want to be responsible for returning you home late."

"I'm an adult."

"And I respect your father," he says. "Do it for me."

"But…" I turn my lips into a pout, my hands reaching for him. "It's not fair! I want to make you feel as awesome as you made me feel."

"I feel just fine," he says. "Although I can't promise I'm not hoping we can do this again sometime."

"There are a lot of negatives in that sentence."

"That's the Minnesota coming out of me," he says. "Let me put it bluntly: I loved touching and feeling you, Andi, but I want more. What are you doing tomorrow night?"

"I have a show."

"It's my brother's bachelor party. We're doing a joint thing with Lilia and a few of her friends. Come with us. We need more people; a few of my brothers can't make it to town."

"I'm sorry, I would, but I can't," I say with a wry smile. "I can't miss my show. I made the commitment already."

"Come out after. I need to see you."

"You know what it's like from hockey," I say, my face rife with apology. "It's just like hockey—if you had a game, you couldn't miss that either, could you?"

"No."

"Well, this is the same thing except I'm not chasing a hard little black circle around on ice skates."

"Well, when you put it like that, hockey sounds pretty pointless."

I shrug. "I stand on stage and make myself look like a fool in the hope that other people will laugh. I'm not sure who's gotten the short end of the stick in this deal."

Shaking his head, he laughs and stands. "Can I drive you home tonight? It's late."

"No, my car's here. I have class in the morning, some deliveries, and then my show. Maybe this weekend we can meet up if you're free."

He looks disappointed, but he does a decent job hiding it as he nods. "I'll give you a call tomorrow."

I glance at my watch. If I rush, speed through every traffic light and jump a few medians, I just might make it home on time. Before I leave, however, I reach for him, kiss him lightly on the lips, and then pull back. "Thank you for everything tonight. I had a lot of fun, more fun than I've had in quite a long while."

"You need to get out more—specifically, with me, tomorrow night. Lilia wants you to be there."

"I'll call you when I'm done with the show. That's the best I can do." I wave and take a few steps down the front lawn. "I promise if there was a way I could get out of the show, I would. I'm sorry."

He remains silent, a hand coming up to return my wave in a stiff gesture.

There are no more words to be said, but the entire drive home I'm thinking about the look on his face as I stepped into my car. I'm almost certain he wanted me to stay.

Picking up my phone, I debate quickly between Angela and Lisa, decide on Lisa, and hit dial.

"Hey," she says. "What's up? Everything ok?"

She was obviously sleeping, and I realize how late it is. At the same time, I'm realizing that maybe I want to keep this moment private, a secret between Ryan and me, at least for now. "Sorry, butt dial," I say. "Goodnight Lisa."

"You woke me up for that?"

"Sorry," I say. "Go back to bed."

"Asshole."

"Love you too."

Chapter 22

Andi

When I push open the door to our small home in a deteriorating neighborhood on the almost-east side of Los Angeles, my dad is there, sitting at the kitchen table in full alert mode. The slight scent of marinara sauce lingers in the homey kitchen, which hasn't changed a lick since my mother died.

The scent suggests my dad didn't feel like cooking tonight. The beer in front of him suggests he's had a long night of waiting. I cringe, but there's no going back now.

"Do you like him?" Papa Peretti asks as he looks up from his half-empty beer.

"Who?" It's not a good answer to the question, but I don't have anything better to say.

He gives me a look that tells me he knows I'm full of it, and I flinch. "The boy, Andi, the one who called here today. Do you like him?"

"He's nice," I say. "Tips really well."

"That's not what I meant."

"I don't know Dad, it's too early to tell."

"Sometimes you just know these things."

I remember the feel of Ryan's lips on mine, his fingers squeezing

118

my hips, the look of those chocolatey brown eyes as he said my name. Then I change the subject. "If you could go back and fall in love with Mom all over again, knowing she wouldn't be here today, would you do it?"

His eyes close for a brief minute.

"Sorry." I take a seat at the table and squeeze my dad's hand. "Forget I said anything."

My dad and I are not ones for serious heart-to-heart conversations. We're hardly ones for conversations at all unless they involve yelling at each other over pizza orders.

"Forget I said anything," I say. "I know you don't like to talk about it."

"Her," he says. "I'm always willing to talk about *her*."

I hang my head, the somber moment seeping throughout the room. The ache in my heart comes back, stronger than before. My dad hasn't figured out how to live without her yet, not successfully at least. I'm not sure any of us have.

"I'd do it all over in a second," he says. "A hundred times, a million times."

"But this heartache…"

"Is a sign that I did at least one thing right in my life." My dad has these furry brown eyebrows and they crinkle, his expression filled with pain mixed with joy as he looks at me. "Your mother was the best thing that ever happened to me, and I'd never have known what it meant to love unless I'd met her."

"But—"

"There are no buts," he says. "That's it. I loved her, love her still, and that's all. She's the best part of me, even if she's not here physically. She's still *here*, Andi."

I fall silent, lost in my thoughts, wondering how on earth we even got onto this subject. I'm not in *love* with Ryan; I'm hardly in *like* with him. We've just met. "Ryan asked me to go to a wedding with him, as friends. Sort of like a date, but…it's complicated."

My dad swirls his beer around and looks at me. "Are you friends?"

"I suppose."

"Does he treat you well?"

"I hardly know him, Dad."

"Do you want to go?"

I pause, considering everything, and I finally nod. "I don't know why, though. It'd be easier not to go."

"Go," he says.

I blink at him. "What?"

A smile turns his lips upward, and for the first time since my mother's funeral, I see tears smarting in his eyes. "Go. What's the worst that can happen? You have a horrible time and come back to your family, your studies, your work?"

"I suppose."

"Have I told you how I met your mother?"

"No," I lie. He's told me many times before, but I love hearing the story.

"It was Christmas, and we were both shopping for gifts for our significant others. I had a girlfriend, she had a boyfriend, and there was exactly one Beach Boys album left."

"The Beach Boys?"

"A joke," he says. "We had the same taste in gag gifts."

"What happened?"

"I let her have it, of course," he says with a wry smile. "I was a gentleman."

"Yeah, right."

"Fine, she was beautiful and I wanted her to like me."

"But you were both dating other people."

"Exactly," he says. "So of course nothing happened. We parted ways until exactly one year later, when I saw her while looking for Christmas gifts again. This time, we were shopping for ourselves."

"Two bad breakups?"

"Within days of each other," he says. "I still didn't know her name when I asked her out to dinner that very night. We were engaged six months later."

My heart warms and aches all at once. My father might be many things—abrasive, stoic at times—but he always loved my mother more than anything. I saw it, my siblings saw it, and that's why none of us has married yet. We haven't found that sort of love.

"The reason I'm telling you this story again—yes, I know you were lying. I've told you this story many times before."

I laugh. "I love hearing it."

"I love to tell it," he says. "It brings her alive again."

"I'm so sorry, Dad." I pull him in for a hug. "I don't know what else to say."

I hear him swallow over the lump in his throat, which surprises me. Of all nights to get emotional, I hadn't expected my night with our star customer would be the inciting incident for our first real talk in a long while.

"You don't have to say anything." He pulls back, takes a drink of beer. "What I'm trying to say is that sometimes, these chance opportunities come along, and you need to take them. Take your chance and run because you never know where the path may lead."

I smile and sit with my dad until he finishes his drink. He stands first, depositing the bottle into the recycling bin. I stand too, pulling my polo tight around me.

"When's the wedding?" he asks.

"The twentieth," I say. "A few weeks away."

"You have that week off work," he says. "Angela will cover, and I'll call your friend Lisa. She does a good job."

"She does a horrible job."

"Don't worry about it," he says with a grin. "Goodnight Andi."

"Night Dad."

That night, I find myself too excited to sleep—excited about my night with Ryan, the upcoming trip, and maybe, just maybe, the possibility of something more.

Chapter 23

Andi

My lack of sleep shows the next morning. I wake up early, too excited to lay around in my bed, so I pass the time working on new material. It's only seven in the morning, and I've already come up with a new bit to test during my show tonight.

As I brush on some foundation to cover the bags under my eyes, a pang of regret strikes when I remember that I'll be missing the bachelor/bachelorette party tonight. I can't be *that* disappointed, however. After all, I'll be accompanying Ryan to the real wedding, which is much more exciting than a night out at the bar.

The more I think about it, the higher my hopes drift, and the higher my hopes drift, the easier it is to forget that this whole thing is a ruse. I'm to be Ryan's fake girlfriend to save him from having to go with one of his mom's picks. Even though he posed it like a date, he meant as friends; both of us were clear that there would be—could be—nothing more.

On the positive side of things, after last night, there is no doubt in my mind that he wants me just like I want him—physically, all of him, all the time.

Maybe we could do this thing in a way that meant we could have awesome sex and then call it quits after the wedding, no strings attached. People do that all the time, right? Not *me*, necessarily, but I bet Ryan has done it plenty of times before.

That's what puck bunnies are for, if I'm not mistaken. I might not be very familiar with hockey, but I know the meaning of the term: girls hanging around the rinks, throwing themselves at the men for a chance at their beds. Maybe he thinks *I* wouldn't want that, I realize as I swipe on some mascara. Maybe if I bring it up to him, he'll be interested in rearranging our deal to include sex.

If he can use the stick in his pants like he uses his fingers, I'll be in for a treat. Plus, it isn't fair that he got me off and I have yet to return the favor. I pull out my phone, intending to call him and ask for an update to our agreement.

As soon as I hit the dial button, however, I cancel the call. *No,* I tell myself. That's not a phone call to make at seven thirty on a Monday morning; it's probably something we should discuss in person, anyway...or maybe we could just have sex first and talk about it later. I am all about ignoring problems until they can't be ignored any longer.

If we both enjoyed the sex enough, why would we need to *have* a problem? Like my dad said, worst-case scenario is I come home from Minnesota and resume my daily life here in Los Angeles. No harm, no foul.

Whether or not Ryan actually gets traded doesn't make a huge difference. The way I see it, if he does move out here, I'll never see him...unless he keeps ordering pizzas from me; then I suppose we'd have to talk about things. Maybe. If he doesn't move, well, we'll be thousands of miles apart.

My phone rings, cutting off my wandering thoughts. I look down in horror to find Ryan's name on the screen. *Shit.* He saw me dial him and hang up. I can probably blow it off as a butt dial on my way to class.

Speaking of class, I'm about to be late, and I can't take another tardy in my econ class. I grab my backpack, shove my legs in some jeans, my feet in some booties, and my arms into a black t-shirt. It's my go-to uniform—it takes me from school to work to the comedy clubs without having to change more than my shirt and the amount of mascara on my lashes.

I take the steps two at a time. "See you this afternoon, Dad!"

"Andi, there's—" my dad yells back, but I'm already out the door.

I feel a little bad, but he can text me if it's that serious. I am *late*, and I'm planning on walking the half mile to school since it takes longer to find parking on the stupid campus than to hoof it on foot.

My phone rings again when I'm halfway to the sidewalk—Ryan again. *Shit.* My finger hovers over the accept button. It wouldn't take all that long to explain about the butt dial, but at the same time, I'm *really* late.

I press the ignore button.

Somehow, I still hear his voice.

"Blowing me off?" Ryan asks. "Nice to see you, too."

My head jerks up and around after I first check my phone. The call isn't connected, so I turn my attention to the sound of his voice, and that's when I see him. There, in all its glory, is his gorgeous body perched against a car, his t-shirt form-fitted around sexy, strong arms. In his hands—those hands that made me feel amazing just last night—he holds two coffees.

"What the hell are you doing here?" I ask. Then I raise a hand to cover my mouth. "I'm sorry. I mean, what brings you around on this fine morning?"

"You didn't answer your phone."

"You couldn't possibly have gotten here since I didn't answer..." I trail off, realizing he's joking. "Funny. I'm running really late to class. I promise I was going to text you as soon as I got there."

"Get in." He shifts, pointing to the car behind him. It's a third car, neither the BMW nor the Ferrari. I'm not sure where he got this one, but it's probably best if I stay away from moving vehicles with my track record.

"Oh, I was just going to walk. It's not far."

He grins a cheeky smile that compels me return it. "I brought you coffee."

"What?! You drove across town, in morning rush hour, to give me a cup of coffee?"

"You've delivered plenty of things to me, and I figured it was my turn."

"But..." I trail off. "You're nuts."

"I wanted to see you," he says. "You're late to class. Get in the car and let me drop you at the doors. Parking sucks around there."

"Well, if you're sure."

"If I get five more minutes with you, it's worth it."

"Who turned you into Romeo?" I give in, taking quick steps toward the car. I grin to make sure he knows I'm kidding, and then accept the proffered coffee.

He kisses me on the cheek as I take the cup from him, the sweet scent of espresso and frothed milk rising to meet my nose.

It's a familiar scent, and I raise my brows at him. "This is from your favorite little coffee shop."

"Tell me it's not your favorite now, too." He opens the door for me, assists me inside like I'm some fragile doll, then presses a kiss to my forehead before he closes the door. "Keep your hands and arms inside the vehicle for this *wild* ride."

I think he's kidding, but he slides into the driver's side and the *wild* part starts. He pulls away from the curb, and I realize he definitely wasn't kidding. He drives like a maniac, but this is not a bad thing. In fact, he not only gets me to class on time, but he drops me off at the door seven minutes early.

I feel like my hair is a little windblown as I turn to him in shock. "Quite the ride."

"I've been training," he says with a smirk. "I heard the traffic out here was horrible."

I laugh. He's funny, kind, and smart. I remember my dad's words from last night, and I turn to face him. "Hey," I say more softly, my voice taking on a slightly serious tone. "I have to talk to you about something."

"Of course." He tries to hide it, but his face sinks in disappointment. "I expected you to change your mind, Andi, don't worry. Minnesota is a long way away. I just met you, and if you don't want to come, I totally understand. It was..."

I rest a hand on his arm, squeezing tighter and tighter until he stops talking. "It's not that at all." I set my coffee in the cup holder, and then I do the thing that feels most natural in the world. I slip my hand around his head and pull him in for a kiss—a deep, lingering kiss that makes my chest heave something more than lust. When I pull back, I wait for him to open his eyes. "That's all I wanted."

He blinks, surprised. "That is significantly better than what I hoped you were going to say."

"There's one more thing, but it's not bad," I add quickly, before he gets that crumbly, disappointed face again. I hate that face on him—it ruins the sparkling, beautiful one I've come to adore. "I think we should have sex."

"What?"

"Sex."

"I understand the word," he says, running a hand over his forehead. "Do you mean...right now?"

I look at the students flooding around our car in the drop-off lane, and I blush. "No, of course not! I'm talking about our agreement."

"Agreement?" He seems a little lost, and I can't say that I entirely blame him.

"You asked me to come to Minnesota as a friend, to get out of your mom's date choices."

"Yes," he says.

"And I want to add an amendment to that agreement."

"An amendment?"

"Let's be friends who have sex. I don't want to go as your *friend*, I want to go as your...well, friend with benefits."

He raises his eyebrows. "I have to say this a surprising development."

My face flames red. "Unless you don't want to! I didn't mean that we have to, I just thought after last night, maybe—"

He leans so close to me that I stop talking. "After last night, how could you think I would have any objection to this arrangement? I want nothing more than to take you to bed..." He trails off, his hand landing on my thigh and inching higher and higher. "I want nothing more than to kiss you, taste you, take my time with you."

My core is about to spontaneously combust, and if I don't get out of the car soon, I'm going to be dry humping him again, and that just wouldn't be classy—not in the parking lot drop-off lane. "So that's a yes?"

A flash of something in his eyes makes me nervous. "Andi, you're gorgeous. You know I want you." He slips his hand underneath my shirt, his fingers brushing against my stomach. "But I like you too much to not be honest."

"I'm not asking for anything more," I say, feeling the sting of rejection before it hits. I try to ward it off. "I'm just volunteering my opinion that we should have sex. If you don't want to, just say no. It's not a big deal, honestly."

"I don't know if I'm going to get traded or not. Jocelyn hasn't even decided if she wants to take me on as a client, so everything's up in the air. I just can't get into a serious relationship right now."

"I understand that. I don't want one either."

"I know you say that, but—"

"Look," I interrupt. "I have to get to class, but I'm an adult woman. I make my own money, follow my own passions, and sleep with whomever I want. If you don't want to get involved with me, that's fine. I was just offering because based on what happened last night, I thought we might have a good time, but if you're not interested, just say so. I'm a big girl."

"I am interested—"

"Hold on, please," I interrupt. "I know you don't want a girlfriend, and if I *say* I don't want to date you, I mean it too. This is a two-way street, got it?"

"Understood." He nods. "To be clear, whether or not I end up in Los Angeles, we are not agreeing to do anything more than hang out and have some fun together."

"Exactly," I say. "We'll have some fun until the wedding, and then I'll come back to LA and focus on school and comedy while you focus on hockey. No pressure for anything."

"No pressure."

I extend a hand, and eventually, he extends his own with a smile. As we clasp hands, he hesitates. "What is it this time?" I ask. "Don't tell me you're backing out now."

"I completely forgot one of the reasons I showed up this morning."

"It *wasn't* to bring me coffee?"

"It was, but…I came to tell you that my flight home is tomorrow. Yes, I realize this is horrible timing, but when I saw you, I forgot everything I'd come to say. I have to head back to the Cities for preseason training."

"Oh."

"I want to see you again," he says. "Are you sure you can't come out to the party tonight?"

"I'll call you after my show," I tell him again. "That's the best I can do, sorry."

He shakes his head. "I understand, I just…" He looks down at his lap, where there's a distinct outline of his magical staff, and it is raring to go. "Do you see what you do to me? I *need* to see you tonight—or better yet, skip this class. We only have twenty-four hours left together until I leave. After today, I probably won't see you until the wedding."

"Crap!" I glance at the clock. "I'm late again!"

I fling open the door, wave, and hightail it toward the building. My brain isn't thinking. I realize once I near the doors that it might've been rude to leave him like that, all ready to go after driving all the way over to see me. I run the few steps back to the car, knock on the window, and gesture for him to roll it down.

He does, and I stick my head in there. "Sorry to run," I say. Then I point to the outline in his pant leg. "Hold that thought, okay? We'll find time. I promise."

"We'd better," he says. "Or I'm taking you with me tomorrow."

"That's kidnapping."

"Get to class before I kidnap you right now," he says with a wink.

I laugh then wave as I make my way to the front doors.

I walk into the room five minutes late and receive a death stare from my professor.

Worth it.

Chapter 24

Ryan

That girl catches me off guard more than anyone in the country. On the planet. In the whole damn universe.

Last night after Andi left, I went upstairs to take a shower—a cold one. It didn't work, even after I took care of myself *twice*.

This morning, it happened again. Another cold shower, a frustrated breakfast in which both Lilia and Lawrence told me to pull the stick out of my ass and stop acting like a jerk, and I knew I had to see her. I didn't care if I had to drive across town; the only cure for my mood was the sight of her smile, the curve of her lips, those lights blinking on in her eyes when she caught sight of me standing at the car.

I hadn't bargained on her updating our entire arrangement, but what can I say? Maybe my fingers are magic. I'm sure her mouth and her hands are magic, too. I certainly intend to find out.

Currently I'm sitting in traffic with a hard-on that won't quit and the image of her smile burned into my mind.

Friends with benefits, I think to myself. I like the sound of it.

Except the friends part. I don't want her as a friend; I want her all to myself. I'm possessive, and having her part time just isn't going to work for me.

So, I have between now and the wedding to find a way to prove it to her.

I'll start with tonight.

Andi can't come to the party because she has a show; well, I'll bring the party to her.

"Lawrence," I speak into Lilia's bluetooth—she let me borrow her car today since mine's still dented and damaged, but I won't tell Andi that. "How do you feel about kicking off the festivities at a comedy club tonight?"

"What?" he asks.

"Trust me, you won't be disappointed."

Chapter 25

Andi

I'm standing backstage and my nerves are shot.

I can hear people out there. Real, live people.

Something is wrong. There are never *people* at my shows.

"What the hell is happening out there?" I ask Lisa, who's primping next to me backstage. "Did a group of tourists get lost and end up in here?"

Bartender Rick calls backstage. "Andi, are you almost ready to go on? You've got a full house tonight."

"Why, Rick?" I turn to him, throwing my hands up in the air. "Why do we have a full house tonight? I didn't bring anyone. You didn't either, did you, Lisa?"

"No," she says, crinkling her eyebrows. "Why are you so nervous? You *want* an audience. That means you're successful. Who knows? Maybe some agent heard about you and is coming to see what the fuss is all about."

"Maybe that's it!" I shriek with understanding. "It's *your* fault. You did so well at the Laugh House the other night that everyone is coming to see you. It's free, and maybe they wanted another show. God, Lisa! Why are you so good? I can't handle this sort of pressure."

"Sure you can," she says. "I've heard your material before. How many times have I told you it's a great set? All you need is to catch the right person's attention, and it'll blow up. I guarantee it."

"I'm not doing my usual set!" I whimper. "I couldn't sleep last night, so I wrote all new material. It's not tested at all. I haven't even tried it on Angela."

She winces. "Can't you revert to your old stuff?"

"I think the new stuff might be good," I say. "Or it will be. It's just a little rough right now, and I usually prefer to try it on Angela first because she always laughs and then tells me what's stupid. She's very blunt."

"Get out there, Andi," Rick says. "I'm serious. This is the most customers I've seen in this bar since we opened our doors. If you bomb and send them all running, you're never doing a show here again."

I crumple onto the couch. "I can't. I give up."

Lisa sits down next to me and then hits my thigh with enough force to leave a mark. "Get out there. He's just kidding, aren't you, Rick?"

There's no answer, but he's only two feet away; he definitely heard.

"Rick, you asshole, tell Andi you're kidding," Lisa says. "Or we'll never bring our business here again."

"I give you free drinks," he grumbles. "I'm kidding, Andi. You know you always have a place here. Just go out there and do a great job like you always do."

I burst into tears. I can't help it. I clasp big, burly Rick into a hug. "Thank you, buddy."

Rick peels me off of him; neither of us are much for touchy-feely-ness, but these last few weeks have been an emotional rollercoaster. What with my morning sex confrontation with Ryan, the news that he is leaving tomorrow, and my desire for more of him, my poor hormones are a mess—a mess that came out all over Rick's shirt in an unusual display of emotional tears.

"Can you…fix her?" Rick asks Lisa. "Please."

"I'll go first," Lisa says, handing me a towel and a tube of mascara. "But I swear, woman, if you're not back here when I get off stage, I will hunt you down. Understand?"

I smile, wipe my tears away, and wave the tube. "I'm fine. I just needed to explode in a crying mess on Rick, I guess. I feel better already. Go get 'em, tiger."

Lisa gives me a half-sympathetic, half-threatening look before she takes the stage. As I apply my makeup and clean my face, I hear her killing it out there. It makes my insides war with themselves; as much as I'm happy she's a hit, it adds extra pressure—if I go out there and suck on stage, it'll be made doubly worse by following Lisa's winning set.

Lisa's ten minutes go all too fast.

The thing to understand though, is that onstage, three minutes takes a year. A ten-minute set is like winning the lottery in showbiz; it is a big deal—maybe not *such* a big deal at a tiny bar like Rick's, but at some of the bigger stages, anything over five minutes means the comic has made it.

So when Lisa passes the mic off to me, I drag my feet on stage, paste a smile on my face, and try not to stare directly into the lights. I fail, and it gives me an instant headache, but I blink a few times and introduce myself. "Hey guys, I'm Andi Peretti, and—"

I stop speaking because the hoots and hollers are too loud. Even with my microphone, their whistles are drowning me out. It's even louder than the rambunctious applause Lisa received at the end of her bit.

I frown, still blinded, trying to make out the shapes of people sitting in the audience. "Wow, I haven't even done anything yet. You guys are a great crowd."

I smile to more whistling and screaming. The only explanation is that they're drunk—out of their minds drunk. That's when I catch sight of a lick of white fabric draped over someone's head, the end dusting along the gross floor—a veil. It's a bachelorette party.

Crooked chairs line sticky tables, and Rick moves between them. He's not used to having to maneuver around customers, so he knocks more than one person in the head with his tray. Even as I watch him clumsily dish out the drinks, I don't put everything together until I hear his voice.

Ryan's voice. "We love you, Andi!"

In that moment, everything goes clear. The darkness adjusts and suddenly those dark forms resemble bodies...bodies I recognize. Lilia's in the veil, obviously. Lawrence is on one side of her, fingers in his mouth as he lets out an ear-splitting whistle. Ryan's next to his brother, and beside him are a few guys with tattoos on their arms and the beat-up look of professional hockey players. One of them is missing a tooth.

"Holy shit," I breathe.

"Go," Lisa says behind me. "I don't care if it's the Queen of England, do your bit!"

I take a deep breath as Lisa's words echoing in my head. Then I lock eyes with Ryan and nod to him as my heart beats in a suspicious way, as if it's happy...happy to see him. He probably brought the party here as a joke, a gag for everyone to get a kick out of, but it means something to me—even if he's here in hopes of sex. This thought gives me the strength to go on, to do the best I can.

The best I have is pretty decent, as it turns out. I don't perform at my absolute best since I'm too busy weaving together new material with the old, but it's certainly not the worst. By the time the red light flashes in the back of the room signaling the end of my time, I wrap the last joke with a bow and blow it into the audience with a kiss.

"I'm Andi Peretti. Thanks for coming out tonight." I raise my microphone. "And congratulations to Lilia and Lawrence. Round of drinks on me!"

Rick leaps to attention as I turn to face Lisa. It's a habit, me looking to her after a show. We always give each other a thumbs up or a thumbs down, lovingly rating each other, and we're both harsh and kind, all at once. If I bomb, she'll let me know. If I nail it, she'll tell me that too.

Judging by the two thumbs up and her shit-eating grin, I nailed it.

I thank the heavens. I'm finally about to make my way offstage when a figure comes up from behind and sweeps me into a hug. Ryan's scent is spicy and his cheeks are freshly shaven and smooth as they brush against my neck while he nuzzles into my body.

"You killed it," he says. "I loved every second. We all did."

"Ryan, you didn't have to do all this—change your plans, bring everyone here…" I turn to face him, his arms slipping to rest just above the waistline of my jeans. "It's too much."

"I wanted you at the party. You couldn't make it, so we brought the party to you," he says with a grin. "Everyone loved it. They can't stop talking about it. One of Lawrence's agent friends wants to get your card."

"My card?" I say faintly.

"Business card."

"I, uh…"

"Don't worry," he says. "I'll take care of it and get him your information, if that's okay?"

"Of course it's okay," Lisa says from behind me. Her eyes are in shock, but she pulls it together and sticks out her hand. "I'm Lisa."

"You killed it, too," Ryan says. "But then again, we met the other night, and you already know I enjoy your work."

She retracts her hand. "Right. Sorry. Autopilot."

He clasps her in a one-armed hug, and she gives me a look over his shoulder as if she's not sure what to do with it. I can't help but laugh. The night is already one for the books.

It's now that I realize I can never be *just* friends with Ryan.

Already, the tenderness in my heart is too much for a casual acquaintance. That scares me, but I remember my dad's words—that it's better to fall in love, no matter the cost—and I forget my worries. I let myself sink into the moment, and when Ryan plants a kiss on my lips, I let it happen. I kiss him back despite the hoots and hollers from the crowd, and when he pulls back, we can hardly breathe.

"Will you come out with us?" Ryan whispers in my ear. "I need you tonight—alone...after."

He presses against me, and I can feel just how much he needs me. I let my finger brush against the front of his jeans. "That's a lot of need."

"Sweetheart, you don't even know."

I take his hand. "Do you guys have a place in mind that you want to go next? If not, there's a great Mexican spot a few doors down."

"Do they have beer?"

"And a mechanical bull."

He nods his head and grins. "Lead the way."

Chapter 26

Andi

If there's life on Mars, I'm pretty sure the folks there can hear my screams.

The mechanical bull is way more vicious than I remember from my twenty-first birthday. Then again, I was younger, more flexible, and less sober than I am right now. I can barely hold on to this mother-bucker.

My jeans have slipped a little too low, and I'm sure my pink lace undies are peeking over the top. My tank is tight enough that I'm not flashing the *entire* population of the bar, and that's a small miracle considering the amount of bouncing and jiggling going on.

However, when I'm finally thrown from the bull, it's all worth it. There, waiting to help me up, is Ryan. His eyes twinkle as he extends a hand, pulls me to my feet, and squeezes me to his chest.

"You kicked Boxer's ass," he says. "Shit, if I'd known how good you were at riding bulls, I would've invited you to the farm a long time ago."

"The farm?" I'm dizzy in my post-mechanical bull haze. "*Oh*, right. Minnesota. You know, I've never seen a farm."

"Never seen a farm?" This is from Boxer. Danny Boxer is the biggest, meanest guy in the league, according to Lilia. He plays for

Los Angeles. He's also freaking hilarious. "You've never seen a farm?!"

I glance at Boxer's arms, which are slathered in tattoos. He was the one with the missing tooth in the audience at my show, and there's a scar above his eyebrow. I asked him if it was from hockey and he grunted. I don't know what that means.

"Sorry," I tell him. "I'm from the east side of Los Angeles. Can't go more than a few blocks without seeing a 7-11. The most farming I've seen is the one time my brother tried to grow his own oregano."

Boxer snorts. "Oregano, right. Teenage boy? Not oregano."

I don't know why I've never thought of it before, but Boxer has a point. My dad did throw that plant away mighty quick, but I was too young to understand. "I never realized! Do you think my brother was growing *weed*?"

"You're cute," Boxer says as Ryan tightens his grip on my arm. Then he shakes his head and repeats *Never seen a farm* several times before Ryan shushes him.

"Never have I ever," Ryan says. "Let's play."

"Never have I what?" Boxer looks confused. He's probably not the smartest bulb in the box. "I've seen a farm."

Ryan is patient with him, almost adorably so. "Hold five fingers up," he instructs Boxer. "We go around in a circle. Everyone says something they haven't done, and if you've done it, you put a finger down. First one out of fingers has to take a drink."

Once Ryan rounds up the gang—Boxer, me, Lawrence, Lilia, and a few other teammates—he points at me to start.

"Never have I ever seen a farm," I say.

Everyone puts a finger down. "If I weren't marrying *him*," Lilia says, elbowing Lawrence, "I'd still have my finger. That damn Pierce farm."

"Never have I ever delivered a pizza," Ryan fires off next.

My finger goes down and I glare at him. "Not fair."

"Two can play that game," he says with a smirk. "You want to snipe me, I'll get you back, sweetheart."

"Never have I ever been engaged," Tommy says. Tommy is another of Ryan's teammates, and from what I can tell, he's the team captain. He's tall, handsome in a clean-cut sort of way, and the most responsible of the group at first impression—possibly because he's the sober driver of the group. "Put 'em down, Lawrence and Lilia."

They each put a finger down, which leaves them with only three left. I sneak a glance at Ryan and find he's watching me. I leave my finger up, and so does he. The plot thickens.

"Fine, if we're attacking people, then," Lawrence says as he snaps his finger down, half joking, half annoyed. He's probably had one too many beers, and we've started serving him water. "I guess it's my turn."

We wait patiently as he scans the group, his eyes circling past everyone, as if digging for dirt to use against one of us. On his first pass over the circle, he comes up empty. His eyes flick again to my face, and then to Ryan's, and then back to mine. His eyes widen, and I know what's happening before Lawrence opens his mouth.

Ryan does too, and he acts first. "Come on, man," he starts. "Leave Andi out of—"

But Lawrence lets out a slurred sort of smile, a bit saggy at the corners of his lips, his eyes a little hazy. "Never have I ever fallen in love with my delivery girl."

Everyone falls silent. Around us, the cheers of the bar crowd sound as yet another rider saddles up on the mechanical bull. All eyes at our table flick between Ryan and me. Why? I'm not quite sure. Obviously he's not in love with me. We just met. I shouldn't care that he leaves his finger up. I shouldn't care at all.

Dammit, I care, I think as Ryan's hand flexes. His finger twitches as if he's going to put it down for sympathy to spare me the embarrassment. I decide I don't want a pity finger, so I take action.

"Well, we all know my finger's staying put," I say with a polite smile at Lawrence. "My dad has some fantastic delivery girls, but I'm not into that sort of thing."

A round of titters helps to dispel some of the awkwardness, but not all of it. Ryan's still shooting daggers at his brother. Lawrence is oblivious, but Lilia's not. She mouths *I'm sorry* then tries to hook her arm in her fiancé's. "Let's go, buddy," she says. "I think you need to snooze."

He grabs for her, misses her arm, and squeezes her boob.

"All right then," Lilia says. "Someone's handsy. Here, have some water."

"We're still playing," Ryan says, his jaw tense. "Nobody's upset here."

"Ryan, please, let it go," I murmur. We're close enough that nobody *should* be able to hear, but since everyone is paying such close attention, they can probably read my lips. "It's his bachelor party. He's allowed to overindulge. Forget about it. Leave your finger up. Boxer, do you want to go again?"

"Never have I ever fallen in love with a delivery girl." Boxer snorts dumbly. "Good one."

Ryan turns his gaze to his teammate. "Really, Boxer?"

"Ryan…" I rest a hand on his arm, but that only serves to set him into motion.

He puts his finger down solidly. In fact, he puts down all of his fingers except for the middle one. Turning to me, I catch a glimpse of something in his eyes—lust, longing, desire, whatever it was that drew us together—and beneath it I see a hint of something more. It's not love; it's too soon for that, but it could be friendship, maybe.

I don't have long to analyze what's going on in those beautiful brown eyes of his because the next thing I know, he's leaning in, breath spicy with the scent of his gum, his hands sure as he grips the back of my head. He kisses me, in front of everyone, a scorching kiss that causes Lilia to suck in a breath.

When Ryan pulls back, he's wearing a smug expression as he glances around the table. He slides an arm around my shoulders, hugs me to his body, and smirks. "Who's next for the game? I've got a finger or two left."

Lilia exhales. "*Never have I ever* been kissed like that! *Damn.* Come on, Lawrence. We're going home. You're going to sober up and kiss me like that."

"Like what?" Lawrence is staring somewhere between Ryan and myself, his eyes not fixated on anything.

"You're right." Ryan stands, pulling me with him. His hand slips over my ass, cupping it possessively. "It's time to go home. Tommy, can you drive these guys home? We'll find our own way back."

Chapter 27

Ryan

"I wouldn't have been brave enough to try this place on my own." I inhale another taco and pray it doesn't wreck my intestines tomorrow. "How'd you find this thing?"

Andi laughs, a sound that makes me smile back at her involuntarily.

"My dad's always been a big foodie—you know, before it was cool. I know Peretti's doesn't seem all that fancy—it's not, really—but my dad cares a lot about food. He worked for years to get a recipe for pizza sauce that he was happy with."

"My brother recommended your dad's place," I say. "That's how I found it in the first place. According to Lawrence, it's the gem of the pizza world in LA."

"We get a lot of local business," she says happily. "Repeat customers. We're not a big name chain, but we try to make sure our customers are happy with what we serve. My dad might be blunt and seem a little emotionless—he loves playing the *tough guy Italian* card—but really, he's sweet. He cares more than anyone I know."

Listening to her talk about her family is equal parts fascinating and heart-wrenching. The way she speaks about them makes it easy to see the love, the connection. Though she doesn't talk about it much, I can sense how much she misses her mother, and I hate that she's lost someone so important to her.

My own family is close-knit back home, even though my brother is a dick sometimes. My parents are great, truly, and I can't imagine losing my mom like Andi has. When my brother isn't being a drunken asshole, he can be decent, too—unlike tonight. I'm still pissed at him for putting Andi and me on the spot like that.

Luckily, she doesn't seem all that fazed by it. After we loaded Lawrence and posse into Tommy's huge rental and sent them home, I asked Andi to grab a bite to eat with me. Since she knew the area well, she suggested a local place that sold tacos.

I love tacos, I just hadn't expected to love them from a sketchy-ass cart on the side of the road. Seriously—there's a small guy behind the cart flipping meat and other various substances that resemble food, and if I had to guess, one could catch salmonella from simply breathing in the scent of sizzling meat.

But Andi insisted they were great, that she comes here all the time after her shows, and that she hasn't gotten sick once. One bite in, and I was sold.

"If I get sick tomorrow," I say to Andi, swallowing a mouthful of taco. "It will have been worth it…almost."

She laughs again and steals one of my tacos. I lean in to snag a bite, but she moves the taco at the last minute and puts her mouth there instead. I let my other hand find her waist, my fingers sneaking a squeeze of her glorious hips as her lips play over mine.

The girl is heaven. She tastes like it, looks like it, smells like it… I can't imagine what it'll feel like when we finally give in to temptation and put Andi's new amendment to use. The tension is crackling through the roof now, hotter than the sizzling pan next to us.

"You're good," I murmur, reluctant to pull my lips from hers. "I would've fought you for that taco, but it seems you've traded me for something I like better."

She gives a shining grin, then pulls back with a teasing wink and bites into the taco. "*Aha!* You fell for my trap."

I reach for her as she shrieks loud enough for half the street to hear. I don't give a damn—I'm having too much fun to care. She tries to run away from me but I scoop her up by the waist, toss her over my shoulder, and snag a bite of taco as I run my fingers along her ribcage.

She squirms, shouting good-natured expletives as I carry her fireman style. She's light; I'm pretty sure I've carried burritos heavier than her. The whole situation sends my mind spiraling toward the bedroom.

I imagine my hands squeezing her hips, sliding into her softness, bending her over the couch, the counter, the…hell, anywhere. She's light enough that I could hold her with one hand against the wall.

The thought has me bursting at the seams of my boxers while marching down the street with her over my shoulder. She's given up squirming and now rests her elbows on my back, her chin in her hands, probably a pout on those lush lips of hers.

"Hey," she says after half a block. She taps the top of my head. "Want a bite of my taco?"

I freeze. "What did you say?"

"I have one left." She laughs. "Want a bite? I'm full."

I need to see her smile more than I need to breathe. The urge to hold her, to kiss her is more than anything I've ever known. I swing her into my arms, my eyes locked on hers as a brush of surprise sweeps across her face.

She holds the half-eaten taco with both hands as I cradle her in the middle of Hollywood Boulevard for all the bums, tourists, and late-night streetwalkers to see. I don't care who sees us. Bring on the paparazzi. Let *Jocelyn* watch.

I can't be friends with this girl. I haven't laughed like this, had fun—*fun!*—like this since I was five years old shooting dart guns at my brothers. Being friends is not an option. I need more.

I'm just getting ready to tell her that when she puts her arms around my neck and gives me the softest, sweetest kiss I've ever tasted. It's honey on marshmallow levels of sweetness, and I can't handle it. I need her so badly it's painful, and I groan.

"Sweetheart, can we go somewhere else? Preferably somewhere private."

Her eyes burn, smoldering with desire. "Please."

I wiggle out my phone, not daring to set her down, not daring to let this moment pass. I hit the call button for an Uber. It gives me an estimate of three minutes. *Three frigging minutes—I can't wait that long*…but I guess I'll have to, because she slides out of my arms.

"One second," she says. "How long 'til the Uber comes?"

I tell her a few minutes then watch as she runs back to the sketchy-ass taco stand. She forks over a few bucks, gets another load of tacos, and brings it back. I don't comment because I love—and I mean *love*—the fact that she eats whatever she wants. Despite weighing half of me, she's put away the same number of tacos. I'm impressed.

"These aren't for me," she says, glancing at my face.

Obviously I don't hide my surprise very well.

She jogs easily over to the mailbox in front of her comedy club. "Here you go," she says, handing over the plate of food to the man living next to the mailbox. "Have a great night, Phil."

"Good show," he says. "That boyfriend of yours is a keeper."

"Good*night* Phil," she yells, walking back to me. "Mind your own business!"

I pretend I didn't hear their exchange.

However, she can read my face again. "Ignore him," she says. "He's full of it. Thinks he's got everyone figured out."

"That was nice of you," I say. "You two seem like you get along."

She waves a hand. "He's my biggest fan. It's the least I can do."

"So he's my competition?" I raise my eyebrows. "What do I have to do to become your number one fan?"

She leans in, gives me a wink. "Take me home tonight. I'll let you figure out the rest from there."

I believe I've died and gone to heaven. She's hot, funny, and unafraid to say what she wants—hell, this morning she added an *amendment* to our contract, stating that she wants to have sex. If I don't propose to her now, some other bastard will, and he'll be the lucky one.

"Why are you single?" I ask instead.

Lilia would have my ass if I proposed right now anyway. She wouldn't want anyone encroaching on her wedding plans. Also, it's too soon…right?

"Oh," she says, a light going on in her eyes. "Don't get me started. We could be here all night."

"Bullshit."

"Ryan…"

The way she says my name has me watching her eyes, waiting for her to find the words she needs to say. I reach out and cup her cheek in my hand. The skin is soft, so very soft, and I let my thumb brush over her lips. "Yes?"

"You didn't have to do that back at the bar." She raises a shoulder. "Really, I can roll with the punches, take a joke. You didn't need to make a thing about what Lawrence said."

"He didn't need to be a dick."

"He was just having a good time," she says. "I'm around a lot of dicks, anyway. I'm used to it. Lots of comics are awesome, hilarious people, but there are a few…"

"In any profession," I add. "There are some great hockey guys, and then there are…"

"Dicks," she finishes, and we share a smile.

"Exactly."

"Well," she says. "I guess I owe you a thank you, but just know, I didn't expect you to do that, or to say anything. I can stand up for myself."

"It was nothing," I say. "I don't mind showing everyone how I feel about you."

"But *love*..." She says the word quietly, with reverence, as if she's in church. "It's too soon for that. And when I—er, well, this morning when we talked—"

"When you asked for sex, you mean," I say with a wink. "Yes, I remember that vividly."

Her face colors, but she nods. She wasn't lying—this girl can roll with the punches.

"I honestly meant it. I don't expect anything from you, and you shouldn't from me. We're just having fun." She flashes a quick smile that doesn't quite reach her eyes. "I want to make that clear."

"Of course," I say. "Fun it is."

"So..." She hesitates, kicking her toe against the ground. "Speaking of fun...where's that Uber?"

Chapter 28

Andi

"Is this weird?" I ask as we sneak through the doors of the guest house like two teenagers. "We can go someplace else."

"Like your house?" Ryan raises an eyebrow at me. I've already explained that I live with roommates—more specifically, my dad.

"Point taken," I say.

Even if my dad has been strangely encouraging about my new relationship-sort-of-thing with Ryan, that doesn't mean he'd welcome Ryan into our home with open arms at three thirty in the morning, especially smelling like whatever mechanical bulls mixed with tacos smells like.

"This is my home away from home." Ryan steps through the door, exposing a quaint space fit with everything one might need to live.

It's the guest house behind Lawrence and Lilia's place, but it's hardly tiny. In fact, it's nicer than ninety percent of the *full*-sized houses in this city. A small kitchen is visible past the living room, a coffee maker and beans sit on the counter, and a bowl of fresh fruit is centered on the table. "Sometimes I sleep in the extra bedroom at the main house if we're hanging out there and I don't want to walk back, and because Lilia's a great cook."

I laugh. "Makes sense. It seems like such a shame that this sits empty all the time."

He grabs my hand and pulls me toward the back, to a clean, plush, modern bedroom that's just the right combination of minimalist and luxurious. "It was part of the agreement when Lawrence moved out here."

"Agreement?"

"With my parents." He cringes a bit. "My parents are great, and they love us a lot—maybe too much. They wouldn't let Lawrence move out here until he could afford a place with a back house for them to come stay whenever—and for however long—they'd like."

"No such thing as a parent loving their child too much," I say softly. "I think it's sweet."

"Yeah," he says, slowing his pace as we enter the bedroom. "I suppose it is. Anyway, my parents never use it much; they prefer to stay in the main house. But who knows? My mom's hoping Lawrence and Lilia will be converting the guest bedroom into a child's room soon, so…I suppose she wants a place to stay when she comes to visit her grandkids."

"No pressure."

He laughs. "Lilia is vocal about wanting kids, so she's not annoyed by it. My mother gave them her blessing to get married on their third date when Lilia mentioned she was one of three girls and wanted at least that many kids herself. My mom loves babies."

I shake my head, smiling, and I let Ryan guide me to the bed. We perch on it. "They're a great fit for each other," I say. "I love watching them together. It's adorable, but, I don't know, it doesn't make me gag like some couples. Know what I mean?"

He nods. "She's great for him. He's really lucky to have her."

"It takes two to make a great couple," I say. "She's lucky too."

"In some odd way, I guess you're right," he says grudgingly. "But I'm still pissed at Lawrence, so I'm not feeling as generous as you."

"You need to let it go!" I lick my lips playfully, resting a hand on his chest. It's firm and solid; the beat of his heart is strong underneath his shirt. "Maybe I can help distract you?"

He falls back at my feather-light touch, as if I have the strength of the Hulk, and collapses on the bed. "Ravish me."

I swing one leg over his waist, so I'm straddling him. He's got on jeans and a button-down shirt that's open at the neck may be the sexiest thing I've seen him in yet. My fingers reach for the buttons and flick them open.

When his t-shirt is revealed, I pause for a moment and admire.

"Like what you see?" he asks, teasing.

"Shut up! I'm ogling you."

His eyes crinkle with a smile, those chocolate eyes lined with devilish thoughts, his hair playfully mussed, hanging just a little too far over his eyes. "Ogle away, but first, let me do this."

This turns out to be a pretty great surprise.

His fingernails dig into my skin and pull me toward him. I'm situated on his lap, and I can feel every inch of him beneath me. It's erotic, even though our jeans are a barrier between us. I grip his arms hard enough to leave a mark, a gasp hissing from my lips as I adjust so that we're fitted perfectly through the fabric, but it's not enough.

"I need you," he says. "I can't wait any longer, Andi."

"Okay, I'm done ogling," I say. "Take your pants off."

"Your wish is my command."

I rest a hand against his chest, pushing him back. "On second thought, you can wait for me this time."

He closes his eyes as my hands go to the button on his jeans. I pop it open, my hands itching to touch him. He's wearing black boxer briefs, and I rest my hand against the impressive bulge.

It's his turn to sizzle a breath between his lips, his head rolling back against the pillow. "Shit."

"Shit bad or shit good?"

"Shit don't you dare stop, sweetheart," he says. "Take off your shirt."

"I'm not done—"

"I didn't ask if you were done." He moves into a sitting position faster than I can blink, corralling me as he links my arms behind my back. "I asked you to take your shirt off. Please, I want to see you...all of you."

My chest rises and falls. I've never been so turned on in my life. All at once he's commanding, decisive, and then playful again. I'm realizing I have never known good sex—not yet.

Suddenly, I'm worried that nobody will ever live up to Ryan. He's worked more magic with his fingers than any man has done with my entire body combined. It'll be impossible to date again after Ryan.

Then again, I haven't even *had* Ryan yet. I focus on him now, pushing thoughts of what's next into oblivion. The way he's looking at me feels a bit like a lion watching its prey, and if I don't get moving soon, I bet he'll take my shirt off with his teeth.

I reach down, wiggling out of his grasp, and pull my shirt over my head. I'm wearing a simple, black bra—I hadn't expected to go out after my show tonight, so I was dressed for practicality.

Ryan, God bless his soul, doesn't seem to care about the bra at all. It hits the floor one second later, and then his mouth is on my collarbone. Hot and tender, he leads a trail of kisses down my chest, brushing his lips over the tops of my breasts.

I'm on fire. The touch of his lips against my skin is enough to set me off, but I refuse. This time, I'm bringing him with me. Then, his lips clamp around my nipple, and I forget about everything else. His mouth moves in ways that have me writhing, pulling him closer and pushing away all at once.

Ryan reaches out, grasps me, holds me to his chest. His arm

guides my back onto the soft comforter as he lays me down, exposing every inch of me. It's his turn to fumble with my jeans, and he struggles. I don't blame him—they're from high school and thus a little too tight around the waist.

"Shit," he says, throwing his hands up in the air. "Damn jeans."

I help him, my hands guiding his as he peels the pants away from my legs until they're nothing but a memory. All I care about are Ryan's hands—they're running up my legs, just the tips of his fingers making contact, sending goose bumps prickling over my skin.

"Ryan…" I say, but that's all I can manage as his fingers pass the insides of my thighs.

All I have on now is a thin pair of panties. They're lacey and pink, something fun I always wear when I perform. I wear them for luck, to remind me that I can be fun and flirty if I really want to, and they're an even better reminder of that now.

He rests a possessive hand there, one of his fingers straying along the outside of the fabric, testing for my reaction as he watches my face, the pressure almost too much to handle. It's overwhelming, and I mumble nonsense.

"You like that?" he murmurs in a husky, lust filled voice "I'm just getting started, honey …"

Next, he dips his head and plants a kiss next to his fingers, and it makes me burn with pleasure. Lava—I am *lava*.

Thankfully, he pauses there, giving me a moment to breath. "You are ready for me," he says, almost in awe.

"Not yet," I grit out. "Lay down first."

He doesn't listen, his hand clamping down as he leans in for a kiss. This time I'm ready for it, and I take advantage of his one-armed stance to shift him over onto the bed. It pains me to shift his fingers away from working their magic, but I do it before he can stop me and lower myself against him.

Now it's just me, a bit of lacy material, Ryan, and his boxers. I can feel him for the first time without denim between us, and it's more pleasure than I've ever known. I close my eyes, adjusting until his fingers come up to grasp my waist.

"What do you think you're doing?" he murmurs. "I wasn't done with you."

We're somewhere between playful wrestling and passionate sex, and I like it. I love it, actually. Especially when he starts rubbing again, tracing small circles around my sweet spot. My eyes are still closed, and I'm lost in the moment, moving against him, until I realize it's enough to set me off. I raise my hips from him, pausing the momentum.

His hand clasps my wrist, but it's not enough to stop me from slithering downward and sliding his boxers off. He springs free, sort of like a jack-in-the-box, and the analogy makes me giggle in my head. I do another second's worth of ogling, and then I lower my mouth to him, clasping my lips firm enough to draw a sharp breath.

He had started to argue, to reach for me, but he loses all will to fight as I begin to move. "Oh, shit," he says. "That feels incredible."

I hide my smile. Never did I ever think I'd meet Ryan Pierce in person, let alone be here, in his bed, making him hiss with pleasure. My life could be so much worse.

Judging by his moans and his fingers gripping my hair and pulling tight, whatever I'm doing at the moment is working.

"Stop," he says, breaking the rhythm. He's on the verge, I can see it in his eyes. "Lie down."

"But—"

"Lie down," he says again. "*Please.*"

It's difficult to argue with a demand like that, so I roll onto my back. Somehow, the undies have disappeared. He perches on top of me, one arm easing around my back so he's holding my chest to his, our skin slick with heat, want, need. He's produced a condom from somewhere unknown and rolls it on, and the next thing I know, he's nudging into me, slowly, cautiously.

"You're a tease," I gasp. "Freaking tease."

He reaches around, grasping at my back, my bottom, my hips, pulling me tighter. He's barely inside, and already he's filled me. His hand joins the party, rubbing in circles and bringing sensations to the table that I've never before experienced.

Finally, I can't handle it anymore, and I yank his hips toward me. We sit there for a moment, stilled, almost in shock at how good this feels. I've never felt so complete, so on fire, so needy for more.

I can tell he feels the same, and only a second later he puts his hands on either side of my body and begins to rock. It's not enough to just *be*; I need everything he has to give, and he needs me too—I can sense it.

I move with him, my hips arching, my mouth pressed to his neck. He kisses me, but I can hardly think, can hardly feel, and all I know is the sense of exhilaration as if we're on a rollercoaster that's about to fly off the rails.

"You feel incredible," he murmurs. "Thank the Lord for amendments."

I murmur an agreement as my hands dig into his back while his fingers cinch me tight, and I feel the racing of his heart. Our mouths clash in a tangle of heat. Then, just when I'm ready to go over the edge, he pushes me back, pulls almost out, and hesitates, his eyes locking on mine.

We pause there, my core aching for him, his hand fisted through my hair as he holds on tight. The moment is shattered as he thrusts in, long, hard, fast, and from there we're on a bottle rocket sailing toward space.

His name falls from my lips as he rocks us to a climax, and when we finally take off, I learn the meaning of seeing stars. Tiny little shimmering things I never knew existed in reality fill my field of vision.

We continue sailing, feeling, gasping, until long after the stars have blinked out. I collapse against him, satiated. I'm spent, completely, and in a post-sex drunken bliss that makes it impossible to speak.

He strokes my hair, whispers gentle words against my ear, and runs his fingers down my spine until finally, I feel somewhat human again. The first thing I do is look up, smile, and kiss him hard on the lips.

"Wow," I breathe when we break. "That was…"

I decide to let him fill in the gap.

"Out of this world?" he murmurs, his hand sleepily pushing my hair back from my face.

We manage to disconnect, but neither of us are in a hurry to go anywhere. I roll into his chest and his arms hold me tight to him. I'm exhausted and completely, utterly happy, and I decide I want to have sex like this all the time. It's *awesome*.

With each of my previous partners—granted, there weren't a *lot*, but the number is higher than one—sex has been this sort of vanilla thing we did to fill the time if we were moderately attracted to one another. It has never been about love, passion, or even lust.

I have no clue *what* just happened with Ryan, but it was *not* vanilla, and it was *not* boring. I want more.

"Fantastic," I add. "That was fun."

"Let's do it again." he says. "Once wasn't enough."

I curl in against his body. "Good thing we can do it as many times as we want."

"Very good thing."

His hand runs along my naked back, his touch gentle, the opposite of our furious motions of moments before. It's the first time

I've ever had the urge to cuddle, but since we're friends with benefits, the situation is a little confusing. Is cuddling expected? Required? Frowned upon?

"So," I say curiously. "What happens now?"

"Now?" He glances up at me, mischief in his eyes. "My, oh my, Andi, you're insatiable."

I feel my cheeks flame. "I just meant like…what do we do? Do we cuddle? Should I go home? This friends with benefits thing doesn't come with a handbook, you know."

He turns to the ceiling, his bark of laughter startling me. Shaking his head, he faces me. "You are truly one of a kind."

"Fine, can I take a shower then?" I smile, pleased that our hookup hasn't changed the easy atmosphere between us. If anything, things seem even easier now. We don't have to pretend we aren't looking forward to a repeat session.

He runs a hand leisurely along my leg, stares at my boobs, and then grins. "Towels are in the bathroom," he says. "But first, come here."

"Where?"

His answer is a kiss, a breathtaking kiss that has me thinking we are going for round two. But, just as his hands skim over my stomach and down to my hips, he stops, giving my butt a firm pat. "Shower's that way." I give him a look of frustration, and he merely raises his eyebrows. "Is there a problem?"

"You know what you're doing to me," I say, stomping off to the bathroom. "And I expect you to deliver on your promise, buddy!"

I step into the bathroom and find a smile reflected back at me in the mirror—a smile and real, true sex hair. I'm actually proud of this wild 'do—I look like quite the maniac.

I snap a quick picture of my new hairstyle and text it to Lisa. I have to share this moment with someone, and she'll appreciate it.

My phone beeps with a text two seconds later. It's Lisa, and she's sent me five eggplant emojis. I don't quite understand it, but I understand it enough to send her a turd image back.

And then the thumbs up.

Finally, I climb into the shower, lather up with the expensive soaps lined up along the ledge, and wash my hair with delicious-smelling shampoo. By the time I climb out, I'm feeling like a new woman. This time when I look in the mirror, I see a makeup-less face that is smiling, happy, and refreshed. Sex works wonders for my skin.

Unless…maybe this is more than sex? Already, I find myself dreading Lawrence and Lilia's wedding. As excited as I am to be invited, I don't want the date to arrive, because once that date passes, Ryan and I will no longer have a reason to see each other. I don't want to think about that.

Instead, I leave the steam-filled bathroom and head to the bedroom where, at least for now, my fantasy has become reality.

Chapter 29

Ryan

I'm ready to fall asleep. She's been in that shower for so long I actually debate knocking on the door to make sure she is still alive, but when I put my ear to the door, I hear her humming.

Fucking adorable.

She's humming in the shower, and it sounds happy, so I return to bed and now I'm lying here, waiting for her to return and sprawl out on the sheets next to me.

She exhausted me. I've been with plenty of women before—hockey players are rarely at a loss for options—but none of my options have been anything like Andi, nowhere near as satisfying, as intelligent, as goddamn sexy. Whatever she did with her mouth, those hips—I'm hooked. That's not to mention the fact that I enjoy *talking* with her, too, before and after.

Suddenly I can understand why Lawrence left behind his dickhead ways when he met Lilia. If she makes him feel anywhere near as good as Andi makes me feel, well, shit—I'd give up my dickhead ways too.

Even though that's not an option for so many reasons. We both want to enjoy this for as long as possible, but at the end of the day, our relationship is going to grind to a halt in one way or another, no pun intended.

If I get signed here, Jocelyn will have my balls in a vice-like grip, especially my first year with the Lightning. I won't be able to get away with anything. If I don't get signed, well, there goes any hope for continuing our little agreement. Two thousand miles sure puts a kink in the friends with benefits amendment, and not the good kind.

I'm running a hand over my forehead, debating when I should bring this up to Andi, when she waltzes into the room and I forget all logical thought—or illogical thought, for that matter. All thoughts fly out the window at the sight of her wearing my fluffy-ass towel.

I'm sure she's naked under there. She left her clothes by the bed and stumbled to the bathroom in nothing but a pair of socks. Now the socks are gone, and so is her makeup, and damn if she isn't even more beautiful with a plain face.

"Do you by chance have a t-shirt?" she asks, a hint of shyness creeping into her smile. "Unless I should leave now? I don't really know the etiquette here. I've never been a friend with benefits before."

I'm speechless. *Leave now?* When I find my words, I gargle something that doesn't make any sense.

"What?" she asks. "Was that English?"

I might've thought I was completely spent—it's been a long day between training early this morning, enough sexual tension to break a lesser man, and finally the most insane release—yet somehow, I'm ready for her again.

I stand, the sheets falling off of me as her eyes land on a gigantic sign that I'm ready to go again.

She holds a hand up to her mouth and stifles a burst of laughter. "I guess that means I'm not getting kicked out yet?"

Luckily the condoms are already out and ready. I slip one on, watching her eyes for any sign that she's not looking for a repeat.

On the contrary—she lets her towel fall to the floor.

I was right. She's naked under there.

"You are stunning," I find myself saying. Normally, I'm not one for compliments and touchy-feely shit—girls get too attached when I start saying that stuff—but this isn't a conscious choice; I'm just blurting out whatever's on my mind. "I need you again."

Her *yes* is more of a needy groan, and I know before I even touch her that she's ready. When my fingers find the warmth between her legs, she inhales a sharp breath. This time, there's no foreplay, no dicking around—it's urgent.

I lift her up and wind her legs around my back. We move forward, her back crashing against the wall harder than I'd intended. "Sorry, sweetheart," I say, watching her eyes. "Did I hurt you?"

Her eyes shine with need and she shakes her head as she pulls me harder against her. I catch the back of her head as she throws it back, just before she hits the wall, her hair soft and damp against my fingers.

"I thought about you in the shower," she whispers. "Daydreamed, really."

Hot damn. I lower her hips, closing my eyes, savoring that first moment as we join in a mesh of limbs. This time, it's about need, raw, dangerous need, and I don't hold back. I want her to be mine, mine alone, and that thought is terrifying, so I thrust harder, faster, her moans growing louder and wilder with each passing second.

I can't last much longer—she feels too good. Her teeth bite down against my shoulder as we hurtle toward the finish line, and when we reach it, I explode. Together, we sag against the wall, my hands holding her up, small puffs of her breath against my neck are sending jolts throughout my nerve system.

When I finally let her down, she's grinning.

"God, you are insatiable," I say, running a hand through my hair. "Was that good for you, sweetheart?"

She nips my lip. "What do you think?"

I laugh, holding her against me, loving the way her naked body feels against mine. I've never been a cuddler—again, it leads to attachment too quickly—but Andi is different. Perfect.

"I'm going to shower," I say, maybe a bit too abruptly, needing some space. "Make yourself at home, climb in bed, raid the fridge, whatever."

"Is everything okay?" Her eyebrows crinkle in concern.

She heard the shortness in my voice. *Shit*. I give her a long, lazy kiss to show her just how *right* everything is. "Some of us need a break, that's all. We're not all as energetic as you," I say, heading to the shower. I stop in the doorway to the bedroom. "And Andi?"

She's climbed into bed and looks up in surprise. "Yes?"

"I'll be thinking of you."

She turns red, but doesn't let the embarrassment get to her. "Let me remind you that *I'm* not the one who needs a break, Mr. Pierce."

I turn away, at a loss for words.

For the second, or third, or fourth time today, Andi Peretti has made me speechless.

Chapter 30

Andi

I'm woken by a kiss on my cheek.

"Sweetheart," a voice murmurs against my ear. "I have to get going. You can keep sleeping if you'd like."

I pull the pillow over my head out of habit. I'm a college student—resisting mornings is what we do.

"Babe, my flight leaves in just over an hour, I've really gotta run."

The urgency in Ryan's voice draws me out from under the pillow. The most emotion I can manage on my face is a raised eyebrow. "Why?"

He laughs, even though I'm not trying to be funny. I'm simply not a morning person. Apparently I'm *especially* not a morning person after a night—and morning—of fooling around in bed.

It didn't help that we slipped in one last go-round before the sunlight came up, a new record for me. Turns out I like setting new records, I just don't like returning to real life afterward.

"No…" I moan. "Stay."

I've never felt so exhausted. I feel like I've been hit with a sack of bricks—a big, beautiful sack of brick abs attached to Ryan Pierce.

"Babe—"

"Oh, *flight*!" It finally registers. He's leaving for Minnesota today, and I'm holding him up. "I am so sorry. I forgot!"

I fumble with the sheets, which is less than productive. My feet tangle, and I'm a hot mess as I fall out of bed and land in an oddly contorted yoga pose on the floor.

"Sorry," I say. "Not a morning person."

"Wouldn't have guessed," he says, reaching over to scoop me up. Once he plants me on my feet, he kisses my forehead. "I promise I didn't plan things this way; I really, really wish I could stay."

"It's fine. We're friends with benefits." I rise up onto my tiptoes to kiss him back. "Breakfast not required."

"Breakfast is *desired*, however."

While I'm standing there with hair that appears to have been electrocuted, he apparently wakes up looking ready for a media interview. If I'm not mistaken, he's showered again—his hair is damp and curly, falling in soft loops onto his forehead. He's wearing jeans and a sweater that make him look like a cross between a Ralph Lauren model and the hockey player he is.

I look down in horror. Apparently I never found that shirt of Ryan's, or if I did, it ended up on the floor with the rest of my clothes. I dive for my underwear first, shimmy into those, and then begin the search for my bra.

After a moment, I look up from examining the underbelly of Ryan's bed to find it dangling from his fingers.

"Looking for this?" he asks. "Come and get it."

"I thought you had to leave...*urgently*."

"I do, which is why I was about to tell you to take your time, but then you bent over and I got all distracted. Don't blame me."

"My car!" I exclaim. "It's in the parking lot on Hollywood Boulevard."

"It's fine there," he says. "Boxer will take you up to retrieve it."

"Boxer?"

"Big guy, missing a tooth—"

"I *know* who he is," I say. "But why is he bringing me to my car?"

"Because I called him and told him to get his ass over here because I don't want you paying for an Uber when it was *my* ass who dragged *your* ass back here."

"I didn't mind the dragging," I say with a shrug. "Fair's fair. I can Uber."

"He's waiting outside. Just leave the keys on the table when you're ready to go, and Lawrence will lock up—"

"I'm ready," I say, one leg still outside of my jeans. "Or I'm almost ready."

"I'll just leave you the keys—"

"Nope, I'm good!" In all honesty, I don't want to be trusted with the keys to Ryan's apartment, even for a short time. Too much could go wrong—I could lose them, break something, decide I love his bed and shower more than mine and never actually leave this place... "Let's go."

He clears his throat.

I glance down, realizing that I put my arm through the head hole of my shirt and things are all off balance. I make the necessary adjustments, ignore the fact that my hair looks like a bird's nest, and march out of the room.

Ryan locks the door, and I see a huge SUV on the street—Boxer, I'm guessing.

"Is he here for both of us?" I ask.

"No, I have someone picking me up. They'll be here in a second."

"Are you sure you don't want to go with Boxer? I swear I can get a ride."

"It's fine," he says. "Really. I'd love to see you longer—I mean, you can ride with me to the airport if you want, but I figured you have things to do."

"Right," I say, even though I don't really have things to do. It feels too clingy to say otherwise. Even so, I have no classes, nothing until three this afternoon when I have to report to Peretti's for work. "Well, have a safe flight."

"Andi…" He pauses. "I had a really nice time last night."

"Me too."

He takes my hand in his, looking at the back of it as if there's a message written there. Apparently he sees nothing because he sighs and brings his eyes to mine. "You're coming to the wedding, right? Without a doubt?"

"Of course," I say. "I owe it to your Ferrari."

At first he looks dismayed, then he must realize that I'm joking because he smiles. "Whatever the reason, I'll take it."

There's a moment of silence, a heavy moment in which both of us try to decide if there's something else to say—at least, that's what I'm doing. Do I tell him I'll miss him? It's the truth, but I'm not sure what the protocol is for our agreement.

"I'll miss you," he says. "I hope you don't mind me saying that."

I let out a breath. "I'll miss you too. I mean, after last night…I'll *definitely* miss you. Let me just say, I had no clue what I was going to be missing."

He looks proud of himself, and for good reason, too.

I follow his eyes as he watches my face, trails his gaze down to my lips, and then opens his mouth to say something else.

"Don't worry," I say before he reminds me that we're *just friends* again. "I'm not attached or whatever. I just meant I had a good time."

"Just friends?" He frowns, his grip on my hand growing tighter and tighter until he's squeezing me so hard there's a red mark from his fingers. "Andi, I—"

I hold my breath and wait for whatever he's about to say, whatever is so difficult he's having a hard time getting it out, but the words never come.

Behind me comes the honk of a horn, and I turn to find a sleek black Porsche pulling up to the curb. Behind the wheel is a slim blonde; she's gorgeous in an ice queen sort of way. She's dressed in an outfit that I'm sure was more expensive than what I pay in a month's rent, and she looks pissed.

"Oh, I'm sorry," I say, backing away, confused. "Is that your...ride?"

"Andi, no," he says, seeing the look on my face. "It's nothing like that. She's the agent I'm hoping to sign with, and she's ticked because we're late going to the airport. It's not your fault though, it's mine. I called her last minute for a ride so I could send Boxer with you."

"She's going with you to Minnesota?"

"We have a meeting this afternoon with my coach. She'll fly back out afterward," he says. "And if you're wondering, no—there is nothing, has never been anything, and will never be anything between her and me."

"Did I look that desperate?"

"Not desperate," he says with a flustered look over my shoulder. "But I didn't want you to wonder, or worry, because—"

"Friends with benefits," I finish. "I get it, and I appreciate it. Look, have a great flight and enjoy your time. I hope you get whatever it is you want the most out of all this."

"The most?"

"Minnesota, LA, the Stars, the Lightning, anything else that I don't understand in your little hockey world. I hope it all works out for you."

"My little hockey world," he repeats with a ghosted smile. "I'll miss you. Call me sometime."

He leans in, brushes a kiss against my cheek, and then he's gone.

I watch as he climbs into the car. His potential agent pulls away from the curb with tires squealing. She looks pissed at me, pissed at him, pissed at the world. *Yikes*. That woman is wound tight enough to pop a vertebra when she sneezes.

"Hey, you ready to go, Andi?" Boxer calls from the car. "Pierce told me to bring you to your car, but there's a problem: I don't know where he put your car."

Big, lovable Boxer, I think as I make my way to the car and give him directions. As we take off into the horrible traffic, I can't help but watch the cars around me and think that of all people in Los Angeles, Ryan Pierce has chosen me to miss.

We might never be able to make things work in any sort of permanent way, but at least for now, I can enjoy the little moments we have together.

Chapter 31

Andi

My phone rings just before we turn onto the highway that'll lead us to Hollywood Boulevard, Phil, and my car. I look down, my heart racing with all sorts of insane thoughts going through my head.

In the split second before I glance at the screen, I wonder if it's Ryan calling to tell me he changed his mind and wants to stay here for just a little while longer. *Friends,* I mutter to myself. *We're friends.*

"Friends?" Boxer looks over. "We're friends?"

"Sure," I tell Boxer as I answer the phone. "Hello?"

"Hello," Boxer says.

The man on the other end of the phone clears his throat. "Hello, may I speak to Andi?"

"This is Andi," I say, and Boxer looks over, finally putting the puzzle pieces together. "Whom am I speaking with?"

"This is Nick Bennett," he says. "I'm a friend of the Pierce family."

"Oh," I say. "Are you looking for Ryan? He's not here."

He laughs, a soft sound. "Ryan didn't tell you I'd be calling?"

"Um…"

"Let me start this over," Nick says. "I'm an agent for VWA, and I represent stars such as Andrew Flemming, Adam Thomson, Lila

Montenapoleone, and—"

"I know who you are," I say stiffly. I'd recognized the name when he'd first said it, but for some reason, the dots didn't connect. "I sent you headshots about three years ago."

"Yes, I remember," he says. "You were young. Twenty?"

"Good memory," I say, trying to remain calm. Nick Bennett is the best of the best—he's gotten at least three comics their own shows in the last year alone. Signing with Nick is like receiving Willy Wonka's golden ticket in the world of comedy. "I'm older now, more experienced."

Just as I'm about to smack my head into the car-seat in front of me for sounding so stupid, he laughs again. "I've been following your career closely, and it seems like you've built up a solid resume."

"I've tried," I say. "Sorry, did you mention Ryan asking you to call? You really don't have to—"

"No, you've misunderstood," Nick interrupts. "Ryan didn't tell me to call. I asked for your information when I realized y'all were dating."

"Oh, well, we're not dating."

"Right," he says, sounding unconvinced. "Well, Lawrence is one of my closest friends. I was at his bachelor party the other night, not realizing we'd kick the whole thing off with a comedy show."

"You and me both," I say. "I didn't see that one coming."

"Lucky me, it was the best show I've seen all month."

"You're kidding."

"I hounded Ryan all show to get your number. He finally broke down after asking you if it'd be okay."

"Are you lying?"

"Sorry?"

"He didn't put you up to this, did he? You're not doing him any favors by calling me?"

"No, absolutely not. Ryan seemed hesitant to share your info, if anything."

"Oh."

"Now that we've cleared up that matter, I have to say, Andi, I loved your stuff." He moves the conversation along, for which I am grateful. "I'm calling because I may have an opportunity for you. How soon can you get to Studio City?"

"An hour?"

"I'll see you then. Do you need the address to VWA headquarters?"

"I'm not…" I look in the mirror at my sex hair, about to tell him I'm not ready for a meeting, not ready for my career to get a break, not ready for the pressure.

Then I realize…I'll never be ready.

"Problem?"

This might be my only chance in the world to get a meeting with Nick Bennett. I straighten my shoulders, tilt my chin a little bit to the sky, and force a smile on my face. "Absolutely not. See you soon."

No sooner do I disconnect than my phone beeps with a text. It's from Ryan.

> Ryan: I forgot to tell you—I hope you don't mind that I gave your phone number to Nick Bennett. He's been a pain in my ass about it ever since he heard you at the show. If you don't want him to call you, let me know. I'll take care of it.
>
> Me: I just got off the phone with him.
>
> Ryan: And?
>
> Me: Are you sure you didn't force him to call me? If you're lying, I'll find out and hunt you down.
>
> Ryan: I promise. He asked me.

Me: Pinky swear?

Ryan: On my life.

Me: Well, I'm on my way to see him now.

Ryan: Lucky bastard. If he hits on you, I'm going to be upset.

Me: Jealous?

Ryan: I wouldn't say jealous.

Me: What would you say?

Ryan: Possessive.

Me: Same thing.

Ryan: I don't care what you call it, the fact is, I want to see you again. Can I book your tickets for the wedding?

Me: You don't have to pay. I'll book them. Payment for the car, or the meeting with Nick.

Ryan: Absolutely not. I'll send you the confirmation information in a few minutes. Two days around the wedding sound good? I know you'll have to be back for work.

Me: I've asked my boss for some time off.

Ryan: Is it too much to say that I miss you?

Me: No...I miss you too.

Ryan: Good luck with Nick today, but you don't need it. If he doesn't sign you on first sight, he's an idiot.

Ryan: I'm going through security, going to turn phone off soon. Call me after?

Me: Safe flight!

I almost catch myself typing *Love you* without thinking about it, but not because it means anything. I say those words to Lisa all the time, and she says them to me too—even if she's a little more crass and adds a few curse words in there just out of habit.

While thinking about Lisa, I text her the news about my meeting with Mr. Bennett.

She responds immediately.

Lisa: No way! Good luck! I love you, bitch!!! You'll do great. Call me after—drinks, my bed, tonight.

Chapter 32

Andi

"So? How did it go?" Lisa's voice sounds through the speaker. "I've been on pins and needles over here."

I'm making my way out of VWA agency headquarters, still spinning from the interview with Nick. My sex hair has been somewhat tamed, and I'm lucky that the comedy business is casual by nature. My black tank top and jeans worked great with the leather jacket and high heels stashed in my trunk.

"He asked me to do a five-minute bit," I say, my breath coming in gasps. "I think I nailed it. We didn't agree to sign anything yet, but he's interested. He's sending in the footage for some new show."

"One of those *Last Comic Standing* type things?"

"Yeah, but a brand new Netflix edition," I say. "They have their male roster set but needed a few females. He's going to call you next!"

"Shit, you're kidding."

"He loved our show!"

"Shit."

"Stop cussing! This is exciting!"

"Damn."

"That's a curse word, Lisa. Say something else."

"Bitch, I don't know what to say!"

"Okay, well, at least we're getting somewhere." I reach my car, unlock it, and slide inside. "Plans for tonight?"

"My house at nine."

"I have to work."

"Well, I'll order a pizza," she threatens. "And make you come over."

"Lisa, I really have to work."

"Ryan got to hang out with you when he ordered pizzas!"

"Ryan ordered twenty pizzas."

She blew out a breath. "Come over when you're done. I'll be waiting, but I can't guarantee there will be any wine left."

"I'll bring a bottle."

"Good girl," she says. "Bye."

As I pull away from the parking lot, I debate calling Ryan to tell him about the meeting. It truly felt like it was a success. Nick Bennett listened, explained in no uncertain terms that he thought both Lisa and I had potential, and offered to put our footage in front of producers.

Even if they didn't opt to take us for the show, he thought the two of us had potential for a joint show at a big, local theater. I am positively buzzing with excitement, and of their own accord, my fingers dial Ryan.

When he answers, his voice is quiet. "We're about to take off," he whispers. "How'd it go?"

"Success!" I shout. A driver looks over at me from the next lane, and I realize my windows are cracked. "Success," I say more quietly. "At least, I think so. Too early to tell, really."

"I didn't have a doubt in my mind," he says, and in the background an airline attendant tells him to shut off his phone.

"I'll hang up," I say, "I just…well, I wanted to share the good news with you."

"So glad you did," he says. "Congratulations."

"Ryan." This time it's a closer female voice, clipped and short, and I am willing to bet big money it belongs to the ice queen who picked Ryan up from his house. "Didn't you hear the attendant? We're taking off."

"I've gotta go," he says. "I'll talk to you later."

"Bye," I say, hearing the click of the ended call almost instantaneously.

I focus on driving home, but my mind is somewhere else, somewhere distant. I'm on top of the world one second, thrilled about the opportunities for my career, Lisa and I going places... If Nick's prospects are serious, this could change our lives.

On the other hand, Ryan Pierce is flying away from me with a beautiful woman by his side. I trust him, and I know he wouldn't lie to me, but...we are friends with benefits. We aren't exclusive, we aren't married—we aren't anything, really.

Even if he promises nothing will happen between him and the agent, what happens when he spends time with her day after day while I'm thousands of miles away? And if not her, then someone else.

While one part of my heart is thrilled, the other is aching. Unfortunately, I can't do anything about either of them at the moment.

Only time will tell.

The problem is that I'm impatient, and I don't feel like waiting.

Chapter 33

Andi

"Andi, for the third time, will you bring me the freaking—" My dad pops his head out from the kitchen at Peretti's and cuts himself off midsentence. "Andi?"

I'm sitting on a barstool at the counter staring deep into the flames of the oven, oblivious to the customers around me. I only vaguely hear my dad's voice calling my name to bring him something or other to fix the leaky faucet.

"Is everything okay?" he asks, his voice a little gruff as he rounds the counter and takes a seat next to me. "What's on your mind?"

"Nothing," I say, forcing myself to snap back to attention. Neither my dad nor I are big in the way of talking about our feelings. We prefer to grunt and argue with each other until the problem has passed or otherwise fixed itself. "Sorry, just distracted."

"I'll say. I've asked you for the screwdriver several times."

"Where's the screwdriver?" I stand. "Sorry, I didn't get a lot of sleep last night."

It's the truth, but that's not the only reason I'm off balance. The adrenaline has eased from the morning's meeting and the previous night's thrills, and now Ryan's far away and I'm waiting to hear from Nick. This odd limbo has me in some weird funk, and I can't decide if I'm excited or sad, happy or depressed, tired or alert. Somehow, I manage to be none of the above, which is why I'm floating around in a fog of uncertainty.

"I recognize this, whatever it is," my dad says. "I've been there. Something's bothering you."

"Comedy stuff," I say. "Don't worry about it. I won't let it affect my schoolwork."

"Is that all you think I care about?" he asks. "Your stupid grades?"

"Stupid grades?" I face him. "You're the one who makes it sound like it's the end of the world if I get a B+."

"Nobody should get a B+ in art class, Andi. Draw something on a page and turn it in to your teacher."

"It wasn't an easy art class," I mumble. "I suck at drawing."

"But you don't suck at comedy," he says. "And that's an art."

I frown. "How do you know?"

My dad looks at his fingernails. They're clean, but he plays with them anyway. "I just know."

My dad has never been to a show, never supported my dreams of being a comic. He still wants me to be an accountant—stable job, stable pay, stable everything. "What aren't you telling me?"

"You know that thingy with videos?" He glances at me, his cheeks reddening ever so slightly. "The tube or whatever."

"YouTube?"

"Whatever. Where they put videos of you?"

It starts to click. "You've seen me on YouTube?"

"Rick has a channel and he puts all your stuff on there," he says. "Your sister showed it to me once."

"I am going to kill her," I say through my teeth. "I thought you didn't know how to use the internet."

"I don't," he says. "But there's only one button I have to click in the little bookmark tab and it just pops up for me. Magic."

"Magic," I mumble. "So you've seen me perform once?"

"Once?" He shakes his head, a smile playing on his lips. "I've seen every one of your shows, kiddo."

My jaw drops open. "But I thought…" I can't even finish my sentence. "What about accounting?"

"I wanted you to get your education while you're young. I didn't go to college, and I wanted you to have that opportunity, to be able to get out of the restaurant biz if that's what you desire."

"Dad, I love working here. Peretti's is great, and—"

He waves a hand. "I have no regrets about how my life turned out, but I want you to have whatever opportunities you may desire. I thought you were too young to decide whether or not you needed a college degree when you graduated high school, so I made you enroll."

"Yeah, I know."

"You've got talent, kid."

"For accounting?"

He meets my eyes, and I realize we have the same forest green coloring there that lightens in the sun and darkens under the stars. "You're going to make it in the comedy business, sweetheart. You're talented, really funny, and smart too, not that stupid humor."

I'm not sure what qualifies as stupid humor, but I'm glad my dad doesn't think I have it. "Wow, I had no idea…"

"You'll be graduating this year, and I guess…" He shrugs, returning his gaze to the countertop. "It's time I am honest with you. I want you to go after your dreams. Get that degree first, like I ask, but then go for it. You're young, and you've got grit. If anyone can make a living from their dreams, it's you."

"Dad—"

"Whatever news you got that has you in a funk—good or bad, I don't care—you're going to succeed at this, Andi, and I want you to know I'll be there for you."

My eyes sting. As I mentioned, we're not an emotional family. Then again, we've never talked like this, not even at my mother's funeral. "That means a lot, Dad."

I lean over and put my arms around his shoulders. He squeezes me back, and dare I say he blinks a little faster than usual? I've seen my dad cry twice, that's it—once when my mom got sick, once when she died. I hate seeing him cry more than anything.

"Maybe you can come to a live show once," I tell him. "I'd love that."

"Me too," he says, his voice gruff.

We hesitate a moment longer, both of us in new territory. It's clear that neither of us is quite sure where to go from here.

"Is there anything else going on?" My dad's face crinkles as if he's not sure whether or not he actually wants me to tell him. "Did you want to *talk* more?"

I shake my head, but after one more look at him, I find myself spilling the details about my day. I tell him about the audition, about the morning with Ryan—only the part about him leaving, not the good stuff from the previous night. Mostly, I just mention that he flew home.

"He's gone, and I don't know how to feel about it."

"Feel however you want, kid," he says. "The heart wants what it wants, even if your mind thinks it's stupid."

We sit together and I think about his words. The more I think about Ryan, the more I realize my heart wants to be next to his. My heart, my soul, my body—all three pieces agree on one thing: that Andi Peretti is happier when she's around Ryan.

The phone rings, breaking the silence. My dad answers. "Hello?" he asks. The other person begins speaking and my dad glances at me. "Uh-huh. Uh-huh. Uh-huh."

I blink up at him, trying to read his expression. I can't.

"Uh-huh, uh-huh," he says a few more times. "A smiley face?"

My heart beats faster.

"You don't want a pizza, do you?" he says to the person on the other end of the line. "Sure, I'll send her over."

"Who was that?" I ask, trying to be calm. Ryan's not even in the state—it can't be him.

Sure enough, I'm right.

"That was Lisa," he says. "She misses you."

I try not to show my disappointment. "Ah."

"She mentioned you had a rough day," he says, watching me cautiously. "She also mentioned that she's got a bottle of wine with your name on it, and said if you could bring over a pizza, that'd be great."

"I already told her I'd be there after I finished up here," I say. "Sorry, Dad, she's persistent—"

"Go," he says before I can finish. "Angela will be arriving any second, and we can handle it."

"But—"

He reaches into the cash register and hands me a hundred. "Here are your tips. You can take the extra sausage I made by accident."

"Are you sure?"

"Go."

"I'm scared of Lisa, too," I say with a smile, and my dad laughs. "Thank you."

"I love you, kid," he says.

"I love you too, Dad."

He hands me a pizza, and I head out to the car. I've begun parking in the alley again, even though the vehicle is still missing a few pieces. Either my dad hasn't noticed, or he doesn't care.

When I slip into the car and the GPS guides me toward Lisa, a sense of calm falls over me. I have family. I have kickass friends. I have a potential breakthrough for my passion, and I hooked up with Ryan Pierce last night.

Life could definitely be worse.

Chapter 34

Andi

"You really didn't have to bail me out early," I say as soon as Lisa opens the door. I grabbed a bottle of wine on the way over, and it's balanced on the pizza. "It's nice of you to offer, but I could've stopped by later."

"I was being selfish." She reaches for the wine, and then leaves me to trail behind her carrying the pizza into the apartment. "I was out of wine, and you'd promised me a bottle."

We both know she's lying, but that's how Lisa rolls. She's the most loyal friend a girl can ask for; she might swear like a sailor, but she's got my back, and I've got hers. That's how it's always been, and it's how it'll always be. I force her into a hug to show her I appreciate it.

I take my shoes off since I'm well acquainted with her home. It's a tiny place that she shares with a roommate, but he's rarely home. He's one of our mutual comedian friends, and he's gay—or so we think. I'm not sure it's ever been confirmed.

"Derrick's gone. Hamptons," she says. "I think he's found a *friend* out there, but what do I know? Sit down. Tell me everything."

I follow her abrupt change of subject easily. We've been doing this for years, and Lisa has a cadence to her speech that I've grown accustomed to.

"I'm not sure there's much to tell."

"Uh, how about we start with the first question: why the hell did Nicholas Bennett call you?"

I wince. "He saw our show?!"

"I know." Lisa sticks a hand on her hip. "I heard that *from him*. He called me after he finished with you!"

"Did you get an audition too?"

She squeals, a sound I never expected to Lisa make. She hates teeny-bopper, high-pitched girly noises, but in this moment she has her Justin Bieber-fangirl impression down pat. "Yes. Tomorrow. Hence the reason I'm drinking heavily tonight."

I eye her glass. "You're cut off."

"I'm kidding. I haven't had a thing to drink tonight except for whiskey, and that doesn't count." When I start to argue, she waves me off. "Moving along because I can't talk about Nick any more without freaking out. So, tell me about Ryan."

"Ryan..."

"Pierce."

"I *know* which Ryan," I say. "I'm trying to figure out what to tell you."

"Did you kiss?"

I hesitate a moment too long and she inhales the hugest of breaths.

"Maybe I slept over."

She smacks me with a pillow, clearly too wired to formulate a thought.

"I sent you a picture of my hair!"

"I thought you were making out! You *never* sleep with guys this quickly."

"Oh, don't worry...we didn't sleep." By now, I'm grinning. "It was *ah*-mazing."

She falls back onto the bed. "You're a goddess. Ryan Pierce. *Ryan Pierce.*"

"He's just a normal guy," I say, remembering our shared laughs, the way he touched my hair, caressed my skin. "And I hate to say it, but…"

"You like him."

I nod. "A lot."

"Well, you're going to that wedding with him, right?"

"As a friend…with benefits."

"When is it?"

"Just under a month away."

"You won't see him until then?" she asks. "How does this whole thing work? I usually don't *date*, I just…well, I have one date and that's it. So what's the protocol? Does he call you, or do you call him?"

I shrug. "We're figuring things out. I don't want to put any pressure on him. I went into this agreement knowing full well it's not going anywhere."

"Don't say *agreement*, it seems so formal."

"I sort of demanded sex."

"Who are you?" Lisa asks, forgetting about the wine glass in her hand as she stares at me. "*I'm* the one who has irresponsible one-night stands. You're the responsible one who dates guys for seven years and then takes a break for three."

"That happened once, in high school, and it was hardly serious. He didn't even ask me to prom."

"Yea, because he was a douche."

I ignore her commentary, hugging the pillow she throws at me. "Last night didn't *feel* irresponsible. It felt like the best thing in the world."

"Ohmygod."

"What?"

"Are you in love?"

I swallow hard. I've been wondering the same thing, but I can't admit it. It's too crazy. "I can't be. It's too soon. We only met a few weeks ago, and we just had sex for the first time last night."

"And the second?" She's fishing now.

"And maybe the third," I say. "Like I said, awesome."

"I need to get laid."

"Yeah," I agree. "Probably."

"What happens next?" she asks. "Are you just supposed to stay a free bird while you wait for the wedding?"

My phone rings, interrupting the conversation. I look at the name. *Ryan*. "One second."

She peeks at the screen then gives me a conspiratorial wink. "I want to listen. Let me listen, please."

I roll my eyes, but I answer it in front of her. "Hello?"

"I booked your tickets," he says. "Confirmation will be in your inbox shortly, sweetheart. I'll see you in a month, and not a day later."

"Okay," I say, my heart thumping at the sound of his deep, rolling voice. "I'm looking forward to it."

"Nervous?"

"Yes," I admit.

"Me too," he says. "I miss you."

In the background, I hear a woman saying Ryan's name, louder and louder until finally, I say, "I think someone's calling you."

"I told you I'll be right there," he says, his voice carrying over a little distance as he speaks away from the phone. "Sorry, I had a meeting with my coach and Jocelyn, and we grabbed some drinks after."

"I thought she was flying out earlier," I say, and then realize that sounds as if I'm jealous—which I'm not. I'm definitely not jealous that she's there, next to him, and I'm not, so I quickly add, "I mean, things must have gone well if she's sticking around, right?"

"Great!" he says, and his voice is light and excited. "We won't have the contracts finalized until, well, after you're here, but it's looking like I'll be playing for the Lightning next year."

"That's great news," I say, my heart soaring at the idea of him being in the same city as me. "I'm happy for you."

Jocelyn calls for him again, and Ryan lowers his voice. "I'm sorry, I've gotta go. Jocelyn's flight is leaving soon, and she asked if I could drop her off."

"Okay, well, thank you again for the tickets. You didn't have to buy them."

"I need you there." He says the words, but sounds distracted. "Call me tomorrow. Goodnight Peretti."

"Night."

Before I can ask in what exact capacity Ryan Pierce could ever need *me* in his life, he hangs up. It was probably a slip of the tongue, and I try to push the thoughts away.

But the thoughts persist. Maybe Ryan wants me to keep his mother off his back, or he just wants an easy hookup with no strings attached. Maybe he wants company out here until he can make real friends. As much as he made me feel wanted this morning—and last night—I can't shake the thought that it is all so temporary.

When I work up the courage to look at Lisa, she has a gentle, almost kind look on her face. "You're falling for him, aren't you?"

I throw the phone on the bed and fling myself backward into the pillows. "Dammit."

Chapter 35

Ryan

"You're falling for her, aren't you?" Jocelyn asks as we cruise toward the airport. "What's her name?"

"Andi," I say before I can stop myself. I can't help it. She's always on my mind, ever since she left my side. She's been on my mind for days—even before she wrecked it with fantastic sex.

Then, after, when she didn't turn all clingy and call me a hundred times on the first day, I was almost ready to propose. Even as I drive to the airport, I can't help thinking that a girl who can make me laugh, who looks hot as hell in a stupid red polo shirt, who is ten times smarter than me and can nearly make me explode with the touch of her hand—what more could a man ever need?

I'm already hard again, wishing she were next to me.

"You told me you weren't going to get involved."

Jocelyn's clipped, ice-cold tone kills the mood in my fantasies. My boner deflates faster than if I'd jumped into an ice bath.

"I'm not *involved*."

"You're having sex with her."

"What business is that of yours?" I'm pissed, my hand gripping the wheel tight. If I didn't respect Jocelyn's work as an agent so much, I would call her a taxi and tell her to get out. But, my Midwestern upbringing left me with some manners, and unfortunately manners don't involve kicking a woman out of my car. "Who cares if I'm having sex with her? That doesn't equal a relationship."

"Maybe if it was a one-night thing, but you're calling her. I'm not deaf." Jocelyn's pissed too, and this isn't boding well for our working relationship. "When I asked who that girl was this morning when she was coming out of your house, you said *nobody*."

"And I meant that she's nobody *you* need to care about."

"But she's somebody *you* care about, which makes me concerned. I can't tell you the number of hockey players I've signed who get distracted by their dick the first year of their career. We all look like assholes, and I don't plan on letting that happen again."

"Thanks for your *concern*," I spit out. "But I can control my dick."

"Really? Because it sounds like it's getting away from you."

"What the fuck, Jocelyn? Why does it matter?"

She turns toward me, eyes like blue steel. "You promised me you wouldn't get involved. By default, that means she *has* to be a one-night stand. No strings attached. I don't care how many one-night bunnies you feel like banging; I care when there are strings connected to the same girl. If you're fighting me on it this hard, there are a lot of damn strings hanging loose, Pierce. Tie that shit up."

I hate that she's right. I hate that this thing, this agreement, whatever stupid idea I had with Andi, has turned into something more. I hate that it's already affecting my career, and I haven't even started the season. More importantly, I hate that I'm falling in love with her.

Now's not the time, the place, the...anything. We're a million miles apart, and we're both at insanely important junctures in our careers. Everything about this situation is so wrong and yet, I can't help it. There's more here than I'm willing to admit, and Jocelyn's calling me out on it.

"We have an agreement," I say to Jocelyn. I tell her the truth—well, a part of the truth. "We're fuck buddies. Got it? Sure, there are a few strings, but I don't love her. That's not where this is headed—for either of us."

"How long is it going to last?"

I fix her with a hard gaze. "Until Lawrence and Lilia's wedding. That's how this whole thing started, anyway. We were friends, and I asked her to help me out. My mom's been trying to fix me up with these girls I went to high school with. They're not for me. I don't want them. So, it's easier to appease my mom with a fake girlfriend."

"Good."

"You're changing your tune."

"Not at all," she says, gathering her briefcase as I pull over to let her out at the Sun Country terminal. "If there's an end date in sight, I'm happy. The date to sign contracts is a week after Lawrence's wedding."

I knew where she was heading before she went there. I try not to break the steering wheel as I throw the car into park. Now I've gone and promised Jocelyn something I can't uphold on my end—if Andi wants more after the wedding, I'm going to give it to her.

A chill centers on my spine as I consider the alternative. Andi might just catch her big break with Nick Bennett before my brother's wedding and be so focused on her career she wants nothing to do with men.

In fact, who knows if she'll even show up at the ceremony? I relax slightly, thinking that the chances of Andi wanting anything more than a few additional orgasms are slim to none, and if that's the case, my agreement with Jocelyn is a non-issue.

"I'll have my assistant book your flights for a few days after the wedding." Jocelyn shuts the door, leans down to the open window, and gives me a cold-hearted smile. "You show up at my offices unattached, and we've got ourselves a deal. You show up sniffing around like a lovesick puppy, and everything's off, you're back to Minnesota, and you don't fucking get her anyway. Are we clear? There's only one option, Pierce."

I grit my teeth, which she must take for agreement because she reaches through the window and gives me a pat on the cheek with fingers that grate like nails on a chalkboard.

"I'll see you and your friend at the wedding."

When she leaves, I'm fuming. I slam my palm against the wheel, frustrated that there are no good options before me. I sign with the Ice Queen, and she's going to expect me to drop things with Andi. I don't sign with her, and the chances are high that I'll be in Minnesota another year. I love the state, love my team, but it still puts me two thousand miles away from Andi.

Then again, I'm not even sure Andi wants *me*. She's the one who proposed this whole sex-without-attachments thing. Maybe Nick Bennett is going to make her a huge-ass star and she'll forget about me. God knows she has the talent to do whatever the hell she wants in this world.

If only I'd played by the rules, maybe I wouldn't have fallen in love.

But I broke the rules, and now I want more.

Chapter 36

Andi

My phone beeps as the airplane coasts to a stop. My nerves are shot, my heart is fluttering, and my fingers are trembling. I hardly manage to open the text message without dropping my phone.

Luckily, it's just Lisa. She's texted me another seven eggplant emojis, which still doesn't make sense to me. Do they really look like penises? Peni? I text her back a frowny face, and she sends back hearts and kisses which I interpret to mean *Good luck in Minnesota*.

She and I have learned to read each other's minds, and at this point in our relationship, we can have entire conversations via emojis. It's quite convenient, and a lot more fun than actually spelling out words.

My phone rings before I leave my seat.

"I love your emojis," Lisa says. "But I figured you might need some talking down from a ledge."

"No ledge," I say. "I'm still on the airplane."

"Well, you have a big giant penis waiting for you at the gate, and I know you're nervous about it."

"Lisa!" I glance next to me. The old man in the seat there has clearly heard the words *giant* and *penis* and is giving me a serious onceover. "Quiet. You're embarrassing me from two thousand miles away."

"Well, I'm here to distract you, and I'll bet it's working. Are you even nervous anymore?"

"Not about Ryan," I say, thinking that the old guy next to me is looking too interested in my shirt and what's underneath it. "Nervous about getting off of this plane, maybe."

"What do you have to be nervous about? Ryan has called you every day for a month."

"That doesn't mean anything."

"Bullshit. He's head over heels for you."

"Maybe he just wanted to make sure I'd still hook up with him this weekend."

"If he hadn't called you once, wouldn't you still have hooked up with him? After all, y'all *say* you're friends with benefits, and that specifically means he *doesn't* have to call."

I think for a moment. "I suppose you've got a point."

"Don't kid yourself. You still would've slept with him."

"Maybe," I say defensively. "You don't know that."

"Come on," she says. "You might've tried to resist, but you wouldn't have been able to. All that wedding crap and love in the air, Mr. Charming flying you across the country just to be with him— you would've caved the second he laid a hand on your panties."

I debate arguing with her, but it's probably true, so I let her statement go unchallenged.

"You don't have to tell me I'm right," she continues. "My only point is that he didn't *have* to call. A man doesn't call once or twice *a day* to talk to a fuck buddy. A guy calls once or twice a day to talk to the girl he can't stop thinking about."

"But—"

"Don't be nervous. Just go have a good time. You're probably wondering what the point is, or what's going to happen next, but I instruct you to let your mind be blank. Zen."

"What am I supposed to think about?"

"Getting off! His schlong! The fact that you're going to a wedding with Ryan in the *first* place! I don't care. Just don't worry about something you can't control. No use focusing on the future when you guys have an agreement that specifically says *no future*."

Finally, the aisle begins to clear, and I climb from my seat. "You're right."

"I know it's not easy," she says, her voice a bit softer. "You both have feelings for each other and all of us on the outside can see it, but there is so much up in the air right now—for both of you."

"You're right."

"I'm right?! Of course I'm *right*. You *just* signed on to film a pilot for TV. Television. If that gets picked up, you'll be going places."

"You too," I say with a smile, warming at the fresh memory.

We got the news yesterday, signed the contracts today. Nick Bennett secured us positions to film the pilot of a new female comic-centric show. Nothing is set in stone yet, but it's a better start than we've ever had before.

"At least I know that you and me, we're going places together."

"Damn straight!" She laughs. "I'd handcuff myself to you before I let them drag us apart, but that's not all you've got going for you. Graduation is around the corner. You'll have your degree. You have a job and a family who loves you. We'll find an apartment together so I can get rid of Derrick for good."

"You're right," I agree. Life's really not so bad. "But I'm still nervous."

She lets out a long sigh. "What are you wearing?"

I look down. I have on *everything*. "Everything," I tell her. "Ryan told me to be prepared. Minnesota has unpredictable weather."

She sucks her breath back in. "You know it's August, right?"

"Yes."

"It's too late now, I suppose," she says. "Go. Get off the phone with me, then get off with Ryan."

"Jeez, you're crude."

"I'm honest."

"Bye," I say as my phone beeps with a message.

It's from him.

Ryan: I'm here.

Those two little words have me ready to collapse back into my seat, even if it means giving the creepy old man next to me a peek down my V-neck t-shirt. I can't wait to see him, but I'm not ready, either.

Plus, I'm really *really* hot—literally. Since I didn't quite know what to wear on the plane—Ryan warned me multiple times that the weather in Minnesota is finicky at best, disastrous at worst—I wore everything.

Being a Cali girl, I know exactly two sorts of weather: sunshine, and a little bit more sunshine. Therefore, to battle this so-called 'unpredictable' weather, I wore clothing to be prepared for all occasions: a t-shirt, a cardigan, a rain jacket, knee-high boots over skinny jeans, and a pair of gloves tucked into my pocket. Judging by the attire of other passengers, I am slightly overdressed. Most women here are sporting shorts or dresses.

Damn, I should've checked the weather before getting on the plane, but I was running late after signing contracts, and I don't have any room in my bags to stash additional clothes. Therefore, I'm stuck wearing all of it, and now I'm about to die from overheating.

The line moves along. "Did you come from the North Pole?" The man behind me crinkles his old, fluffy eyebrows and I frown at the amount of hair poking out of his nose. "All you need is a team of sled dogs."

"Funny," I murmur.

"You look good," he says. "Would look better with less clothes, I bet. I have to say, I overheard you talking to your friend on the phone, and—"

"Bye," I say, bursting through the gates of the plane. I'm running down the terminal dragging my carry-on behind me. I'm breathing heavily—between the running and the clothes, it's like a sweat lodge in here.

I don't have the patience to deal with my new-old friend; I'm already rattled enough. Heading to a new state with a guy I hardly know is more than enough to do the trick.

Sure, I've talked on the phone with Ryan more than I've ever talked to anyone in my life. It sort of feels like we've known each other forever, but in the grand scheme of things, we're new, and the feelings are strong.

I don't stop jogging until it's too late, and I barrel into the waiting area. I mean to dodge the other passengers and slow down, maybe use the restroom to reapply perfume and mascara, scrub some of that gross airplane air off of me, but I'm totally out of it. I crash into the first pair of arms I see.

The embrace is familiar, his arms strong as bricks, muscle twined beautifully underneath a simple white shirt. These arms are attached to a sturdy torso, a chest so firm I let out a puff of air as I hit it, losing what little breath I have left.

The legs underneath this torso are gorgeous in a pair of worn jeans, as if someone styled Ryan Pierce for a country fashion catalogue, and of course all these body parts are attached to the sexiest face on the planet.

"You sure are in a hurry to see someone," he says, those chocolate eyes of his melting my stomach to nothing. "I sure hope it's me."

"Yes," I say. "Definitely yes."

His eyes twinkle, and in the next second he's got me dipped, carry-on and all, in front of all the passengers and airline staff. I hear at least one woman sigh, and a man near the back whistles loud enough to pop an eardrum.

The kiss is just as fantastic as I remember, if not better. Our month apart has both of us burning for more, and if I'm not mistaken, one or both of us will spontaneously combust into flames as soon as we're alone.

"Hi," he whispers against my neck as he returns me to my feet.

"Hi," I say back.

"Let's get out of here." He grabs my hand. "Please."

I nod, mute, and follow him.

He leads me through the airport, and I have to admit, I feel like a queen. Ryan Pierce didn't only pick me up from the airport, he showed me off to the world, and by George—whoever George actually is—I want him more than I've ever wanted anyone.

If we part ways after this wedding, my heart is going to hurt.

A part of me wishes I'd played by the rules, had never let any of this evolve into anything more than the physical relationship I requested.

But the other part of me, that little corner of my heart that my dad tugged at with his words of advice—that part of me is content.

Despite all my efforts to remain distant, I am falling in love with Ryan Pierce.

Chapter 37

Ryan

She's even more beautiful than I remember. Despite the odd getup she's got on, she's the prettiest person in the entire airport. We shuffle into my waiting car, which I parked illegally at the curb while praying airport security would be light during the lunch hour.

I hold my breath as we push through the doors.

"Where are you parked?" she asks, scanning the pickup lane.

"Here." I gesture to the truck right before us, its hazards blinking.

"But—" She frowns and bites her lip, and it's the most adorable thing ever. I want to lean over, nibble on that lip for her, but she's too busy glancing furiously toward the man in a security uniform strolling toward my vehicle.

"Ask questions later," I say. "Hop inside."

She lets out a flustered laugh, one I take to mean she's amused at the narrow escape from the parking lot attendant. We pull away from the curb just as the man scratches his stomach, looks toward our car, then to the doors of the airport, and then back again. He waves a hand and continues his stroll.

"You weren't supposed to park there!" She faces me, her face flushed. "You could've waited outside for me so you didn't risk a *ticket*. What were you thinking?"

"I wasn't." I take my eyes off the wheel for a split second to look into hers, hopefully conveying some of my excitement about seeing her again. "You texted me that you landed and you were running early, so I ditched the car to meet you at the gate."

Her eyes blink once, and then she turns to stare out the window. "You didn't have to do that."

I reach over and rest a hand on her leg. I'm determined to make sure this weekend isn't weird in any way, even if she's decided she doesn't want anything physical. Maybe she's met someone, or maybe she's decided this is a horrible idea. Regardless, I've already decided to make sure she has a good time in my home state.

"So, how've you been?" I ask, struggling to keep my voice even.

"Since we talked last night?" She gives me a mischievous smile, and we're back. The awkwardness is gone, the tension dispelled, and we're the two people who have become inexplicably intertwined over a pizza. "Good, except for a creep on the plane who tried to stare down my shirt. Oh, and Lisa says hi."

"Hello to Lisa," I say, trying not to show my annoyance about the creep. "If you got a name, I'm happy to pay him a visit."

"Relax!" she says on a laugh. "He was eighty years old."

I'm grumbling about it, but I back off. Might as well save the frustration for the rink.

"So, this is Minnesota?" She gestures to the green landscape as we drive toward the suburbs where my family has a little farmhouse. "I thought it would be colder than this."

"Is that why you're wearing…uh, whatever it is you have on?"

She looks down at her mismatched outfit. It's almost like something out of a cartoon, but somehow she manages to rock it like a supermodel. She's got a stiff little jacket, tight jeans that show off her gorgeous legs, and boots that go up to her knees, despite the fact that it's the middle of summer.

"By erratic weather, I meant sometimes it rains," I say. "It does snow, but that's in winter. I'm thinking I should have been more clear."

The sun has arrived today, extra bright, sparkling even, as if to show Andi just how beautiful the countryside can be. We pass the huge center where we play our home games, and I point it out to her. Then we pass through St. Paul and continue on I-94 toward our neighboring state.

"You live in Wisconsin?" she asks, her eyes watching the sign.

"Of course not," I say. "I'm not a traitor."

"Didn't mean to touch a nerve."

"We don't joke about these state lines," I say with a smile. "I live near the border."

"And what is our plan for today?"

"My mother and Lilia are out shopping or whatever," I tell her, suggestion heavy in my voice. "So I can show you to your room…"

"You don't waste any time, do you?"

"I see our minds are in the same place."

She gives the slightest shake of her head, but she doesn't deny it. A second later, she slides her soft fingers into mine, locking them there, and I sense a whisper of curiosity.

I squeeze her hand, tightly, letting her know the gesture is *more* than welcome. I step on the gas, floor it, and concentrate on getting us home as quickly as humanly possible.

It's not a far drive, but I can't last much longer. Sitting this close to her, smelling the scent of her still damp hair wrapped into a messy thing on top of her head, is intoxicating.

We're home in ten minutes flat, the fastest I've managed to make this journey. I give her the fastest tour of the house ever. It's empty, which is a miracle in itself with five of us brothers.

We're all back in town to see Lawrence get hitched. He's the second youngest, a little spoiled, but we're all happy for him. I'm also happy we don't see my family right away as I lead Andi straight to my old bedroom.

"I have a condo in Minneapolis," I say. "But my mom wanted us all together for the weekend, starting with dinner this evening."

"It's only…" She looks at her watch. "Three in the afternoon— what time do you eat dinner?"

"Honey." I sweep her into my arms, weird crunchy rain jacket and all. "Dinner's at seven—that's not the problem. The problem is that my plans for you can't be rushed."

Her cheeks turn a little bit pink. "Oh," she says softly.

I lean in, tilt her chin upward, and do what I've needed to do for these past few weeks. I press my lips to hers, long and slow, savoring every moment of her skin on mine.

Neither of us is in much of a hurry; we have hours until dinner, the house is silent, and she is finally mine.

Andi has other plans for how things are going to go, however. She nips at my lip, pulling my head hard in toward hers. A second later she's lost her jacket and both of her hands are wrapped into my hair. I meant to get it cut before the wedding, but at the moment, I'm glad I haven't. I like her fingers holding tight with fervor.

"Slow down, we've got time, baby," I tell her. "We're going to do this right."

"There's time to do it right later," she says, a playful sparkle in her eye. "I haven't had sex in a month, and—"

Her eyes widen suddenly, and she looks up at me as my hands slide under her shirt and luxuriate in the softness of her skin.

"I didn't mean anything by that," she says quickly. "If you've had sex, or whatever, I mean—we're just friends. I just didn't have the opportunity, I guess—very busy with school, you know, and—"

"Andi." I smooth her hair. "There hasn't been anyone else for me, either. I didn't want anyone but you, and I still don't."

"Ryan," she looks at me through her lashes. "I didn't want anyone either. I think…"

"What?"

She shakes herself out of whatever she was about to say, smiling instead. "Never mind. Where were we?"

I'm about to argue with her, demand to know what she was going to say. I have a feeling the very same words were on the tip of my tongue, but then her hand slides down the inside of my pants, and she inhales as she strokes me. My mind is now blank.

"Shit," I mumble, unable to control the words coming out of my mouth. "I need you, sweetheart—*so* damn bad."

"Then we'll do it *right*, later," she says, her breath coming in gasps. "I need you too."

Her chest heaves beneath that V-neck, her breasts pert, in need of attention—which is fine by me, since I've missed her boobs. Desperately.

Our pants are off seconds later and I have her spread on my high school bed. If I'd known back then there'd one day be a girl as hot as Andi in my bed, I probably never would've left my mattress.

Back in high school, I was quieter, a background player. The looks, the girls, the money came later in life, once I matured in college. It would've blown my high-school mind to learn I'd be here now, like this, with her.

She lays sprawled on the bed, her hair in waves around my pillow. Somewhere along the way on our journey home, the thing holding her hair in place got lost, and thank God for that. She looks striking like this, her hair loose and free.

I move over her, holding myself up with one arm while I tease along her panty line with the other hand. I can feel through the fabric that she's ready; I can smell her, and I need to touch her.

The moan that comes from her throat as I slip my finger past the fabric sends a surge of desire pulsing through my veins. I lower myself onto her, just barely brushing skin to skin, needing to feel our naked bodies touch.

She holds me tighter, closer, arching her hips to meet my fingers. Judging by the sounds she's making, she's close already. Her hips buck higher.

"Baby…" I say, and then I feel her clench around my fingers.

I swallow my words, too intent on watching the wave of pleasure wash over her face as she spirals into me, her fingers tearing at my back, my hair, my skin, my—

Suddenly, everything is wrong, and both Andi and I realize it at the exact same moment.

Footsteps.

Right outside my bedroom door.

The handle is opening, we're scrambling to get decent, the door is swinging open.

"No," Andi murmurs, diving for covers. "Oh no."

Lawrence strides right through the doorway without bothering to think. He's engrossed in looking at the screen of his phone while I'm shoving blankets around Andi left and right.

"Asshole!" I yell at him. "Get out."

"Crap!" Andi's scrambling to pull the comforter over her face, and I'm scooping pillows on top of her for some reason. I don't even know why; I'm just trying to protect her from my dickhead brother.

"God, Ryan!" Lawrence covers his eyes with his hand and backs out of the room as quickly as he entered. "You couldn't wait two damn seconds to take your pants off?"

"What the hell happened to knocking?" I stand up and check myself out briefly in the mirror to make sure I'm not flashing my brother. I have my jeans on, my face is red, and my hair is mussed. I probably have scratches down my back, but I don't care. Once I'm sure Andi's covered, I pull the door open a hair. "What did you think you were doing? Didn't we have this conversation about knocking in like, the fifth fucking grade?"

"I just came to say hi to your *friend*," Lawrence said. "I yelled up the stairs, figured you didn't hear me."

"Of course we didn't hear you. We were occupied."

"I see that now."

I run a hand over my face. I don't really care all that much, except Andi seems mortified. Any other girl, and it wouldn't have been a big deal—bunnies tend to like that sort of attention—but Andi isn't a bunny; she is the polar opposite.

Lawrence gives me a little smirk and a thumbs up, his dickhole personality returning. "I suppose I'll leave you two alone to finish what you started."

"Go away."

I slam the door shut and turn to face Andi. She's sitting up in bed, the covers pulled up to her chest. She's doing a magnificent job of pretending she's not bothered.

"I'm so sorry," I say. "I should've known—"

"It was an accident," she says with a wave of her hand. Her nonchalance belies the reddish tinge around her neck. "Don't worry about it."

"I should've locked the door."

"I *said* don't worry about it." She shrugs. "I'm a big girl. If I say I'm fine, I mean it. The only problem I see is that, once again, you made me feel quite excellent, and you didn't get the chance to finish."

"How are you still single?" I ask, moving across the room. "I could marry you tomorrow, Andi." I'm half kidding, but she seems unsure of whether or not it's a joke. "Relax," I tell her. "Kidding."

"I knew that," she says. "Anyway, why don't you lock the door, get over here, and take your pants off?"

"About that marriage proposal," I say, letting my hand cup her cheek as I swoop in for a kiss. "Maybe I'm not kidding."

She nips my lip. "Sounds good to me."

I clear my throat. We're in dangerous territory.

"I'm kidding," she says. "Relax."

"Me too," I say, the tension easing. "But really, we can wait. There's plenty of time tonight."

"Is there?" She lets the covers fall from around her shoulders, exposing silky white breasts in a lacy purple bra. One strap has slid down her shoulder. "Are you sure?"

I reach for her strap, bringing it to the correct position on her shoulder. It's a trap—her hand snakes out, snaps at the waistband of my jeans, and instantly I'm ready.

"You sneak," I say, looking down.

"I thought he might feel differently," she says, nodding toward my crotch. "What do you say we head back to the bed?"

"How can I resist an offer like that?"

She leans backward, spread like a beautiful, exquisite platter before me, filled with all the delicacies of the world. I start to follow her, drawn toward her figure, when she raises a finger and shakes it at me.

I panic. "What? Everything okay?"

"Lock the damn door, Pierce!"

I can't help but laugh. I shouldn't be surprised; she makes me laugh more than anyone else. I make quick work of the lock then join her in bed.

"I've missed this," she says, pushing me back against the pillows. Her lips trail down past my ribs to the sensitive edges of my abs then approach the score zone near the rim of my pants. She teases the zipper down, and then, with a devilish look, frees me from my boxers.

I hiss and close my eyes as she takes me into her mouth. "Andi, baby—"

"I'm home!" a shrill voice yells up the stairs. "Anyone else home? Ryan, is that your car outside? Do you have a friend over?"

"Goddammit!" I bite out. "Not *now*."

"Who…" Andi murmurs, then falls silent as the voice continues to pierce the air.

"Lawrence, is that you making all that racket?" my mother yells from the hallway. "You know how I feel about cursing when you're in this house. Is your brother home with his friend yet? I don't want her first impression to be a houseful of boys with filthy mouths."

I shake my head, my jaw tense as Andi slowly sits up. "I'm so sorry."

Andi has this look on her face that's halfway between disappointment and amusement. Then, the sound of footsteps on stairs reaches our ears, and we simultaneously scramble to pull ourselves into some semblance of presentable attire.

By the time the knock sounds on the door, I've thrown most of the pillows on the bed and Andi's essentially dressed, with the exception of one missing sock and some mad sex hair. I fling open the door.

"Lawrence, why are you in your brother's—" My mother is already speaking before she realizes it's not Lawrence. She stops abruptly and scans the two of us, her eyes going from confusion, to realization, to that *motherly* look that says she knows exactly what was going on before she arrived.

I give Andi credit—she hardly flinches at the intrusion.

"Hello, Mrs. Pierce." She extends a hand, a polite smile on her face. "We were just about to change for dinner. I didn't get a chance to fix my hair yet, and I fell asleep on the plane."

God bless Andi, and God bless my mother. They are both

champions of the highest quality because they completely ignore the situation. My mother puts on her perkiest smile and bypasses Andi's handshake, pulling her in for a full-on Pierce hug.

"It is so great to have you here," my mother says, holding Andi at arm's length. "You are gorgeous. Another girl in the house—another *woman*! Do you know how long I've been waiting for this moment? Lilia has been a godsend, and now we have another. My dreams are coming true!"

"Well, I'm happy to be here. Thank you so much for the generous invitation." Andi bows her head a little, smiles again. "You have a beautiful home."

"Well, then let me show it to you!" Raising five boys means my mother has seen it all, and she isn't about to be played a fool. She knows what we were doing, and clearly, she doesn't want us messing around before dinner. "Come with me, dear."

"Oh, I already got a tour," Andi says. "Thank you so much. I should probably fix my hair."

I feel like it's my turn to chip in and say something, but I'm not sure what to say, so I stand there with a dumb look on my face. I think I deserve a break though, since my mother almost walked in on a sight she should *never* see.

"Oh, Ryan's never been very good at giving tours of the house, except for maybe his bedroom," my mother adds a little pointedly. "Come on, darling, let me show you the kitchen. Have you ever had lefse? Ryan's father is Norwegian, you know…"

"Mom," I say weakly. "Leave her be."

"I'm just being hospitable," she says, a sharp edge to her words. "Did you even offer this poor girl something to drink? Can I get you water, coffee, tea? She's probably starved, Ryan. She's been on the plane for nearly four hours. Look at her! She's tiny. She needs *food*."

"I'll go downstairs and help get dinner ready," Andi says, giving me a look that I interpret to mean everything's okay. "I'll…see you soon."

I nod, and then they're gone.

Apparently the entire welcome committee has decided to pop in and say hello. I sigh, running a hand through my hair in frustration. Don't get me wrong, I love that Andi's happy, satisfied, and yes, welcomed by my family, I'm just not sure what to do now, standing alone in my bedroom with my boner, wishing Andi's transition to the Midwest had gone just a little bit smoother.

Chapter 38

Andi

They live in a fairytale cottage.

Mrs. Pierce, who is incredibly pretty in a soccer mom sort of way, guides me down a hallway lined with pictures of her boys in all stages of hockey careers. She's going on and on about how much trouble they've gotten into over the years, but all I can think about is that this place feels like home.

It's a little bit hard, I admit, to be here—not because Lawrence burst in while Ryan had his fingers doing unmentionable things, and not because his mother almost caught me doing dirty deeds to her son, but because *she's* here—Mrs. Pierce, a mother, and the most motherly mother I've ever seen besides my own.

I miss my mom. I miss the way she smelled of cinnamon and vanilla. While my dad had cornered the pizza market, my mom had baked everything. Maybe it was the soft, gooey smell of chocolate chips wafting from the Pierce's kitchen or the warm, lingering hug she gave me before knowing my name—whatever it was, she reminded me of what life was like before my mother died and things began to fall apart.

On top of all that, their house is yellow with sunshine washing in through generously sized windows to bathe the walls and floor, bouncing its rays all the way up to the vaulted ceiling. Parts of the exterior look Victorian, while other sections appear a little lopsided with a modern spin, as if the Pierce family had made adjustments over the years with each new family member.

Though Ryan's earlier tour was admittedly short, I didn't miss the array of pictures out on every surface, or the little trays of peppermints and candies in easy reach on all the end tables. If my nose isn't lying, a pot of coffee is brewing from the same place as the baking cookies. The whole package is a bundle of warmth and hominess.

"It really is lovely to have you here." Mrs. Pierce pushes up her sleeves. "Ryan hasn't stopped talking about you since he came home *weeks* ago."

"Really?"

She winks. "I know he can come off as…I don't know, a little *resistant* to the idea of dating, but, my dear, it seems you've got him infatuated."

"Oh, well, I don't know about that. It's still early in our relationship."

"I know I'm right, dear." She gives a tinkling laugh, pats my hand. "And it's quite easy to see why."

"Oh," I say again, for lack of a better phrase. I hadn't expected this much *welcome* from Ryan's mother, especially not after she caught us fooling around five minutes after we stepped foot into her house. "Well, thank you. Thank you so much, again, for letting me stay with you. I could've gotten a hotel, or—"

"Any girlfriend of Ryan's is family," she says, cutting me off midsentence. "Make yourself at home. Can you grab me the spoons?"

I must go all dazed and confused for a long minute because she points toward the silverware drawer and repeats the question. I hand over a set of spoons and she takes them briskly, organizing them on a towel.

"If you'd like to join Ryan upstairs, you may," she said softly. "I didn't mean to kidnap you to the kitchen. I just thought... I've never had a daughter, and Lilia's far too busy to help—it is her wedding, of course."

"I'd love to help. Really."

"Are you, by chance, interested in learning to make lefse? I'd love to teach you. The boys always end up throwing it across the room or wrestling each other to the floor."

A sudden wave of emotion rocks my body, and I swallow past a lump. I haven't baked since my mother died. Making lefse might not technically be baking, but it feels close enough. "I'd love that," I say. "My mother was a baker."

"Oh?" She lets the question hang, as if not wanting to press. "And she is..."

"Gone." I clear my throat. "Passed away several years ago."

"Andi..." She shakes her head, the look in her eyes so filled with sympathy, I find my heart cracking in two. "We don't have to do this now. Why don't you find Ryan?"

"No," I murmur. "I'd really, really love to learn."

She pulls me into a hug, surprising me as she holds on for longer than is natural. When Mrs. Pierce lets go, she wastes no time jumping into business, asking me to pull out sugar, flour, pots, and pans.

The time passes quickly, and it's a blast. I can't say I've become a lefse master when we're finished—after all, I am Italian and not an ounce Norwegian—but by the time dinner is ready to be served, my face is red from the warmth of the stove, my fingernails are dusted with sugar and flour, and my heart is full.

In addition to lefse, I helped prepare the sides for the meal—buttery mashed potatoes, crispy asparagus, tender kernels of sweet corn. The whole experience has been far more enjoyable than I expected.

Through the process, Ryan checks on me several times—at first, quite often, as if worried his mother has kidnapped me. After I reassure him I am helping voluntarily and loving every moment, he grabs a beer and joins Lawrence in the garage where athletics of some sort blare on the television.

"I didn't mean to make you prepare the whole rehearsal dinner," Mrs. Pierce says. "I hope I didn't steal you away from Ryan too much. I know he'll have an earful for me later tonight, just as soon as you jump in the shower and he gets a moment alone with me."

"I'll talk him down," I say with a laugh. "Plus, I don't really understand sports, or whatever they've got on the TV. This is much more fun, I promise."

"Really?" She looks so hopeful, so bright-eyed that I'm tempted to squeeze her again.

"Absolutely." I grin. As weird as it sounds, I want to be part of this family. I hardly know them, but something tells me I belong. "I'm going to run upstairs and change quickly, if you don't mind. I have flour everywhere."

"Is everything okay?"

"It's more than okay."

I can't tell her that everything is not *quite* okay. In fact, with each passing step, my mood worsens. As I ascend to Ryan's bedroom, my heart begins to race, and I realize that everything is *far* from okay.

I'd fling myself onto the bed, but I don't want to get flour everywhere, and I probably don't need to be so dramatic. As I head into the room, I can't help but wonder if I'm letting this stupid game of pretend get out of hand. Right now, it feels like I'm going to be hurt at the end of it—and I might not be the only one.

Chapter 39

Andi

Once I've shed my clothes, I suddenly feel too tired for a shower.

I collapse face first on the bed and lie there, a light cloud of flour puffing off of me. I can't bring myself to care about the mess. Sheets can be washed, but my heart cannot be magically fixed, and I'm worried. After this weekend, we don't have to see each other again, and that sucks.

"Hey, honey," Ryan says from the doorway. "Is everything okay?"

"Yes," I mumble into the pillow. "Great."

He moves soundlessly across the room and sits on the bed. A hand comes to rest on my back. "What's wrong?"

"Nothing."

"Don't bullshit with me, Andi. We're friends. Friends don't do that."

I lie still for a moment longer, wishing the smushy bed would swallow me whole. So many of my problems would be solved if I just disappeared into this mattress. Then I start thinking about what he said, and that word—*friend*—grates on me until finally, I roll over.

He's looking down at me, and I almost lose my breath, nearly forget what I'm going to say. His eyes are milk chocolate, dripping warmth. He hasn't removed his hand, and it slides across to my stomach, low, just over my pelvis.

It sends tingles to my sensitive areas, and I'm instantly turned on. I have half a mind to pull his beautiful lips to mine and kiss him senseless, but for once, I'm too upset to think about sex.

"Friends," I say.

His fingers tighten, pressing against my skin. It's tempting, distracting, but I fight the urge to pull him to me. "I thought we agreed—"

"I know what we agreed," I say. "It was my stupid idea to agree to it in the first place."

"I'm the one who came up with the original idea. All you did was throw sex into the mix, and I can't say that I complained."

"Of course you didn't complain! You weren't supposed to *complain*. This was supposed to be easy, simple. Fantastic sex, no strings attached—other people can do it, so why can't we?"

"What's bothering you, Andi?"

His eyes are on me, serious, watching as I consider my response.

Finally, I gesture to his fairytale house, to the warmth, the coziness, the sounds of family showing up downstairs to celebrate the marriage of one of their own. "I don't belong here. I'm pretending."

"I *asked* you to do that."

"We're lying to your mother!" My voice screeches a few octaves higher. "She's a really, really awesome woman."

"Except the whole walking-in-on-us-without-knocking thing, she's okay," he says, trying for a joke. When he doesn't get a reaction from me, he pauses. "I've dated girls before—my brothers have too— and not all relationships work out. I can just tell her we broke up in a few months. She'll get over it."

His words are like a stab to my heart.

"She taught me how to make lefse," I say. "A family tradition. She let me help prepare a meal for the family—a family I don't *belong* to. In ten years, there might be some picture of me with you at this wedding, and she'll be wondering why she wasted any time on me at all, and—"

"Andi," he interrupts my almost manic voice. "Please, you're overthinking this."

"I am not."

"You're here as my friend. I care about you. So what if we tacked on the label of girlfriend? It doesn't make a difference; the label doesn't change anything. It's just you and me spending time together like we have been these last couple months. We don't have to stop being friends after this weekend."

"Friends," I say again. "Sure."

"I'm an adult, you're an adult. As long as we're happy and we're not hurting anyone, then what's the matter?"

"I'm *not* happy."

"What?"

I slap a hand over my mouth. I didn't mean to say that; I'm not even sure it's true. The words just popped out, and now I'm stuck with Ryan, his hand frozen just below my belly button, his eyes locked on mine and asking silent questions.

I take a moment to gather my thoughts, and I sit up in bed, his hand sliding off my waist. I decide to be honest. "I said I'm not happy."

"Which part don't you like?"

"I don't feel right about lying to everyone."

"Then don't lie."

"What?" It's my turn to be confused as I watch him watch me. "Isn't it a little late for that? I don't want to spoil Lawrence and Lilia's weekend."

"Don't lie to them, then."

I shake my head. "I'm not understanding."

"Come with me to the wedding tomorrow as my girlfriend."

I squint at him. "I'm already your fake girlfriend, that's the *problem*."

"I didn't say fake. I said *girlfriend*."

I blink again. "Are you just saying this to appease me? Then you'll 'break up' with me in two days? It's the same thing."

"Maybe I'm not being clear." Ryan stands, his long legs carrying that athletic figure over to the door and closing it. This time, he locks it, and when he turns back, his eyes are ablaze with intensity. "I want you to be my girlfriend. The whole deal. Exclusive. Mine. I'm-not-sharing-you-with-anyone-else sort of girlfriend. No breakups, no fake anything. Be mine, Andi."

"Ryan…" My heart is leaping at the possibilities, but I can't get my hopes up. "Are you serious?"

"Look, I didn't want to get into anything with you, either. I truly didn't. My career's on the line if I fuck up, and your career is just starting to take off—I'm sure of that, too. We live across the country from each other. The timing of us meeting is horrible, but I can't let you go."

"I want to be your girlfriend," I whisper. "I missed you more than I thought it was possible to miss another person while you were away."

His eyes light up, and he's crossing the room before I have time to process what's happening. One of his hands swoops beneath my legs, adjusting me on the bed so I'm spread eagle, my belly exposed as my shirt slides up.

"Say it again," he murmurs against my neck. "Tell me you'll be mine."

"Yes, Ryan, I love you."

He doesn't answer me, but he doesn't need to. He works the button on my jeans free with the other hand. For the second time today, my pants are coming off, and his are still on.

"No," I say firmly. "If you're taking my pants off, yours are coming with."

"You don't have to tell me twice." His eyes flash. "I can't wait a second longer."

"Are you sure *now's* the time?" I gasp, sitting up far enough to help him get rid of his jeans. I nod toward the door. "There are people arriving downstairs, and dinner is in ten minutes."

"I said I wanted to take my time, but I can't wait. I need you now. I'll make it up to you later. Slow, sweet, whatever the hell you want, but now—"

"Now," I say, urgent with my need. "There's no time for slow."

He agrees by kicking his pants to the floor. We survey each other for several long seconds before everything bursts into a rush of desire, need, and latent sexual tension that's been burning since the morning I left his house weeks ago.

As I reach for him, he's pinning me to the bed. Somehow, he's gotten a condom on again, and it takes him all of one second to feel that I'm ready.

He slides in, slow, steady, exhaling a loud breath. "You are so perfect, sweetheart."

I raise my hips to meet his thrusts, incapable of speech. His hand grips the back of my head, his mouth tears at my lips in a fusion of need and hunger, and we begin to move together.

My hands are on his back, nails digging into his skin as I hold on for the ride. His breath swirls with mine until it's impossible to tell where his ends and mine begins. I've never felt more on fire. The only things I'm aware of are the tiny waves of pleasure building, building, building in my stomach.

A cry slips through my lips as I reach the ledge, holding on, waiting for him to join me as we catapult off the steepest of cliffs. Ryan groans, his lips pressing hard against my neck, and I let go.

Together, we erupt, fireworks smoldering toward the ground as we let the tremors carry us into a blissful, post-sex haze.

"Holy cow," I say, clapping a hand against my forehead. "That was incredible."

"I was going to say something earlier," Ryan whispers against my ear, launching into a long overdue, luxurious kiss. "And then I forgot."

My mind is destroyed, so I'm not even sure what he's talking about. I close my eyes and enjoy every sensation. "That's okay," I say. "I'm pretty happy with how things turned out."

He waits until I open my eyes, and then meets my gaze. "Actually, I remember now." He cups my cheek in his palm, running a thumb over my lips. In a voice husky, he murmurs, "I love you too, Andi."

I open my mouth to respond, my arms pulling him against me, when we're interrupted for the third time today.

"*Dinner!*" Mrs. Pierce calls from downstairs. "Come eat, kids!"

"They're going to know we had sex," I say, giving him a conspiratorial smile. "They're going to think we're addicts."

Ryan looks completely undisturbed by the thought, nuzzling against my neck, holding my hand tight in his grip. "Who cares? We are dating, after all."

I grin, my smile so bright I feel like an idiot. I want to stay here all day.

Unfortunately, that's not possible.

"Ryan, is Andi in the shower?" Mrs. Pierce calls through the door. "Come down and greet your brothers! We're eating in five minutes whether you're here or not—unless Andi needs more time."

I shake my head *no*, already in motion as Ryan climbs off of me.

"Be right down," he yells back. "She's just changing her..." He looks at me with a blank expression.

"Clothes?" I hiss.

"Clothes," he finishes. Lowering his voice, he looks to me. "I blanked."

I shed the rest of my clothes as I head to the bathroom. Luckily, I've packed plenty of undies and a nice cocktail dress that works for any occasion. I rinse off in record time, shimmy into my dress, throw a sweater over my shoulders, tie my hair into a semi-fancy messy bun, and re-emerge from the bathroom.

"Damn," Ryan says, straightening a shirt over a nice pair of slacks. "You look amazing. We should have sex more often."

"Are you saying I don't normally look great?"

His eyes widen. "No! No, not at all. I just meant—"

I interrupt his babbling with a hard kiss to the lips. "I'm joking. Couples do that you know. Ready for dinner?"

He takes my hand in his and, together, we descend the steps.

At the bottom, a herd of Pierce boys wait for us.

"Anderson, this is my girlfriend," Ryan says with a smile, introducing me to a taller Pierce brother. This one looks older, distinguished, as if he's left behind the hockey ways for more civilized activities. "Meet Andi. She's from Los Angeles."

I smile, basking in the introduction as I shake Anderson's hand.

My girlfriend. I replay the words in my head for the next five minutes as Ryan introduces me over and over to his family members. It's music to my ears, and I know then that I can't be happier than I am right now.

Chapter 40

Andi

"Andi made the asparagus," Mrs. Pierce says, handing it across the full table. "It's to die for. Beck, try it. I promise you'll like it."

Beck, one of the middle brothers, wrinkles his nose. "I've never liked anything green—no offense, Andi."

"Really, it's nothing special," I say. "Just something my mom taught me."

"I'll have some," Anderson says, giving me a polite smile. "Even though I can't believe my mother would put you to work before you had the chance to settle in."

Mrs. Pierce frowns at her son. "We had fun in the kitchen, didn't we, Andi?"

"We did!" I scoop asparagus onto my plate then pass it to Ryan. "It was a lot of fun. I've never made lefse before."

"Did she pay you to say that?" Brody, the youngest, asks. He's got an impish expression, and I can imagine that as the smallest of five boys, he had to learn cleverness at an early age. "One time, Mom paid me to tell Dad that—"

"Hey, now," Mrs. Pierce interrupts. "Civil conversation at the dinner table, please."

Mr. Pierce, a tall, stately gentleman, looks like he's coached his fair

221

share of hockey teams. He has a small scar above his eyebrow, salt and pepper hair, and a twinkle that lightens his otherwise intimidating stature.

He leans in toward his wife. "What didn't you tell me, dear?"

Mrs. Pierce reddens. "Try the asparagus, Daniel."

Ryan passes the plate to Brody who passes it to his father, and luckily, the topic is dropped. Ryan takes the moment of peace to rest a hand on my leg and squeeze. Next to us are Lawrence and Lilia, the Pierce parents are at either end of the table, and the rest of the brothers are scattered in between.

"So, Andi, tell us about yourself." Mr. Pierce folds his hands, ignoring the steaming food on his plate. "We're happy you could join us for the wedding. I hope you don't mind the informality of the rehearsal dinner."

"Yeah, we prefer simple," Lilia takes the question over, her eyes shining. "My parents are arriving just before the ceremony. They were supposed to be here tonight, but their flight was delayed and they'll have to fly out in the morning."

"The wedding is really small," Lawrence says. "We wanted to keep things simple."

"Mostly, we just want to get married." Lilia kisses him on the cheek. "Friends and family only."

"Friends." Lawrence leans heavily on the word, slurring it a little bit, having overindulged again. "You never did say, Ryan, how long the two of you have been dating."

Ryan's hand clenches in my lap. "Long enough."

"Tell us how you met!" Mrs. Pierce chirps.

"Well," I hesitate. "Ryan called Peretti's—"

"Her dad owns the *best* pizza shop in Los Angeles," Ryan interjects. "The best."

"I introduced it to him," Lawrence says with a smirk. "And to *her*."

Lilia frowns at her fiancé. Apparently too much alcohol brings out the dickhead version of Lawrence. He hasn't said anything awful yet, but it feels dangerous, as if we're dancing around dynamite, hoping it won't explode.

"I delivered a pizza and accidentally bumped my car into the back of his," I say. "Ryan was an absolute gentleman about the whole thing, even though I felt *horrible*."

"We exchanged information, even though there was hardly any damage," Ryan says, gliding over the fact that I'd left my bumper behind like a big, fat breadcrumb. "We ran into each other a few more times through Peretti's, and—"

"And he surprised me at my comedy show on the night of Lawrence and Lilia's party," I add. "Didn't see that one coming."

"And she did amazing!" Lilia claps her hands. "The best I've seen."

I blush. I know she's exaggerating, but it's still a little surreal that an entire party changed its course to show up at my show in the first place. "It was nice of them to come."

Lawrence snorts, and Lilia elbows him.

"What?" Lawrence faces the table. "And then Andi slept over and the rest is history."

"You're in comedy?" Mr. Pierce ignores Lawrence. "Would I have seen you in anything? Television programs or Netflix?"

I shake my head. "Probably not. I've been playing at local clubs mostly, although I do have an audition for a pretty big pilot next week."

"Next week?" Ryan turns to look at me. "Is this new?"

"I got the phone call from Nick as we were boarding the plane on the way here," I say with an apologetic wince. "I'm sorry, I forgot to mention it in the whirlwind of today."

"Congratulations!" Ryan says, a flicker of surprise passing through his gaze. "That's incredible! Although, I did tell you this would happen, so you shouldn't be surprised."

Now he's smiling again, clearly happy for me, and I lean in as he gives me a congratulatory hug.

"Andi, that's wonderful," Mrs. Pierce says. "You'll have to let us know when you have a show. If Ryan ends up signed with the Lightning, we'll have two reasons to come out there and visit."

She winks, Mr. Pierce nods in agreement, and the rest of dinner thankfully dissolves into mindless chatter that's interspersed with Lilia stealing Lawrence's wine glass and replacing it with water.

It's well past ten o'clock by the time we finally wrap dinner up. Most of the brothers are staying over at the house, save for Anderson, who doesn't live far away. Lawrence lives in LA, so he's stuck here, too.

Lilia helps her fiancé toward the bedroom, and I offer to help clear the table.

"Sure, dear, that'd be wonderful," Mrs. Pierce says. "Only if Ryan doesn't mind."

"I'll help too," he says. "What can I do?"

"Bring these outside." Mrs. Pierce gestures to the fold-up chairs they pulled in to accommodate the extra guests at the dinner table. "Andi and I can take care of the kitchen."

The two of us sink into an easy silence as the rest of the boys settle near a bonfire out back. The scent of burning marshmallows wafts toward us, and it's an entirely pleasant evening.

"Go on out to the fire," Mrs. Pierce says once we've hauled all the dishes to the sink. "Ryan's probably glued to his skewer. He does have a weakness for s'mores."

I thank her for the lovely meal, wash my hands, and make my way toward the back door. We've made it past the potentially awkward dinner scene, and now we're practically home free. All Ryan and I have to do the rest of the weekend is enjoy the Midwestern summer weather and celebrate a wedding.

Simple.

Resting a hand on the screen door, I stop. Lazy conversation filters through the open windows from the backyard, but it's the second set of voices coming from upstairs that gives me pause. They're in Ryan's bedroom, if I had to guess, and the voices are animated, upset with one another, yet I can't tell who's there.

I consider going outside, but a thought holds me back. What if it's Lawrence arguing with Ryan, or worse, Lilia?

"Hello?" I call upstairs, but nobody hears me—or at least, nobody responds.

I take another few steps.

I'm about to call again when finally, I start to recognize the voices. It's Lawrence all right, and Ryan, and they're arguing about something, someone—*me*, I realize with a start. They're arguing about me.

"—you have to be a jerk at dinner, Law?" Ryan says. "You've known I was bringing her for a month. She hasn't done anything to you."

"Nothing to me," Lawrence drawls. "Why'd you bring your bunny to my wedding?"

"She's my girlfriend, asshole."

"Really? What happened to your little agreement with Blondie?"

Instantly, ice travels down my spine. I know exactly who he means—the agent. I listen for Ryan's response, but it's silent.

"Is the door stuck?" Ryan's mom appears behind me holding a tray. "Can you be a doll and bring these marshmallows out? I have to grab the lemonade pitcher, and I don't have enough hands."

"Yes, of course," I murmur, trying not to show my dismay. It's probably for the best that I don't listen anymore—it isn't my conversation to hear.

I push the back door open with my foot and leave the voices behind me.

"Hey, Peretti! Grab a seat," Brody says with a high five. "Where's Ryan?"

"Probably still inside. I haven't seen him in a little while."

"Do you like marshmallows?"

"I've never roasted one," I admit. "We have lots of burn bans in LA, and we didn't have a pit outside as a kid."

The entire Pierce family freezes. "You've never had a s'more?"

Even though my nerves are rattled, I smile. "Well, I guess I'll have to change that."

Ten minutes, two burned marshmallows, and one devoured chocolate bar later, I've just finished my first s'more and declare it amazing. I'm about to load up on my second one when Ryan appears.

He looks flustered, his hair mussed, t-shirt slightly askew. "There you are," he says to me. Instead of sitting down, he grabs my hand. "Can we get out of here? There's something I want to show you."

A few moans from the rest of the family erupt, and Brody proclaims his big brother to be an *old fart party pooper*, but Ryan's not in the mood to put up with their teasing.

"See you tomorrow," he tells everyone while pulling me away. "Sorry to break up the festivities."

"It's no problem," I say, stumbling as I step onto uneven ground. I right myself and scurry to keep up. "I was looking for you anyway. Is everything okay?"

"Fine," he says through gritted teeth.

"It doesn't seem that way."

His shoulders tense, and then relax. When he turns to me, it's with his lips curved upward. It's a soft, muted smile, but a smile all the same. "Lawrence is being a pain in my ass. I suppose I should give him a break, night before his wedding and all."

"Siblings," I say.

"Yeah," he murmurs in agreement. "Really, I wanted some alone time with you. Mind if I show you one of my favorite places? I really think you'll like it."

"Lead the way," I say, grabbing his hand and following as he leads me farther behind the house to a shed big enough to double as a garage.

As he guides me into an old pickup truck, he squeezes my hand tight. "I meant what I said, Andi. I love you, and I want you to be mine."

"I know." I squeeze back. "I meant it, too."

Chapter 41

Ryan

We're lying under the stars, and it's perfect.

Me, Andi, and the world at our fingertips.

If I could freeze this moment forever, I'd do it in a heartbeat.

This whole night would've been fantastic if Lawrence hadn't decided to push every damn one of my buttons. He's never cared about who I date, who I sleep with, who I spend my time with—until tonight. Now, because it's his wedding, he suddenly thinks he has something to say about it.

Well, I had something to say about it, too.

With my fist.

Luckily Lilia caught me before I could actually hit him. I don't think I *really* would have—he's my brother, he's getting married, and he was drunk—but I came pretty damn close for a minute. I'm glad Lilia stopped me.

"The stars are beautiful," she whispers, and I bask in the feel of her breath dancing across my skin. "They don't make 'em like this in Los Angeles."

I hug her close to me. Usually when I'm riled up, I need to be alone. This time, however, I need her with me, next to me, resting in my arms. I took Andi and the pickup truck, and I drove us until the only sounds around were frogs and grasshoppers in the cool night air.

I prepared for this moment earlier, and I'm glad I thought ahead. While waiting for Andi's flight to land, I hauled out a new mattress and clean sheets and threw them in the back of the pickup. My brothers and I used to take this very same truck to the drive-in theater, sneaking in as many kids as we could underneath a few heavy blankets.

I skipped the theater—too crowded for what I have in mind. Instead, I brought her to this quiet overlook near the river. I've never brought anyone here before.

There are no lights for miles, and it's just us and the stars. The smell of fresh water mixing with the chilly night breeze dances across the roof of the truck, and her skin is kissed by starlight.

Like I said, perfect.

We've been lying here for nearly thirty minutes, neither of us speaking, both of us inhaling the freshness of the air, the scent of each other. She smells like peaches and sunshine, and the closer I hold her, the less I want to ever let go.

"Ryan?" Her voice is small, tender.

"Yeah?"

"I have to ask you something."

"Go ahead," I tell her. "What is it?"

"Was there…" She stops to clear her throat. "Was there ever anything between you and Jocelyn?"

I tense up, wondering if she overheard Lawrence. He spoke loudly in my bedroom, and it would've been easy for her to catch the wrong few words while helping my mother in the kitchen.

"I'm not jealous or anything, I'm just curious," she explains quickly. "I couldn't help but notice that she's gorgeous, and you two spend a lot of time together. I guess…I'm just wondering if you're coming out of a relationship, or if I'm stepping on anyone's toes."

"Oh, honey." I kiss her forehead, relieved. "No, there's nothing between us—nothing but business," I clarify. I'm not going to lie to Andi. I'll tell her whatever she wants to know because I have nothing to hide. "I swear, there's never been anything there."

"Okay."

"Believe me. You are *the most* gorgeous woman I've ever seen."

She giggles as if I'm lying, but I'm not. Jocelyn is all prim and proper and toned muscle, none of the soft curves of Andi, the delicious light in her eyes, the whimsical, carefree attitude. Jocelyn is a woman to do business with; Andi is a woman to spend my life with.

I debate telling her about the stupid agreement I made with Jocelyn, but I decide against it. I made that promise before I knew how much Andi meant to me.

Now that I have Andi, my decision is an easy one. Jocelyn will be at the wedding, and I plan to have a word with her there. I'll be declining her offer of representation.

I'll play for the Stars another year. I like Minnesota.

In fact, I have been planning on asking Andi to stay longer—a month, if she can, at least until her classes start for the fall semester. Then at dinner, she dropped the bomb about her pilot audition.

I hope she didn't see the disappointment in my eyes at her announcement; I'm happy for her, truly, but selfishly, I want her here, with me…for good.

I curl into Andi, her hand dangerously high on my thigh. I press a kiss to her head, liking where this moment is going. I roll into her, slipping my hand down to pull her closer, my fingers lingering on the curve of her back, toying with the edge of her panties, until—

She snores.

It's a cute, light snore that sounds like a baby puppy.

I examine her more closely and find that, sure enough, her breathing is steady and her eyes are closed. She's asleep.

Tucking her into me, I wrap the blanket around her body as she sleeps. The stars blink down on us, and the moon washes the dark of the world away, leaving a sparkle behind.

Before I met Andi, the world never sparkled.

Now, there's no going back.

Chapter 42

Andi

The lazy, warm fingers of sunlight wash over my face, the scent of summer pulling me from a soft, comfortable slumber. I sigh, filled with delight, and pull the fluffy comforter closer to me, resisting the urge to open my eyes.

I roll over, and before I can fall back to sleep, something touches my face…a light wisp of something, almost like air. I raise a hand and press it to my cheek, feeling the item crumple beneath my fingers.

It's familiar: a leaf.

"*Shit*!" I fly into a sitting position, slowly realizing that my whereabouts are not my bedroom, as I first thought, but the back of an old pickup truck. Glancing at the figure next to me, I fall silent, watching him sleep.

When those enchanting chocolate eyes of Ryan's are closed, he has enough boyish charm to make my heart ache. Curly locks droop over his forehead, and as I reach over to push them away, his lips curve upward in a sleepy smile.

"Ryan," I whisper while looking for my phone. "I think we have to go."

"Mmmm." He lets out a groan, turning so his butt is pressed against my legs. "Sleep."

I can't even remember falling asleep the night before. We were talking and cuddling, the stars winking overhead, and I can't pinpoint the exact moment I slipped into unconsciousness. The whole thing was a blur of warmth, pleasure, and the sensation of utter safety while nestled in his arms.

"Ryan," I say, finally locating my phone. "It's nine o'clock! What time do we have to be at the church?"

"Church?"

"Wedding. Your brother, Lawrence," I say. "He's marrying Lilia…"

"Lilia—" Ryan's eyes shoot open. "Shit!"

"What time?"

"Ten!"

"That's plenty of time." I'm not at all convinced, but he's got this wild-eyed, still-in-a-nightmare expression on his face. "Let's get moving."

We're like two of the Three Stooges trying to get everything in order. He climbs over me, I accidentally elbow him in the cheek, he forgets to call my name before tossing me the pillow, and it catches me in the gut.

By the time we're in the cab of the truck, we're spending equal amounts of time laughing, gasping for air, and cussing out the slowest drivers in the state of Minnesota for not knowing we have a wedding party waiting on us.

We reach Casa Pierce before nine thirty, are showered in the next ten minutes, and dress next to each other in his childhood bedroom. It's almost comforting, this ritual. It's not as if we've had much practice with the whole sleepover thing, but it seems we're naturals at it.

I'm pulling my dress over my head, realizing too late that I forgot to undo the zipper. I'm stuck. "Oh no."

Ryan doesn't respond. Peeking through an armhole in the dress, however, I see him watching. He's got his eyes focused on my thong, and the lack of coverage it provides.

"Sweet Jesus."

"A little help here?"

"No," he says, biting his lip. "I'm good."

"Come on!"

"What time did you say we have to be at the church?"

"I didn't say anything. *You* said ten."

He frowns. "We can be late."

"No, we can't. It's your brother's wedding."

"He's an asshole."

"And you're the best man."

"I'm not feeling like being the best right now." He moves across the room and shoots a decidedly dirty glance between my legs. "I'm feeling—"

"I can *see* what you're feeling," I say, staring pointedly at the tent in his boxers. "But I'm stuck in this dress, and we need to get moving."

"Just one kiss." He bends a knee, locks his fingers onto my hips, and pulls me toward him. Gently, ever so gently, he runs his fingers over me and, even though I'm wedged in a dress, I can't help but suck in a hard breath.

"There's time," he murmurs. "We managed it yesterday."

It takes everything in my power to grind out a sound that conveys the word *no*.

"Fine," he says. "Then I'll leave you with this…"

His lips press to the outside of the lace, and I shudder. It's a whisper of friction, but plenty erotic to leave me wanting more. I push my arms through the dress using sheer willpower, and then my hands find his hair, weave into it, and pull his head up toward me.

"You're welcome." He laughs, sending warm puffs of air against my skin. After pressing one last kiss against the fabric, he stands and runs a finger up my skin. A cocky grin has appeared on his face. "You wanted help getting unstuck, didn't you? Well, you're in your dress."

Glancing down, I see that sure enough, the dress is all but perfectly situated over my body. I give a noncommittal harrumph of frustration. "Thanks, I guess."

He laughs louder, pulls me closer, and brushes the damp hair from my neck. "Let me remind you that you're the one who said there was no time for fun."

I reach down, stick my hand on his tent pole, and watch as his eyes roll toward the ceiling. "Two can play this game," I tell him.

It's his turn to groan as I return to the bathroom to style my hair into some semblance of an up-do. When I'm ready, I open the door and find Ryan waiting on the other side.

He blinks once. His hand moves slowly, subconsciously to his throat, where he straightens an invisible tie. "You look…insanely beautiful. Stunning, Andi."

The way his voice is soft, almost unsure, makes me look down. No man has ever complimented me in such a sincere, almost reverent way. I've seen it before in movies, in those truly lucky couples, like my father and mother's relationship, but never in my own.

With a tender kiss, he grabs my hand. "Are you ready to go?"

Squeezing tight, I nod and follow him out of the house. The church is only a few miles away from the house, and we arrive exactly four minutes late.

"I thought we'd lost the two of you," Mrs. Pierce says as we arrive. The photographer is setting up behind her. "Did you have a nice time last night? You look rested."

Ryan hugs me close. "Took her to the river."

She stares at him. "You never take anyone to the river."

The surprise on her face registers deep in my belly, and I'm suddenly reeling with the thought that this is real. No longer are we playing some fantastical game. What we have is *real* and new and exciting.

"It was special," I agree. Ryan shows his own agreement by sliding his hand low on my back. I clear my throat, all too aware that Mrs. Pierce is standing right in front of us. "Anyway, how are Lawrence and Lilia doing?"

"Actually, Lawrence told me to send you back as soon as you arrived."

"What does he want?" Ryan pulls me closer. "I'll head back there now."

Mrs. Pierce reaches out, rests her fingers on her son's arm. "Not you. He wants to see Andi."

Ryan freezes. "Why?"

"He didn't say."

"I'll go with you," Ryan says, turning to me. "See what he—"

"No, just Andi will be fine. Ryan, come help with some chairs," his mother says firmly.

"But—"

"It's okay," I say, offering a smile. "I'll be right back."

Ryan pauses, and then realizes that between me and his mother, he's fighting a losing battle. "I'll be waiting out here…with the chairs. Come back soon, or I'll find you."

I make my way through the beautiful old church, the stained-glass windows giving off a colorful sheen on the white walls, the carpeting red beneath my feet. I let soft footsteps carry me to the area behind the altar where Mrs. Pierce directed me.

"Andi." Lawrence sees me before I can reach him. "I wanted to talk to you."

"The church is beautiful," I say as he pulls me away from the small crowd of men in suits around him. "I can't wait to see Lilia."

He pulls me to the last pew in the side section and sits down next to me. "Listen, I need to apologize."

I shake my head. "No, of course not."

"I had too much to drink, and as I'm sure my brother told you, I can be an asshole now and again."

"I really didn't think—"

"You don't have to stick up for me," he says. "I can admit when I screwed up, and I did. I'm sorry I said any of that at dinner."

"Really, it's okay. I'm over it."

He has similar brown eyes to Ryan, and staring into them is almost eerie. "I didn't realize how serious the two of you are."

"We weren't all that serious," I say, struggling to explain. "It's new, and you couldn't have known. It was an honest mistake."

"He really likes you, Andi," Lawrence says. "I've never seen him act like this with a girl before."

"I really like him too."

"I know, and that's why I'm apologizing." He offers a smile, and in it, I see the charm that Lilia must see too. "I'm trying not to be a jerk, but I fuck up now and again. I just wanted to say, well, welcome to the family."

I swallow over a lump in my throat. "You didn't have to apologize, but...thank you."

He opens his arms, a bit timid, and I laugh.

"Friends?" he asks. "Please? Lilia would kill me if she knew I didn't apologize to you. She likes you too."

I open my arms and give him a quick hug, pulling away with a smile of my own. "So that's the only reason you apologized, huh? To keep Lilia happy?"

He looks alarmed at first, but my voice is teasing, and so is my grin.

"You're good." He points at me, a broad grin on his face as he shakes his finger. "You know what they say: happy wife, happy life. Now, let's go get me married to the most beautiful woman on earth!"

I'm giddy watching Lawrence stride back through the church, clasping hands with his groomsmen as he passes. I'm so occupied watching the reunion that I don't realize Ryan has sat down next to me until he eases his hand into mine.

His face is unreadable. "Everything all right?"

"It's perfect," I say, giving him a kiss on the cheek. "Lawrence isn't so bad."

Ryan looks surprised, sits back against the pew. "He apologized?"

"Let's just say, I think we're friends now."

"I didn't think he had it in him."

"Get up there." I playfully smack Ryan's butt. "Be the best man you can be."

"And then later…" He leans over, his lips pressed to my ear. "I'll make you feel the best you've ever felt."

I shiver as he walks away, goose bumps on my skin despite the warm summer day.

When the wedding bells chime, I stand with the rest of the congregation, the world a bright and sunny place, at least for today. Then Ryan waves at me from his place on the altar, and my heart stutters, racing at the thought that finally, I've found what my dad was talking about.

Chapter 43

Ryan

"May I have this dance?" I whisper in Andi's ear, my hand on the bare skin of her back.

She startles, halfway into reaching for one of those miniature hot dog appetizer things. They're good, I know—I ate about ten of them.

She turns to me, eyes wide with surprise, the little hot dog in her hands. "Dance?"

I laugh. Her mouth is full, and she is obviously going for her second one. "Hungry?"

She swallows. "These are delicious. I need to convince my dad to sell some at the restaurant."

"You didn't answer my question."

Her eyes darken. "A dance?"

I extend my hand and wait as she sets the appetizer on a napkin, wipes her hands, and joins me on the dance floor. By the time she twirls into my arms, my heart is pumping as if I'm about to play for the Stanley Cup.

I haven't made it to the finals yet, which is a big part of the reason I'm looking to transfer. LA is rebuilding their team, and they have a strong bunch of up-and-comers. I want to be one of them—at least, I did until I met Andi.

"Where'd you learn how to dance?" she asks, leaning her head against my chest.

I cinch my hands tighter across her back. "Prom."

We're slow dancing, spinning in a circle and barely moving our feet. It's not as if I'm talented or particularly skilled in this arena; I just try not to stand still or twirl too quickly. There aren't that many ways to screw up a slow dance.

As I inhale the vaguely familiar scent of her shampoo, it's impossible not to get turned on; I can't help it. Her hands, tiny in comparison to mine, clasp my shoulders a bit more firmly than necessary. She takes these little breaths that make it sound like she's excited, and when she looks up at me, it's like I'm the only person she can see.

Without a doubt, I know I'm the lucky one.

"What are you thinking?" she murmurs. "You look so serious."

I blink, and let a smile come to my lips. "I must have been concentrating."

"On what?"

"The way you look."

"Oh?" It's neither a question nor a statement, simply an exhale of breath in the shape of an O.

"You're gorgeous."

"You're pretty handsome yourself," she says, her hands tightening around my neck. "Kiss me, handsome."

It's the easiest request. My arms slide around her back, holding her close, my hands barely skimming her lower back. I'd try to cop a better feel of her ass, but my parents are in the room, and I know it'd make Andi uncomfortable. So, I settle for a peek of her cleavage instead.

Then I lean into her. Her lips are soft, tasting of strawberries, cream, a hint of champagne, and I'm lost in the kiss for the rest of the song. We make out straight through the break between songs, and when the next song starts—a fast-paced rap number, probably by Kanye—we continue slow dancing.

She lets out the smallest moan, and it's nearly enough to make me take her into a closet and have my way with her. I haven't had so many uncontrollable boners since I turned fourteen. That was a rough year because I had a smoking hot biology teacher, but this is worse. A million times worse. That biology teacher couldn't hold a candle to the woman in my arms now.

"Andi," I whisper, pushing her up-do away from her ear, dotting tiny kisses across her neck. I've never understood the phrase *wanting to eat someone up*—it sounds weirdly cannibalistic—but right now, I want to eat her up, she smells so good. "I want to take you home, or to the car, or…you name it. I want you."

She flicks her tongue in the most erotic kiss, and I forget that my parents are in the room. I'm ready to lay her on the buffet table and have her for dessert.

"You're going to have to wait," she says, a hint of a tease, a giggle bubbling in her throat. "I like this game."

I grip her hips firmly and pull her close to me. We're disguised somewhat by the bobbing, throbbing group of dancers grinding around us. I let her feel me against her, and I hold nothing back. "This isn't a game, honey."

Her eyes are beacons of light on the dance floor, and her face flushes with desire. "Wow," she murmurs. "That is…"

"You don't even understand," I say. "We need to get out of here. It's not safe."

"But—"

"You don't understand. I *need* you."

"Where can we go?"

I press my mouth against hers, sliding my tongue between her lips. That simple answer is the sexiest thing she could've said. As much as we need to get out of here, I can't resist making her mine for the world to see. It's hot, a lightning strike of passion.

"Come on," I say. "I know a place—"

"May I have this dance?" An ice-cold voice cuts through the pulsating music. "Good to finally meet you. Andi, isn't it?"

Jocelyn. In this moment, she's *The Bitch.* No offense to ladies everywhere, but I've been cockblocked so hard I'm aching in the most sensitive places. Jocelyn knows what she is doing, too; I see it in her eyes.

She's *pleased* with herself, the monster. Doesn't she understand the meaning of blue balls? Anyway, it's more than that. It's not about my dick, for once; it's about Andi. It's about me needing to be with her, to satisfy her every desire. I want to get the hell away from the public, this wedding, and most of all, Jocelyn.

"Oh, sure," Andi says, her eyes cloudy with lust. She shakes her head, presumably to clear her thoughts, and takes a step back. "You're... You must be Jocelyn."

"I am." She says this as if everyone should know who she is. "Thanks, Andi. I'll return him to you shortly."

"We were about to leave," I tell Jocelyn, giving her my best death stare, holding on to Andi's hand so she can't leave. "I'm sorry, this will have to wait until another time."

"It's okay, really," Andi says, wiggling away from me with a quick smile, one that doesn't reach her eyes. "I, um, I'm hungry. I'll grab another appetizer."

I take a step around Jocelyn to follow Andi and reach for her hand. "Wait."

"I *really* think this is the best time," Jocelyn calls after me. "Surely whatever you were planning to do can wait one minute?"

The song changes to a slow song right at that moment. "No," I growl. "Unfortunately, it can't wait."

Jocelyn gives a pointed look at my crotch. "Really?"

I'm on the verge of exploding from the frustration, anger, and sexual tension. It's all I can do to clamp my mouth shut and not tell Jocelyn what she can do with her manipulative little tricks.

"Really, Ryan, it's okay," Andi assures me. "I'm going to congratulate the new Pierce couple. Find me by the bar afterward."

I begin to argue, but she raises her eyebrows and shoos me away with her hand. She's a champion for putting up with Jocelyn, and she's handling it better than I would if some guy asked her to dance. I'd punch him in the face and ask questions later. That's why Andi's a better person than I'll ever be.

"What the hell?" I turn to Jocelyn. "You need to talk to me *right fucking now?*"

She very lightly puts her hands on me. Her fingers are long, slim, and feel like tentacles of ice on my shoulders. I grudgingly put the tips of my fingers on her waist—too high to insinuate anything sexual, too low to be considered a hug. I feel like I'm in friggin seventh grade, trying to slow dance without getting screamed at by the teachers.

"Language," she says. "When I sign you, you'd better learn to control it. I'm not signing you so I can run around cleaning up your—pardon my French—fucking messes."

"I was busy."

"I see that. It's quite obvious."

I grit my teeth. "Why are you here?"

I know why she's here. She and Lawrence are friends, and it's because of their relationship that I got a meeting with her in the first place.

"I know your brother, obviously. Don't ask stupid questions. Do you see what I mean? When you start thinking with your dick, you lose track of your brain."

"Shouldn't you be over talking to Lawrence and Lilia?"

"I paid my respects. I have a flight to catch in several hours, and I wanted to say my goodbyes first."

"Goodbye," I say, turning away.

Her nails clench into my skin, digging through the fabric. "You're letting her go tonight, aren't you?"

I turn back, frozen. I meant to talk to her tonight but here, in the middle of the dance floor, I can't do it. I can't make a scene in the middle of my brother's wedding. I'm his best man—I'd have to be a complete asshole to turn this evening upside down with a fight between his best man and his colleague.

So I remain silent.

"I take your silence as a good sign." She reaches up, pats my cheek. "Good boy."

I catch her wrist in my hand, hard. "Don't touch me, Jocelyn."

Her eyes glint. She knows she's getting to me. It's no wonder she's the best agent in the business. She's shrewd, beautiful, smart—and cutthroat. She can smell a person's weakness a mile away, and she has no problem exploiting it.

"I can only imagine your display tonight is because you want one last lay," she says. "And I can understand that, believe it or not—"

"Don't you dare talk about Andi like that." I cinch my hand tighter around her wrist. The more frustrated I get, the more fun she seems to have with it. "She is my girlfriend."

Jocelyn's eyes flash. "I see how it is."

"We're not discussing this here."

Finally, a glint of anger streaks across her face. "When you fly to my offices next weekend, you'd better be single, Mr. Pierce. Understand?"

"Why?" I challenge. "Why does it matter?"

"We've discussed this." She pulls her hands off of me and

straightens her elegant black dress. "Those are my terms. If you want your chance at the big leagues, you'll agree to them. I'm offering you a once-in-a-lifetime opportunity. If you lie to me, I will ruin you."

I watch as she storms away, my spine rigid, as if her very touch has turned it to ice.

She *could* ruin me, too.

Jocelyn doesn't play nice, and she doesn't play fair, and I don't doubt that she gets whatever she wants.

She might control the game, but this time I'm not playing by her rules.

Chapter 44

Andi

I try to ignore the tendrils of jealousy creeping over my skin.

Jocelyn looks beautiful in that black gown of hers, so polished, successful, professional. She's all sleek muscles, reeking of finesse and money and all things elegant—things Ryan could have in a second if he wanted them.

Not for the first time, I wonder what he sees in me when he has a woman like Jocelyn feeling up his chest. I eat another hot dog thing without even realizing it while I watch in the reflection of a vase as they talk on the dance floor.

They're hardly moving, and Ryan looks pissed—furious even. I wonder what she's said. What could make him so upset? Did they have a relationship before, or an almost-relationship?

Ryan said no, and I trust him, but she is obviously saying something to piss him off, and Ryan doesn't seem like the type to lose his cool over something trivial.

So what is she going on about that has his feathers all ruffled?

I swallow the hot dog and reach for a glass of champagne, suddenly pretending to be busy as I see them breaking apart. Whatever they were doing, one could hardly call it dancing. They basically stood and shot daggers at each other with their eyes.

Ryan looks up, searching for something—me, probably—and I'm careful to be surveying the high-quality selection of desserts. I don't want him to think I was creep-watching his interactions with that woman. I want him to think I'm over here, all confident and unbothered by the situation as I enjoy a big, sprinkled cupcake.

I've just chosen one with pink frosting and a tiny picture of Lawrence and Lilia's faces on it when I feel a tap on my shoulder and drop the thing back onto my plate.

"You're a doll, you know that?" Jocelyn is standing there, an odd sort of expression on her face. She's smiling, but it looks painful, stilted. When I don't give any sign of understanding, she continues. "For putting up with Ryan's strict social requirements."

"What?" I take another sip of champagne, mostly to calm my nerves. "Social requirements?"

"Playing along as his girlfriend."

Something about the way she says this, as if it's her doing, brings out the cat-like claws I've been trying to hide. I smile sweetly. "Oh, we're not playing. It's real. New, of course, but very, very real."

"Ah, I see." She looks behind me, wrinkles her nose at the cupcakes. "You're quite talented at playing the smitten girlfriend."

"I love him," I say. I'm not sure where it comes from, but it pops right out of my mouth. It's true, I feel it in my gut, but I didn't plan to admit it to a stranger this early in our relationship, especially not her. "We are very real, Miss—"

"Jocelyn." Her voice is a piercing icicle, and it sends shivers down my back. "Is that why you're doing this? Because you love him?"

"Doing what?" I'm starting to get frustrated now, and I hate that she looks excited by that fact. "I have no idea what you're talking about."

She *tsks*, shakes her head. I equally want to know what she's dancing around and don't care at all. If I punch her in the face, maybe she'll spit it out. Then again, I've never been the aggressive type. I deal with everything—conflict, sadness, happiness—through humor. At the moment, however, I'm not feeling very funny.

"Ryan Pierce has the opportunity of a lifetime to sign with me," she says. "I'm going to secure him a spot on the LA Lightning, and he'll win the Stanley Cup in the next few years. He's a talented young man, and he has potential to be MVP, to really make something of his career."

"I know he's talented," I say. "I'm *dating* him."

"Of course you do," she says soothingly. "But apparently he hasn't told you the terms of him signing with me."

I'm silent, and that seems to be answer enough.

"He's flying out next weekend to sign papers, and he will be single."

"No, we're—"

"You think you're together, but it can't last more than a week." Jocelyn's cold blue eyes show the first signs of humor. She's horrible, thriving on my confusion and the pain that accompanies her words. "So if you do truly love him, you'll let him go without a fight."

"No, that's not how this is going to go," I say. "Why does it matter if I date him?"

She leans in, practically spitting with cool rage. "Did you see the way he talked to me out there? He's got a hard-on for you, and suddenly he can't find a second to talk to the agent who's going to give him everything, open every door, give him every opportunity. I don't deal with players who have their minds, dicks, or hearts elsewhere. If a player is signing with me, they're going to focus on their career, and that is it."

"I'm not a distraction," I say. "I support his career. I want him to succeed."

"Yes, until you want to get married, and have a family, and suddenly he needs—"

"Plenty of players are married with families. And anyway, you don't even know that's what I want, what *we* want, together."

"I don't care what either of you want. I care about my reputation, and I care about making Ryan a star," she says. "If you care about him, you'll let him go, because if he shows up to my offices next week and hasn't broken up with you—and trust me, I'll know—I'm not signing him. Then he'll be back in Minnesota, playing for the Stars, and you won't have him anyway."

I swallow, hating that she's touched on the root of my anxiety, the cause of my only worry about being with Ryan. How can we be together if his career is here and mine is in Los Angeles?

"If I were you and I couldn't have the man I loved, I'd at least want to see him happy, successful." She reaches over me, picks up my cupcake, and takes a bite. Then she tosses it in the garbage and turns to leave. Over her shoulder, she offers one last, tight smile. "Goodbye, Andi. It's been a pleasure."

I'm fuming, positively infuriated. My hands are shaking too much to eat. Out of the corner of my eye, I see Ryan talking with Lawrence. He looks up then and sees Jocelyn walking away from me; I can practically feel him burning with anger. In the reflection of my glass, I see him break off the conversation with Lawrence and head across the crowded dance floor to find me.

I'm not ready to talk. I need a minute to think, to process, to calm down. Pretending I don't see him, I make my way quickly, casually across the dance floor and slip into the ladies' room just as he reaches the dessert table.

I poke my head out of the door and watch as he runs a hand through those gorgeous locks, his eyes scanning the crowd, likely searching for me, and my heart pangs with longing. More than lust, more than desire, it's something deeper.

Ryan, as a whole, fits me. He matches me, and I match him, but the timing is all wrong, and that fact breaks my heart.

The first tear slips down my cheek, and I recoil into the restroom, locking the stall door behind me. I put down the toilet seat and collapse onto it, my chest breaking open with sobs. Maybe there's a way to make this work; nothing is impossible, as they say, but it sure feels like it in this moment.

I want everything—my career, Ryan, and Ryan's career.

However, those three things don't work together in any sort of logical semblance. He signs with Jocelyn, and he breaks up with me. He doesn't sign with her, and we live with some sort of doomed long-distance relationship. I could move here, but what about my career? My family, Lisa...the life I've built is there.

As my tears dry and my sobs expire, I'm left weak, tired, and exhausted by the entire evening, but at least I've come to some sort of conclusion.

It's early enough in the relationship that it shouldn't hurt too much to call things off with Ryan. We've only been dating officially for less than twenty-four hours. I'll call it off now, let him sign with Jocelyn, and maybe down the line, things will work out for us. One can hope.

In the meantime, I'm going to spend my last night enjoying Ryan, his presence, his comfort, and then tomorrow, I'll leave with clean-cut ties. My flight is early in the morning, so I'll tell him then.

I wonder, as I leave the stall, if I'd have come here in the first place if I'd known the goodbye would be so hard.

Chapter 45

Andi

The ride home is a quiet one. After I gathered myself in the restroom, reapplied some mascara and lip gloss, and wished the smiling newlyweds a good night, Ryan and I left.

He holds my hand tight throughout the drive. I ask once if he's okay, and he grits out a short yes. I wonder what happened between him and Jocelyn tonight, if he tried to change her mind. It doesn't matter anyway—her mind obviously wasn't changed.

Clearly neither of us are in a chatty mood, so I pass the time by watching the stars fly by the window.

The previous night, the stars had seemed so bright, so warm, so hopeful in their very nature. Tonight, however, they look like icicles pricking through the black night sky, poking holes in what was pure happiness just hours before.

"Do you want to shower?" Ryan asks once we're in his room. He's busy taking off his tie, and though I suspect he's not upset with me, he's too frustrated to untie the knot. "I'll get in after you."

I move across the room and silently help him out of the tie, then the jacket, and rest them both on the bed. He watches my motions in the mirror, his eyes soaking in every detail. It's almost uncomfortable, as if he can see through me, straight to my core.

When he's free of his troublesome outer layers, I offer a smile and make my way toward the bathroom.

I turn at the door and pause to watch him for a moment. He's sitting on the bed, head in his hands. The look on his face nearly rips my heart out of my chest, and I know what he's thinking.

It's me or the game.

Well, I'm not going to force him to make that choice.

"I'm sorry," he says when he sees me staring. "I'm not upset with you, it's...Jocelyn, she's—"

"I know," I say. Then, I lie. "It's okay."

"It's not okay."

I rest against the doorframe. I can't wait until morning. "I don't think we should do this."

His head jerks up. "What are you talking about?"

"Us. Me and you."

"What the hell are you talking about, Andi?"

"Look, Ryan, I came out here as a joke. This whole thing started as a joke. If I weren't such a crappy, clumsy delivery girl, none of this ever would have happened. Let's just call it what it is: a good time."

He stands, his eyes blazing, hard now, unlike the melted chocolate look that takes over when he is aroused, happy, or otherwise pleased. "That's not what this is at all. I love you, Andi."

"You think you love me," I say. "It's not real. We've been pretending so long that it's easy to say."

"Do you love me?"

I remain silent. Of course I do, but I can't tell him that. My heart is heavy, a stone in my chest as I look him in the eyes. "It doesn't matter. We're not meant to be. Those are the facts."

"What did she say to you?"

"She?"

"Jocelyn." He stands, moves across the room. "What did she tell you tonight?"

"Nothing," I lie again.

"It was about the deal, wasn't it? That I have to give you up to sign with her? Well, I'm not going to do it."

"It's not about that."

"I should have told her tonight. I just didn't want to cause a scene at my brother's wedding." He looks down, shaking his head. "I'm an idiot."

"I trust you." Despite my words, he looks so flustered. I reach out and cup my hand against his cheek. "But that doesn't change the other things. So what if you turn her down? You live here, and I live there."

"Stay."

"I…" It takes a second to register. "What?"

"Stay here, with me. I'll decline anything with Jocelyn—that doesn't matter anyway. I'm happy here, playing for the Stars. Stay by my side. Live with me in Minnesota."

I swallow, and the words that come next are hard. "But what about *me*, Ryan? What about my dreams? My dad, my friends, school, my career—I have a real chance at making comedy work. If I stay, I'm giving all of that up."

His eyes are hollow. "I can't ask you to give any of that up."

"And I'm not asking you to give up hockey for me."

"Where does that leave us?"

My eyes smart, and I blink back tears, my soul splitting as I step toward him. My hands clasp his face, and I bring my lips to his in a tender moment.

The kiss is soft, full of all that could be, but never will…full of memories we'll never make, full of the relationship we'll never have, the laughs we'll never share. Instead, stung with its sweetness, strands of pain seep into my very essence. We are right for each other, so very right—but at the wrong time.

When I pull back, his eyes are still closed, his lips pursed in the lingering semblance of a kiss, as if his very world will shatter when he opens his eyes. The illusion will be gone, and the painful truth of reality will set in and drag both of us down with it.

I rise up on my tiptoes, rest my hand on the back of his head, and leave one last brush of my lips against his forehead.

When I close the bathroom door, there are tears on my cheeks.

By the time I'm in the shower, the tears have grown to full-on sobs, my shoulders shaking as I try to remain silent. The last thing Ryan needs is to hear me crying; it's hard enough for us both already.

My eyes are closed when the door to the bathroom opens, and I'm focused on the warm rush of water on my shoulders. I don't realize Ryan is in the bathroom with me until the door to the shower opens.

He's there, shirtless, looking incredible. His cocoa eyes are soft with hurt, his hair curling in disgruntled waves from fingers wrestling through it. "Andi."

It's one word, but it's enough. I push the door the rest of the way open, and he joins me under the steaming warmth. Already, the bathroom is foggy with heat. My hair is damp with conditioner, my body lightly scented with the lilac body soap I imagine his mother left just for me.

"Let me," he murmurs, spinning me around so the water courses between my back and his chest. His hands come up to massage my scalp, working the conditioner through the ends of my hair.

Then his hands slide down my neck, slick with soap. He rubs small circles on my shoulders, loosening the tense knots that have developed there. Then it's my back, my ribs, my hips. His fingers run in sensitive lines across my skin until his hands are circling my waist.

I feel him, smooth and firm against my back, the water slick, the steam making it difficult to breathe, yet somehow, it's more sensual than anything I've ever known.

Then he wraps a hand around me and presses his palm to my stomach. He eases it down, below my belly, to a place where warmth and desire curl under his touch.

One of his fingers begins to stroke, slow, gentle movements that have me biting down on my tongue to keep from crying out. His lips press against my neck as he sucks gently and then eases my head around so he's kissing me.

Stroking, kissing in the heat, I moan into his mouth. His other hand holds my hips so my back is pressed to him. I'm on the verge, and I tell him so.

He murmurs my name, holds me steady, urges me over the wall until I don't have anything left. When his name finally spills from my lips, I sink against him.

He hooks an arm around my waist, the other resting against the wall. "Andi…"

"Mmm?"

"I love you."

"I love you too," I whisper. "Don't stop."

I reach out, my fingers pressing against the shower wall as he slides in, achingly slow at first, so I can feel every whisper of movement.

Arching my back, I silently ask him for more, for everything. He seems to understand my need, and he begins to move faster and faster. He's grasping hard enough for me to feel the indents on my hips, until he releases one hand and brings it around, stroking me at my core.

It's more than I can handle. I feel the wave coming harder, faster, and there's nothing I can do to stop it. We're connected now, our motions intertwined as one, and when he grits out my name, it just about pushes me over the edge.

But he has other plans. Ryan pulls out, leaving me wanting, needing, gasping at him with threats.

"What are you doing?" I turn to face him. "You can't stop like that."

He's standing before me, smoking hot, soaking wet, his eyes ablaze. "I need to see your face."

Before I can react, he picks me up and rests a hand behind me to hold our combined weight. My legs wrap around his back, the shower walls shuddering as he rocks into me. Neither of us notice or care; we're too wrapped in the moment, the heat of it all.

This time, he doesn't stop. He pushes us to the cliff, and together we sail over the ledge. I'm gripping his shoulders for dear life as he eases every last bit of energy from me, and when the last of the tremors stop, the water continues to rush over us.

We stare at each other for a long moment. In our nakedness, we're raw. There's love and lust and desire. There's also hurt, frustration, and something else, something more…despair, maybe.

"Let me finish what I started," he says, and at first I think he's ready for another round.

I'm about to tell him I need a minute to recover when his fingers reach into my hair and continue massaging out the conditioner. I close my eyes, let his fingers work their magic, and then I help him. Beneath my fingers his abs ripple, and for a moment, he twitches alert when my fingers graze his thighs. There's a moment of devilish want in his eye, but then it fades in an instant.

The moment is too sweet to do anything but towel off and climb into bed together.

He wraps me in his arms, and I lean into him, both of us too exhausted to put on clothes. If the night weren't so bittersweet, I'm sure we'd go again and again until the sun arrived and lulled us to sleep.

But as we are, it's too dangerous. To have sex is to invest more in each other, to deepen the relationship ties that will surely break. So instead, we hold each other like the very world will vanish if we let go.

I don't remember drifting off to sleep, but I know that when I did, I was in Ryan's arms.

And when I wake, I'm still there.

My flight is early. His alarm goes off five minutes after mine, and I silence it before he so much as rolls over.

I dress, grab my clothes, and head out of the room. I stop in the doorway, my heart tugging me back to bed. I return to the side of the bed, but only for a brief moment. Inhaling the soft scent of Ryan's shampoo, I press my lips to his forehead.

His eyelids flutter, and my heart nearly stops.

But then he merely rolls over.

I'm free to go.

I sneak out of the house without seeing anyone else, and by the time I've arrived at the airport courtesy of a taxi, I've gathered enough composure to text Ryan. I write out the message eleven different times, and I don't settle on the final one until the wheels of my plane have lifted.

We're just about to lose service when I hit send.

Never in a million years did I think a single order for a smiley face pizza could send my world spiraling off its hinges. As I close my phone and shut my eyes, I pray that my world— which is currently off kilter, lopsided, upside down—can find a way to right itself.

It doesn't work.

At least, not immediately.

When I land at LAX, I'm a mess.

I text my dad to pick me up, and I'm waiting on the curb by the time he arrives, pulling to a stop under the Sun Country sign.

He takes one look at my face and opens his arms. "It'll be okay," he tells me, gripping me tight around the shoulders. "I promise."

Chapter 46

Ryan

Sunlight pokes at my eyes like a knife. I roll over, reaching for Andi's body, but my arm falls flat onto the bed. I feel around for a bit, resisting pulling my eyelids open, wondering if she's in the bathroom.

I can't hear anything, so finally, I peek one eye open.

My heart races the second I see the empty bed.

I know I set my alarm last night, so it can't be later than eight o'clock. I don't sleep through my alarm as a general rule. We have early practices often, and being late to them means more than a slap on the wrist. Old habits die hard.

I reach for my phone, fumble around with it, and blink. This can't be right. Ten a.m.? That would mean I overslept by two hours. *Two hours?*

I pull myself out of bed, throw on a pair of sweats, and leave the room. I make my way downstairs where my mom is sitting by the fire reading a newspaper, a pot of coffee ready. I ignore both of them and look at the clock above the stove. It's never wrong—my mom is militant about keeping that thing clicking along at the right time. She even waits up 'til two or three in the morning, or whenever the hell daylight savings clicks into effect, to adjust it.

Ten-oh-four. My heart ices over. Her flight left at ten.

I take the stairs two at a time, ignoring my mom's calls to come have breakfast. While I was downstairs, a message came in on my phone. It's from her.

> Dear Ryan,
> I love you.
> Goodbye.
> Love,
> Your delivery girl

I let out a stream of curse words that have my mom checking on me from downstairs.

"I'm fine," I yell back to her, even though I'm not. I'm fucking pissed—not at Andi, but at Jocelyn, for starting this whole thing, for running Andi off.

Andi's selfless, and there's no doubt in my mind that Jocelyn said something to force her away from me, somehow guilt-tripped her into thinking she'd be the reason for my lack of success, or whatever—and Andi would believe her because she's a saint with a heart as big as the Pacific Ocean.

Well, I'm not letting Jocelyn ruin the best thing that's ever happened to me.

I shove whatever I can think of into my backpack. I don't even know if I packed real clothes—I could've packed fifty pairs of boxers and no shirts for how much I'm paying attention.

All I know is that I need to get out of here. I double-check that I have my wallet, credit card, and license; they're the only things I really need.

Well that, and Andi. If one thing is clear this morning, it's that I need her like I need my arm. Maybe, *maybe* I could survive without her, but it would be pretty painful and really fucking annoying. I certainly wouldn't be very happy about losing her if there were any other options.

"Where are you going?" my mother asks when I return

downstairs. She takes one look at my backpack and, without moving from her chair, twitches her slipper-clad toes. "Where's Andi?"

"Los Angeles."

"I thought your flight wasn't until next weekend?"

"It wasn't."

She nods. "I see. Do you need a ride to the airport?"

I manage a smile at my mother. Sometimes, mothers are an annoying pain in the ass—it's just a fact of life—but other times, they are the very best thing. This morning, she's the very best thing.

"I wouldn't say *no* to one." My frustration fades slightly. "I was going to drive, but—"

She leaps to attention. "Let me take you. Your father says I drive like a maniac."

"Well, you do."

She smiles. "That's good, because I have a feeling your business can't wait."

I have the best damn mother on the planet. I give her a hug. When we pull apart, she's smiling, pulling me toward the car.

"She loves you, Ryan," she says as we load into her minivan. My mother could easily afford a new car, but I think she likes the old one for nostalgia. "You're doing the right thing."

I swallow, look out the window, and then focus on arranging a new flight on the drive to the airport. I've already hugged my mother this morning, and that's enough emotion for one day. I'm conserving the rest of it to unleash on Jocelyn.

When we arrive at the airport, I have one foot out the door and am shouting my thanks when my mom grabs my wrist.

I raise an eyebrow as I turn to look at her.

"Go get her," she says. "And bring her back. I like her."

"Me too," I say, and then give my mother a kiss on the cheek. "Thanks for…everything."

Then, I'm gone. I make it onto the plane with one minute to spare, and by the time I've landed in Los Angeles nearly four hours later, I'm a bundle of nerves.

One minute I'm pissed to all hell, itching to get face to face with Jocelyn. The next minute, I'm feeling a little insecure, wondering if I've read Andi all wrong. Maybe she really is over me, and I'm chasing her down for no reason at all. Maybe she's just too nice to tell me she doesn't want me.

I hate this. I don't like feeling vulnerable. I have a tattoo on my arm, a scar on my face, and I play hockey for a living—I should be too tough for this shit.

Since I have a carry-on bag full of mostly boxers, I don't wait at baggage claim. I call an Uber, but it's too frigging difficult to find, so I hop into the first taxi I see. It's a minivan.

"This is extra," the guy says. "Big car."

"Big tip"—I hold up my cash—"if you can get me to this address quickly."

It's Jocelyn's office. I send her a text to meet me there immediately.

Jocelyn beeps back in a second that she's already there. I should have known she'd be working on a Sunday morning; she doesn't have a date at church, that's for sure.

The taxi driver does a decent job of getting me there quickly, running only two red lights. I tip him well and climb out. The entire drive, I can only think that Andi's here, too, in this city somewhere, and I need to find her. Unfortunately, she's not returning any of my texts. I can't tell if she's left her phone off or if she's sad, disappointed, angry, and the not knowing is killing me.

Before I head into Jocelyn's office, I manage to score her friend Lisa's number from some comedy website. I call her, and fortunately, she answers. "Hey," I say quickly. "This is Ryan."

"Oh."

I can't read anything from Lisa's tone, and that ticks me off even more. "Do you know where Andi is?"

"Crying in the bathroom?"

"You're kidding me."

"Of course I am," she says, but the soft edge to her words has me wondering if there's not some truth to it. "She's tough. She'll survive whatever the hell you put her through."

"Look, I'm sorry. It was a misunderstanding. I'm here, and I need to see her."

"You're in Los Angeles?"

"Yeah, I got the first flight out here that I could."

"No, I'm sorry. I don't need to ask her to know she doesn't want to see you."

"I know I screwed up. None of this was supposed to happen, and I'm here to make it right."

"Look, I'm Andi's best friend, and I have to deal with the fallout from these things. I'm not letting you make that fallout worse."

"I'm going to tell you this one time," I say, preparing to lay everything on the line. "I am in love with Andi. There was a misunderstanding this weekend, and I'm here to set things right. I really don't think you should be making the decision for her of whether or not she wants to see me."

There's a long pause.

"Just tell me where she is. Home? Working somewhere? I promise if she tells me to take a hike when I find her, I'll leave. I'll never bother you again."

"Promise?"

"Swear on it. I want Andi back, but if she doesn't want me..." I trail off. The threat of her not wanting me is enough.

"She has a show tonight. It's an early one, five p.m. Don't bother

her before then, but you can find her at Rick's bar after."

"Thank you," I say, the relief evident in my voice. "I owe you one."

"Let me give you one recommendation: sort out whatever this misunderstanding is before you see her, because if she comes away worse for wear after you see her, I'm going to cut off your balls and feed them to the birds."

I swallow, the image a vile one. "Understood."

"Great!" she chirps. "Have a super day."

Lisa hangs up, leaving me staring at the phone and fearing for my life a little—and the life of my family jewels. I figure the best course of action is to do what she says—sort out this misunderstanding, once and for all.

Chapter 47

Ryan

Jocelyn's waiting behind her desk. Her eyes are the same icy blue I've grown used to, and they send shivers across my skin the second I walk through her door. I can't understand what drives her to be so cold, so hostile all the time, but then again, that's not my problem.

My problem is Andi, and getting her back.

"Beautiful wedding, wasn't it?" she says as if nothing happened the previous evening. Straightening a stack of papers, she slides them across the desk. "You can get started signing these. I wasn't ready for you today, but I can be prepared in a few minutes."

I stomp across the room and rest a hand on the contracts. "Don't bother."

She freezes. Her hands cup the sides of the stack of paper. My fingers press down on top, and eventually, I win the battle, pushing the papers back toward her.

"Excuse me?"

"I have no interest in these."

"I've raised your signing bonus."

"Didn't you hear what I said?" I repeat. "No interest in them."

"We've come to an agreement satisfactory to both parties. A lot of time, money, legal support, etc. have gone into making this a possibility."

"We had an agreement that worked," I say. "But now there's a third party, Andi. She's the loser in all of this, and I refuse to let that happen."

Jocelyn blinks, as if she's not all that surprised by my demands. "I worried this would happen, but I think I can make you see some sense. Andi is not a *loser* in this scenario. By cutting her free, she's able to pursue her own career."

"Don't twist my words around."

"Andi is talented in comedy. I know—I've watched her videos." She smiles, that smug smirk that proves she's thought of everything. "If you don't sign this contract, you'll be back with the Stars. Yes, it's a great team, and yes, I know you fit in well there, but what about Andi? She'll have to give up her comedy career to be with you. Is that want you want?"

"There's a market for comedy in Minnesota."

She sighs. "You're acting like a child."

I'm silent. I don't want Andi to give up her dreams for me, she doesn't want me to give up my dreams for her, and that's the way it should be. Unfortunately, our individual successes make it difficult to make a success of us, together, as a couple.

"I suppose you could try long distance." Jocelyn shrugs. "I'm sure it works for some couples."

Still silent, I'm fuming. I don't want long distance with Andi. I want her in my bed, wrapped in my arms every damn night.

That's when I have a moment of clarity.

I shake my head and take a step back. Suddenly, I realize she's doing it to me, the exact same thing she did to Andi: guilt-tripping me into thinking everything I'm feeling, everything I want in life, is wrong.

"This is how you did it," I say finally. It's as if the sun has come out after the storm, and I can see the road I need to take. My destination is home, and home is with Andi. "You convinced her that being with me was selfish on her part."

"I didn't have to convince anyone," she says. "I'm just speaking my mind and pointing out the obvious. I'm looking out for your best interests, Ryan."

"No, you're not," I say. "You're looking at the bottom line. You don't know what's best for me."

"I know you. I've watched—"

"Yeah, yeah, you've watched every video of me playing hockey, of Andi doing her stand-up, but that doesn't mean you *know* me. I'm sorry, Jocelyn, for whatever went into organizing these contracts, but I'm done. I'm walking away. It's final. You can look for someone else to play your games."

"These aren't games."

"Fine," I say. "Call it what you want, but just know I'm done."

"Who'll be your agent?"

"I'll stick with Lawrence, or I'll find someone else. It's not your problem."

"Ryan!" She stands, and the stack of papers goes flying as her desk shakes from the sudden movement. "Don't throw your life away."

I pause in the doorway on my way out. "I'm not," I say, my voice soft, even. I'm no longer angry at her, I just feel sad. It's a pity she'll never know why I'm doing what I'm doing.

I understand where she's coming from, trust me—my priorities were different a few short weeks ago—but then I met Andi, and now things have changed.

"Goodbye, Jocelyn."

"Fine."

Her word stops me in my tracks. "Fine, what?" I turn to face her. "What are you saying?"

"I'll sign you anyway." Her nose turns up, her arms shaking as she rests her fingers against the desk. "If you're this serious about her, then I will make an exception for you."

"Exception?"

"Single players sell better. Better advertisement opportunities. The fangirls, the bunnies, the media go crazy for a hot young hockey player with a bright future, but I can make this work. Devoted young hockey player with a sweet, girl-next-door-type girlfriend—we can make this work."

"This is my life, not a story for the media."

"We can make it one. You could earn big on this."

"You know what?" I smile, this time feeling free, finally free from whatever bullshit Hollywood, Jocelyn, and the old Ryan Pierce got roped into. "I love the game. I just want to play hockey, that's all, but there will come a time when hockey's not an option for me anymore, when I'm too old to be of any use on the ice, and when that happens, the world won't care about me. Neither will the media, neither will the NHL, and neither will you."

Her lips are a thin icicle, pressed tight across her face.

"Do you know who will be there if I'm lucky?" My heart pounds harder as I hope what I'm saying is true. "Andi."

"But—"

"I'm sorry, Jocelyn. This isn't going to work for me."

I leave for good this time, my head pounding as I walk away from the best opportunity my career has ever seen. When the Hollywood sunshine hits my face, however, I'm calm. Finally, I know what I need to do. I may not be a saint—far frigging from it—but this time, I'm doing the right thing.

I call another Uber, climb in, and give him directions to Peretti's Pizza.

"Good pies," the driver says. "I love what they do to a sausage."

"Don't I know it," I say, smiling at the image. "Let's make this quick. Big tip if you can get me there in thirty minutes."

"Got a pizza all hot and ready, huh?"

"Something like that."

"Good man," the driver says. "We'll get you there no problem. She'll be waiting for you, man. I can feel it."

I'm not sure if he's talking about a pizza or a girl, but I need the latter to be true.

Anything else is just not an option.

Chapter 48

Andi

I refuse to admit that I've been crying for the last two hours.

After my dad brought me home this morning, Angela agreed to take over my shift, and Lisa swooped by to distract me. We spent the afternoon sipping mimosas and plotting out new material for our pilot audition.

The new material is crap, but it served its purpose—a distraction from *him*. I can't hate him, can't even bring myself to talk bad about Ryan Pierce. I care for him, even after just a short time together. There is nothing wrong with him except timing.

Lisa argued that Ryan should've stood up to the Blonde Bitch earlier, and I understand her logic, truly, I do, but I also understand where he is coming from. He made a deal with her before I ever entered the equation, and it is hard to fault Ryan for being a man of his word.

I also understand his desire to follow his dreams. I have dreams of my own, and I don't intend to roll over on everything I've worked for my entire life. My ovaries might want to drop everything to move to Minnesota and have Ryan's babies, but my brain fights against that urge.

I have a life here, dreams, passions. If I am going to be true to myself and happy—honestly happy—I need to see them through. Otherwise, what sort of mother, wife, daughter, or friend would I be?

"There." Lisa finishes applying eyeliner to my eyes. Minutes ago, she had frozen spoons pressed against my eyelids to dull the post-tears swelling. "You look beautiful."

I glance in the mirror, and it is movie magic at its finest. Lisa, bless her heart, has transformed me into a fox—smoky eyes, seductive red lips, and a low-cut, lacy black tank top over a new pair of dark jeans. She's dressed similarly in black, though her lips are pink and her eyes are dotted with glitter.

"Can you believe it's happening?" She holds my arms and squeals. Finally, it's not forced excitement for the sake of cheering me up. Her eyes sparkle with the same sheen of the glitter on her lashes, and she's squealing. "You and me, together—shit, Andi, we've been dreaming of this day for years!"

My heart speeds up a bit, and it's the first sign I've had all day that my decision to return to Los Angeles was the right one. I smile at her. "I wouldn't be here without you," I tell her. "You are… You mean everything to me."

She blinks, and if I'm not mistaken, there's a hint of mistiness in her eyes. "We're a team. You and me, Andi. We're doing this together—and guess who's going to be in the audience?"

I moan. "I don't want to know."

"Better that way." Lisa winks, but it doesn't help the butterflies flapping about in my stomach.

She met with Nick Bennett shortly after I did, and he told us to start practicing our material for the audition in front of a live audience. This is our first show ever performing stand-up together, as a duo, and it's happening because Nick Bennett worked his magic in bringing the show to life.

There's a crowd out there; I can feel it. Rick was whistling when he came backstage a few minutes ago to announce the ten-minute countdown to show time, and he never whistles. He hates people.

But tonight, people must be making him money, because Rick made his son show up to sling drinks. For the first time ever, Phil (from the mailbox) doesn't have a front row seat. He lives here, and even he didn't arrive in time.

"Agents, other comedians, casting directors, producers, directors." Lisa flops on the couch. "Is this what it feels like right before we *make* it?"

"Don't jinx anything! We haven't made it yet. I haven't retired from Peretti's Pizza, and until I have, I'm not jumping to any conclusions."

"*Capisce*," she says. "Then let's get our asses out there and *make it.*"

We grasp hands for a moment, our fingers squeezing, the excitement zinging between as we make our way toward the stage. Rick is shouting that it's show time, Phil is whistling from the back row, and preshow chatter is at an all-time high as the guests wait for the main event.

Lisa lets go of my fingers just before we head on stage, but not before she takes a second to wink at me, smile, and give a word of encouragement. "You ready to dream big?"

I laugh, because I can't help it. I'm nervous and exhilarated, a feeling I never thought would be possible so soon after leaving Ryan's bed this morning. A pang of longing hits me, and I find myself wishing he were in the audience tonight too, sitting next to his buddy, Nick.

I shake off the wishful notions as we emerge underneath the lights. All thoughts of Ryan disappear as I stare into the crowd. Lisa is laughing, smiling, waving at everyone, but I freeze. It's a full house, a *full* frigging house. I don't care that the house is small in the scheme of things—I've never played a club where there was *standing room only*. People are standing at the back, and every chair is taken.

Thankfully, Lisa has her wits about her and opens the show, cracking a joke about this being both of our first times, and it goes over well. I turn to face her, still trying to make my feet move forward. *This is how it's going to end*, I think. I'm going to die right here of stage fright, and poor Lisa's going to be left doing the show alone.

This isn't how I planned to die.

Then, I see him, and I decide that maybe I can't die yet.

That shaggy brown hair, those fairytale eyes that could melt a woman's heart from across the room, that powerful torso that's built to play, to protect, to hold me close under the shelter of the stars. Ryan Pierce.

In his hands there's a stack of pizzas—at least ten of them—and I recognize the logo on the edge of the boxes: Peretti's Pizza. He's in the middle of handing out slices to all of the audience members, and everyone looks thrilled by the hot and ready pies. He's even given an entire pizza to Phil.

My heart—what's left of it—shatters into little pieces. I think it's breaking for the sole purpose of seeing if he'll be the one to put the pieces back together again. His eyes lock on mine, and mine lock on his, and in that moment, I am ready to give up everything.

But he gives his head a slight shake and flicks his chin toward Lisa. I follow his gaze and find Lisa there, holding the microphone out to me, her eyes expectant. I snap to it, a surge of adrenaline kicking my fears to the curb. My longing for Ryan is replaced by my loyalty to Lisa—at least for now—and I vow to not let her down.

I grab ahold of that microphone, and a beat later, a natural smile finds my face. I step forward to the edge of the stage and, just as we rehearsed, we run through our ten-minute bit. The audience is laughing, chuckling—I think Phil wiped a tear from his eye. I'm on cloud nine, cloud ten if that exists, cloud freaking *nineteen* if I can find it.

Rick flashes the red light at the back of the room, and I catch a glimpse of a grin on his face. We're a hit, I just know it. I pass the mic back to Lisa and she wraps up with our final practiced joke, and the crowd erupts.

Throughout all of it, my eyes scan over Nick—who's giving us a smile that looks like dollar signs—past a casting director that I *know* has worked on big blockbusters, past everyone until I find him. Ryan.

"Thanks, folks," Lisa says. "Enjoy the pizza. Order Peretti's and have a great night!"

Lisa drags me backstage before I can run to Ryan, and I go, but only because she's on the verge of tears. She's jumping up and down, hugging me, and there's nothing I can do about it. I'm in shock.

"We nailed it!" she cries. "We're going to make it, Andi, I know it! Did you see the room out there?"

I manage to hug her back, and her arms are like pythons squeezing the life out of me. I go limp and work on taking deep breaths, but it doesn't work. Then I lose *all* of my breath when the curtain to the backstage area opens and it's Ryan, alone, holding a pizza.

Lisa must hear the catch in my breath because she pulls away, asking if I'm okay.

I nod, and she follows my line of sight.

"Oh," she says softly. "Right. Okay, well, I'm going to go talk to Nick. I'll leave you two alone to…well…"

She squeezes my fingers and, with a final smile, disappears.

Ryan and I are alone, and the air is crackling with tension. I equally want him and wish him away. If we can't make this work, seeing him will only make the pain of losing him ache longer.

"I brought you something," he says with a wink, breaking the silence. He lifts the pizza box higher. "I figured you've delivered me enough sustenance to last a lifetime, and it was time to return the favor."

"Peretti's?" I look at the box. "I don't understand."

He sets the box on the table. "I needed to talk to your dad."

"What?" My heart thumps in my chest. "Why?"

"It's too soon to ask you to marry me, Andi, and we have too much to figure out," he says. "But I wanted him to know my intentions."

I blink, fidgeting with the lace on my shirt. "I'm sorry, I'm not understanding…"

"I want to date you, Andi." He steps forward, takes my fingers in his hands—hands that are large, warm, and capable of so many wonderful things. "But I don't want to date you for one night. I don't want to *fake* date you or have you play some stupid game. I play games for a living. What I want with you is real."

"But your agent…"

"She's not my agent," he says, his jaw firm. "I went to her office this morning to set the record straight. She offered to sign me, and I said no."

"Why? Ryan, you can't! These are your dreams, what you've worked for your whole life. Maybe I overreacted when I left this morning. We can figure things out, make something work—"

"I don't want to make something work, I want to *be* with you— out in the open, for the whole world to see. I just need you to say yes. Tell me you'll give me a chance to make things right."

I hesitate. "But—"

"We'll figure out the details. I want you to have your career, and I'll have mine. We can have a condo in Los Angeles and a house in Minnesota—whatever it takes. I will do anything to be with you, Andi. Anything."

"You gave up the chance to sign with one of the best agents in the business…for me."

"I'm still doing what I love—playing hockey for a career. That's all I need. The rest is bonus, icing on the cake." His long lashes brush against his cheeks as he leans close to me. "You're not the icing, Andi. You're the cake. Without the cake, there is no icing. I need you."

A laugh bubbles up in my chest. "I'm the cake? That might be the most romantic thing I've ever heard."

"Christ, Andi, I'm trying—"

"Stop, Ryan." I raise a hand and smooth it across his face. He's looking pained, and I can't stand the uncertainty in his eyes. "I want to be your cake."

"Andi Peretti." Ryan hooks his arms around my back. "Thank God you delivered that pizza."

"And destroyed your car."

"And pretended to be my girlfriend."

"And ran away from you."

"And most of all…" He pauses, his lips a breath away from mine. "It's a good thing you said yes just now, because I can't live without you."

"Ryan," I say, my voice a low, husky murmur. "Stop talking."

He blinks once, and I watch as understanding sinks in. His eyes darken, he runs his tongue over his bottom lip, and then we both move at once. Our lips meet in a rush of need, his arms sliding around my lower back, his hands gripping my backside as he lifts me from the ground. My legs circle his narrow waist, and my arms slide around his neck.

He stumbles forward from momentum, the pair of us off balance, and we fall onto the backstage couch. The athlete in him emerges, swooping me onto his lap with surprising grace given the fervor of our movements. My arms claw at his shirt, and one of his hands slips into my new jeans.

He nearly rips my new, lacy black undies as he pulls me hard onto his lap, and I feel every glorious inch straining beneath his jeans. I'm perched over him, ready; all that separates us are two layers of clothes.

"I've missed you," I tell him, completely oblivious to any of our surroundings. "I've missed kissing you."

"Baby, we're in public," he says. "We should wait—"

"Public?" My breath comes out as a gasp as I turn and gesture toward the empty room. "The door has a lock."

Ryan stands, takes two steps toward the door, and comes face to face with Rick as he bursts into the backstage area.

"Andi," Rick is saying, "You nailed it out there—*shit!*"

Ryan's standing there, a little awkward, his boner staring big, burly Rick in the face. I think the top button of his jeans is undone, and I know for a *fact* that I'm sprawled on the couch all rosy-cheeked and ready.

"Christ, Andi, not the fucking couch!" Rick storms out and slams the door behind him, still shouting at us. "Get a room—your *own* room."

Ryan, to my surprise, leans forward and slides the lock shut. When he turns toward me, the devil is dancing behind those chocolate brown eyes. "What's this I hear about the couch?"

Epilogue

Andi

Eight Years Later

A soft snow falls outside, coating the world in fairytale white. Christmas lights blink around the fireplace of our bedroom, and the light tunes of carols sound in the background. In the living room of our cozy, three-bedroom house just a few blocks away from Ryan's parents is a Christmas tree laden with gifts.

The only gifts I need, however, I'm watching through the window. Ryan is outside skating with our two rascals. *Three boys.* Resting a hand on my stomach, I think *and soon to be another, or maybe this time it'll be a girl.*

Today is special for a million and one reasons, not least of all because it's our six-year anniversary. Tucker came exactly nine months after we were married; the kid was hardly a honeymoon baby—he was a night-of-the-wedding baby.

Angelo came about a year and a half after Tucker. My cousin Angela had wanted to hold out for a girl to inherit her name, but when it hadn't happened on baby number two, she'd insisted we go with Angelo, and because he's a saint, Ryan agreed.

Since then, we've been trying desperately for baby number three. It's not for lack of trying that we haven't been successful, that's for sure. Ryan's package is as hot and ready as the pizza I delivered on that fateful day years ago, but it just hasn't been happening for us.

I'm blessed beyond belief with my two little boys and one big one, but I can't help feeling that we are meant to have one more, to have three little Pierce children running around. Blinking back tears, I look at the pregnancy test and realize our family is about to be complete.

Ryan doesn't know yet—I found out exactly thirty seconds ago. I'm planning to tell him tonight. It'll be a little wine for him, and sparkling grape juice for me.

I swallow a lump in my throat—pregnancy hormones starting in again. I was a few weeks late this time, but I waited to take the test before I told him. We've had so many false alarms, it's started to wear on my nerves.

I spread both hands over my stomach, joy filling my heart. This little boy or girl is the lucky one, just like me, because Ryan is the most wonderful partner, the most loving husband, and the best father to our children that I could have ever hoped for.

Mariah Carey croons in the background, and I smile as Ryan moves the puck across the icy pond in our backyard. Tucker and Angelo half-run, half-skate after him. They might be little, but they take after their father on the ice, and that's saying a lot. This year, Ryan led his team—the Minnesota Stars—to their first ever Stanley Cup win. I was there, both boys in the seats next to me, and it was magic.

I watch as Tucker takes a tumble and lands hard on his bottom. Ryan lets the puck skid away from him and turns to pull our son up from the ice. Angelo, the feisty nugget that he is, goes after the puck without a glance at his brother and slams it into the net. He throws his stick, punches the air, and then finally decides to see if his brother is okay.

My phone rings, and I look away from the hockey game out back to answer it. "Hey Dad," I say. "How's it going?"

"I saw the show," he says. "You did good, kid."

"Thanks, Dad, it was all Lisa." I can't help but grin. "We have a good time."

My dad still watches every comedy show I perform. Lisa and I have a residency on Comedy Central, and she's married, too, to another one of the Stars players.

She and I do a joint segment, though we're on leave now because Lisa is nine months pregnant with her first baby. We'll resume in the summer. I've found the best of both worlds, truly; I have a family and a career that I love.

"I'm flying in tomorrow. Don't forget to pick me up from the airport," he says. "And by the way, I watered your plants. Your cactus died. Not my fault."

"Thanks, Dad," I say. He takes care of the condo we own above Peretti's newest location in Malibu when we're away. "It'll be a white Christmas here this year. Mom would've loved it."

"She'd be proud of you, kid," he says in a gruff voice. "Anyway, I've got some treats for Tucker and Angelo, and I'm bringing presents from your cousin, too, so have Ryan with you to help me at baggage claim."

"You spoil them too much."

"Damn right I do," he says proudly. "See you tomorrow."

"Love you, Dad."

I hang up, startled for a moment as I look out and see the two youngest boys back on the ice hacking at the puck with their sticks. They have yet to learn the art of finesse. Ryan is nowhere to be seen.

"There you are." His deep, husky voice rolls through the warmth of our butter-yellow bedroom, the fluffy white comforter on the bed crinkling as he pulls a James Bond-style roll across it. "God, you look beautiful with the snow falling behind you like that."

"You're just saying that because I'm naked."

"Not naked enough." He eyes my figure, my stomach mostly flat, not yet showing the signs of our newest addition. "Maybe I can help with that."

I turn and face the window, the sheer curtain preventing the boys from seeing inside. I'm wearing only a black bra and panties, fresh from the shower. I have on no makeup, no perfume, and my hair's still wet, yet somehow he looks at me like I'm ready to walk the red carpet. That's one reason why I love him.

I glance toward the pregnancy test, which I've dropped into the trash bin. Ryan knows how much one more baby means to me, and he's taken it upon himself to utilize every opportunity to make that happen. I won't say no to a little more attention from him before I break the news.

"Don't worry about them." Ryan's lost his shirt, his socks, and his outdoor layers somewhere between our front door and the bedroom. "I told them they could have two hot chocolates if they played a game up to a hundred points."

"What are they on?"

"Five," he says. "We can take our time."

I suck in a breath as he presses against my back. My hands reach forward and grasp the windowsill. It's been over six years, and I can't get enough of him. Every time he walks into the room, undresses me, and works his magic, I'm convinced I'll shatter to pieces from overwhelming ecstasy.

"I don't know how it works, but I love you more every day we're together," he murmurs against my neck. "Happy anniversary, baby."

I throw my head back as his hands slide around my front; they're a little bit cold from being outside, and they unhook my bra in one fell swoop. It falls to the floor, and he drags his fingers over my breasts, squeezing, caressing, massaging until goose bumps skitter across my skin at the clash of warm and cool.

Then he slides his hands down my ribcage, dragging along my sides until I'm writhing with pleasure. All at once, however, he stops. He pulls me into him, his arms cradling me to his naked torso. His jeans are in the way, keeping his gorgeous self from my skin, and I whisper for him to take them off.

"One second, sweetheart," he says. "Let me enjoy."

His hands spread wide over my stomach, almost as if he knows, almost as if he can sense something. He holds a hand there for a long, long time.

Then his fingers turn downward and he lets out a groan as he dips them to my core. It's gentle at first, his fingers exploring with a unique tenderness.

He curses under his breath. "You've been waiting for me."

I spin around, my eyes dark, wanting. I don't dare open my mouth because I want to savor every second. Our alone time is next to nothing with two boys, and it will be even scarcer with the soon-to-arrive third child.

"Ryan," I say in the brief pause of a scorching hot kiss.

I think about telling him the news now, but I can't, yet, mostly because I forget. He has a way of ensuring my mind goes blank in the heat of the moment.

His hair is a mess, courtesy of my fingers running wild through it, and his eyes blaze in a way that means he's got one thing on his mind—the very same thing that's on mine.

I wrap around him as he brings me to the bed, but then he changes his mind at the last second and drops the two of us onto the plush fur rug before the fire. My lingerie has vanished, and I instruct him to ditch the jeans, too.

Once he's naked and I'm spread before him, he looks at me with eyes so full of everything—desire, love, devotion—I'm ready to collapse into his arms, but he's not ready for that. He trails kisses down my chest, lingering on my stomach, and then stops for one last taste between my thighs.

I'm nearly begging by the time he finally eases into me. When he does, I take a moment to enjoy the sensation. Our eyes are locked, and he plays with a curl of my hair, his eyes closed, lips gritted as he, too, savors the moment.

Then he begins to move, slowly, and the friction is intoxicating. I grip his sturdy shoulders, his beautiful arms, and hold tight for the ride.

He slides one hand under my head and devours my mouth with a kiss that sends tingles everywhere. With each swoop of his tongue and nibble of my lips, he's moving faster and faster. By the time we can't kiss anymore, we're rocking hard enough to shake the house. A perfume bottle falls off the dresser, and I raise my hips up to take him in, all of him.

"Baby," I gasp, suddenly remembering the news I have for him. I have no idea why it hits me now, but the words come out in a rush. "I need to tell you something."

He stills, the look on his face pained as he pulls back. "Am I hurting you?"

"No." I put my hands on his shoulders, slow down for a moment, and offer a smile. "I'm pregnant."

Fireworks light in his eyes. "I know, sweetheart. I knew the second I walked into the room."

He runs a hand over my cheek, caresses it gently, and then brings his mouth down for a long, leisurely kiss. The intensity builds again, a slow burn in my belly, until I urge him onward. His lips crash into mine as we both fly toward the edge with renewed fervor.

I burst into a million pieces as he soars with me to an incredible finish, more consuming than anything I've ever known, and when he is satiated, he rolls on top of me, the weight of his body delicious. He turns so his back is to the fire and I am wrapped in his arms.

"Happy anniversary, Andi," he says. "I love you."

My hands rise to rest over his, and I nuzzle in, warm, cozy, hoping today never ends. Life, in this moment, is perfect.

Then...

"Mom!" Tucker yells, the front door crashing open. "I got a hundred and one goals. Can I get my hot chocolate now or what?"

Ryan rolls to his feet, helping me to stand. "I've got this one," he says. "Take a bath, relax, and prepare for the dinner of your dreams."

"I can whip up some turkey chili—"

"No." He wraps me in a hug. "Take a bath, relax, and get in bed—naked. It's our anniversary, and I intend to spoil you."

My heart thuds as I move toward the bathroom and watch my husband pulling on his clothes. "Ry," I say, watching as he slips into a pair of boxers. "What if we order in a pizza? You know, for old time's sake."

He grins at me, those dark eyes taking in every inch of my body. "As long as it's you wearing a towel this time, delivery girl."

THE END

Author's Note

Thank you so much for reading!
I hope you enjoyed Ryan and Andi's story!

For more information, updates, and future release news, please visit my website at LilyKateAuthor.com or find me on Facebook.

***

Stay tuned for more books from the Minnesota Ice series!

Author Bio

Lily Kate writes books filled with heat, heart, and humor. Her debut
novel, *Delivery Girl*, became an instant USA TODAY bestseller.

When Lily's not writing books, you may find her watching
Christmas movies before Thanksgiving, eating whipped cream from
the can, or hanging out with her family.